DOMINION

THE DOMINION SERIES BOOK ONE

S E LUND

ACADIAN PUBLISHING LIMITED

S. E. LUND'S NEWSLETTER

If you would like updates on new releases and sales, special promotions and other news, sign up for S. E. Lund's newsletter. She hates spam and so will never share your email with anyone!

https://www.subscribepage.com/x8t1t7

PREFACE

And death shall have no dominion.
Dead mean naked they shall be one.
With the man in the wind and the west moon;
When their bones are picked clean and the clean bones gone,
They shall have stars at elbow and foot;
Though they go mad they shall be sane,
Though they sink through the sea they shall rise again;
Though lovers be lost love shall not;
And death shall have no dominion.

Dylan Thomas

"That it will never come again is what makes life so sweet." Emily
Dickinson

CHAPTER 1

"WHAT HURTS YOU, blesses you. Darkness is your candle."

Rumi

MY MOTHER never lied to me about the existence of monsters. When I'd awaken with nightmares and dreams of shadows that moved in the darkness, she'd stay with me until my terror passed.

"I'm here," she'd say, stroking my hair. "I'm faster than them and I'll protect you. One day, I'll kill the monsters forever."

My great tragedy was that she couldn't protect herself. A decade after her death when I was only eleven, finding her killer and discovering a way to eradicate all vampires is the only thing that keeps me going. Today I take up the work that ended her life.

THE LATE SPRING evening is rainy and cold so I bring my umbrella and stand at the bus stop outside my building. A professor of linguistics offered to translate an ancient illuminated manuscript I found in my mother's files. My mother started to translate it but never finished, dying the week she received it. The murder was never solved and I need to know if the manuscript had anything to do with her death.

The evening bus isn't crowded because classes and finals are over. I take out my mother's notebook and read it over once more for her notes from the week before her death describe the document that I have tucked in a large manila envelope in my backpack.

By the hand of Julien de Cernay, former Knight, identical twin brother to Michel, former Bishop of Carcassonne, bastard sons of Guillaume, Vicomte de Clarmont. Written 1224 – 1229 A.D. Interviewed on 22 December at Boston University.

Included in the file is a card with a hand-written note to my mother, the script bold, masculine.

Natalia,

I've enclosed this manuscript as promised. It documents my making and that of my twin brother, Michel. I hope it provides you with insight into our existence at a time when life was very different than it is today.

Best regards,

J.

My mother knew this vampire?

That shocks me. She was a vampire hunter, dedicated to killing them off. As a geneticist working for the Council of Clairveaux, she studied genetic diseases, searching for the cause of vampirism – ostensibly so she could find a cure, but I know it was really so she could find a magic bullet and destroy them all. Her files describe the Council – a joint Human-Vampire group appointed by the ruling families involved in its creation. Dedicated to ensuring that the fragile peace between the two species remains in place, the Council ensures that both vampires and humans follow the terms of the Treaty of Clairveaux, signed almost seven centuries earlier.

From what I can gather, the Treaty was created to stop the bloodshed between the two species that had been a constant state since, well. Forever. The Inquisition and the Church's concerted effort to hunt down and kill all vampires under the claim it was after 'witches' and 'warlocks' sparked a desire on the part of vampires to find a compromise. Humans were gaining ground on vampires, beginning to beat them, developing new weapons, and vampires felt under threat. The Treaty was a compromise between extinction of vampires or enslavement of humans. Vampires could continue to exist, but they could no longer kill humans for their blood unless under very specific circumstances. Humans couldn't hunt and kill vampires unless they broke the terms of the Treaty. And above all, like Fight Club, those who knew the truth about vampires and the existence of the secret Treaty of Clairveaux were not allowed to speak of it upon pain of death.

This fragile peace persisted for almost seven hundred years until genetic technology evolved far enough so that it became possible to eradicate all vampires once and for all. Faced with the growing threat to their species, some vampires decided on their own path to ascension - Dominion. Vampire rule.

So, while vampires are still firmly in the closet, some of them don't want to stay there and I think that's why my mother died. The vampire who wrote the manuscript, Sir Julien de Cernay, gave the manuscript to her for a reason and I'm hoping if I can translate it, I'll learn why.

She managed to translate the first paragraph, but then stopped, and it's tantalizing.

"A full moon rises" her hand-written translation starts, "stained red from fires in the village square where five heretics burned at the stake. The Crusades broke my family, estranged me from my brother and now killed me. I died, not on the battlefield as befitting a knight protecting my father's estate, but in a bed in an abandoned castle at the hands of an ancient vampire who bewitched me..."

I can't imagine what it must be like to live eight centuries and despite my hatred of vampires, there's a part of me that wants to meet the writer, Sir Julien, just to see what he's like.

The bus drops me off and I enter the linguistics building's unusually empty corridors, the sound of my boots echoing off the walls. I take the stairs to the third floor, shaking the late spring rain off my umbrella. A tag on room 304 reads Steve Cormier, PhD. I knock and hear papers shuffling inside. The door opens and I'm face to face with perhaps the palest man I've ever seen and for a moment, I'm filled with dread.

Is he a vampire? His skin is so white.

He smiles, holding a mug of coffee in his hands as if to warm them. I stand open mouthed, debating whether to run. I've only seen one vampire before that I know of – the one who killed my mother – but he's just a vague memory of a bloody mouth and white skin. I was only eleven, and I don't even know what he really looked like due to shock, my memory lost into some kind of psychological black hole. I was there when she was murdered, but I have no memory of him or the events. My psychiatrist says I have PTSD-induced amnesia and that one day I will remember. All I know is that I found her lying on the floor, her neck ripped open, blood foaming at her mouth.

That image I can't escape, no matter how I try.

If Professor Cormier is a vampire, he doesn't look like the un-dead of my imagination. Whatever he is, he's wearing an ornate gold crucifix around his neck and now I wish I'd read more of my mother's research. Do vampires really hate religious symbols like crucifixes and holy water?

His skin doesn't look like a corpse, but like he's ill, his skin white like some 17th century nobleman with a powdered face. It's beautiful in a strange way — the way I imagine Keats would have looked before his tragic death.

He's younger than I expected. Thirty at most.

"Are you Professor Cormier?"

"Eve?" he says, extending his hand. I look down at it briefly, reluctant to shake but I don't want to be rude. His touch is a little on the cold side, but not corpselike — not like dead chicken as I imagine a vampire's hand would feel. He holds mine and doesn't let go even after we finish shaking. It's far too forward.

Finally, when my cheeks are hot with embarrassment, he releases my hand.

"Hello. Nice to finally meet you."

Finally? I just exchanged texts with him about this meeting an hour ago...

He has this very soft accent somewhere between continental and Cajun French. He's smiling, one side of his mouth turning up just a bit and I can't tell if it's a smirk or if that's just the way he smiles.

"Hello." I smile back to be polite and hold up the envelope. "I have the manuscript for you to translate."

"Please, come in." He opens the door wider and waves into the interior.

"Thank you." I force another big smile, trying to look like I'm pleased to be here, when what I want is to turn on my heel and run away.

I squeeze past him sideways for he's standing in the doorway and when I walk by I catch a scent of something masculine, and not like the usual cheap cologne I smell on the guys at the university. More like sandalwood or incense. He smells good and not like he's fresh out of the grave the way I imagine a vampire would smell, all earthy and wormy and old blood.

I kick myself mentally. He's probably just got that pale skin you see with some Europeans but given the profession I intend to follow, I'm suspicious of everything.

Inside, it's a typical Boston U junior faculty office – bookshelves on either wall, and a desk in front of a large window looking out over the rotunda. A black leather sofa and chair with a coffee table sit to one side of the office. On the coffee table and on every surface sit piles of research papers and books. There's a chalkboard with words translated from one French dialect to another and into English.

I turn around and he's staring at me, his gaze extremely intense, his blue eyes huge, pupils dilated.

"Please, let me take your coat."

I remove it and hand it to him and he hangs it on a coat tree by the door.

"Have a seat," he says after a pause, motioning to the sofa. "Can I get you anything to drink? It's a damn cold night. There's fresh coffee in the pot."

"No, thanks."

I take a seat and he's staring at me with the strangest expression on his face – half amused and half perplexed. He's attractive, so I don't want to stare at him for fear I'll blush, which I have a bad tendency to do when I'm nervous. But of course I can't help but check him out from the corner of my eye. He's wearing black jeans with a thick black belt and a white button-down shirt. The contrast between his black hair and white skin highlights his blue eyes.

His hair is longish and a bit wild, just below his chin and tucked behind his ears, and his blue eyes are rimmed by thick black lashes. I look away from his intense gaze, and lift up the envelope containing the manuscript and clear my throat, unsure if I can actually speak without my voice cracking.

"Here it is."

He takes the envelope and sits on the chair across from me but doesn't look inside it yet. He's still looking at me with those way-too-blue eyes.

"Eve," he says, drawing the name out. "That's such a lovely name. Is it short for Evelyn?"

I shake my head, surprised at the personal question.

"No, I was named after the biblical Eve. My mother wanted to name me Lilith but my dad said no. Lilith was too defiant, too opinionated, and too independent and he was hoping for a sweet-natured girl." I bite my tongue. I don't know why I'm telling him this except that I'm suddenly nervous.

"And are you?" he says, his French accent soft.

"Am I what?" I say for I've forgotten the direction of the question.

"Sweet natured or defiant, opinionated and too independent? Was his naming you after the biblical Eve successful?"

I frown at his too-personal questions and my too personal answers.

"I don't know," I say. "That's for someone else to say, not me."

"You don't know yourself?" He gives that lopsided grin again, as if he already knows. "I'm sorry. It's just that it would be ironic if you turned out exactly as he feared despite the more innocuous name. Besides, Eve ate of the forbidden fruit and led Adam to his downfall." He raises his eyebrows at that. "Sounds to me as if Eve was a bit too independent as well."

I don't respond for fear I'll say something even more personal.

Finally, he turns to the envelope and opens it methodically, removing the manuscript with extreme care. He takes in a deep breath when he sees it in its entirety.

"Oh, it's very old." He runs his fingers over the extremely fine vellum on which the text is written. "Beautiful," he says in a soft voice. He turns the pages, his index finger tracing the lines as if he's greedy to translate it already and on his finger is a thick gold signet ring. I try to make out the initials, but can't from this distance.

"I should have gloves on to even touch this." He looks up at me. "Where did you get it?"

I look at his nose, at the space between his dark brows, and an imaginary point in the distance – anywhere but in his eyes.

I swallow. "My mother?"

"Is she a collector? How did she come by this? It's priceless."

"She was a researcher," I say and glance away.

"Do you have any idea where she got this?"

"I don't have a clue." When I look back at him, he's staring at me expectantly as if he wants more of an explanation – or doesn't believe the one I've given. "I didn't steal it or anything, if that's what you mean." I'm a bit insulted by his expression, as if he doubts my story – which, of course, he should, since I'm being deceptive.

"I mean no offense," he says quickly, his voice still soft. "I'm just curious how this manuscript came into your hands. It should be behind glass in an archive somewhere in a temperature and humidity-controlled environment."

"That's all I can tell you."

Of course, I could tell him that it belonged to the vampire who wrote it eight hundred years earlier, and that he gave it to my mother a week before she died so she could use it to understand vampires so she could better kill them, but that's not going to happen.

"So, any idea how long it will take to translate?" I say, hoping to move on from personal questions. "I'm really interested in reading it. I think it was important to my mother's research."

"What was she researching?"

I hesitate. More lies. I truly hate telling them, because I don't have a poker face.

I swallow again, my throat dry. "Medieval literature?"

"Of course." He closes the manuscript and replaces it in the envelope. "It won't take long to translate. I can dictate it and have it printed out quickly using new software. But I'm afraid there's a bit of a problem," he says and pats the manuscript. "I have to investigate this a bit more. This document is extremely rare and valuable. I want to authenticate it, just in case it was stolen and given to your mother illegally." He looks at me pointedly. "You must understand."

"No, I don't." I don't want him to take it and start digging into it. For all I know, no one's ever even documented its existence. "I happen to know that the original owner gave it to my mother."

"The original owner?" His voice sounds amused, that grin that could be a smirk starting again.

"I mean," I say, fumbling to recover. "The legitimate owner."

"And how do you know the owner is," he says and pauses, tilting his head to the side. "'Legitimate?'"

"There was a note enclosed with it from the owner. He gave it to my mother to use in her research."

"Yes, but how do you know that this – person – was the legitimate owner?"

I sit silent, my mouth opening and closing like a fish gasping for breath.

"Well..." I stand, reaching for the manuscript. "Maybe I'll just take it back and find someone else."

He shakes his head and grabs the manuscript, holding it in his arms.

"My apologies, Eve, but I really can't give this back to you until I'm certain."

"Listen, Professor, this was my mother's property." I'm starting to get angry. "When she died, it became mine. Give it back to me or I'll have to call the authorities."

He's smirking now but it's not a rude smirk, more of a knowing smirk. Like he knows he's got me.

"I'm curious. Which authorities would these be? The stolen ancient documents authorities?"

His accent is just so superior in its soft Frenchness that I hate him. I reach out to grab the manuscript, figuring I'll just run. Surely he wouldn't chase me like some cop after a bank robber. I get only the corner in my fingers before he pulls it back.

I'm flustered, my cheeks hot. We're standing across from each other, staring each other down, but he's almost a foot taller than me and much stronger, the manuscript in his arms protectively. There's no way I can wrestle it away from him without looking like a complete crazy person.

"I'm not very happy about this," I say, digging my nails into my palms to control my emotions.

"I can tell, Eve. I'm truly sorry."

I stand there fuming, worried that he won't give it back to me and then I'll never know why the vampire thought my mother should have it.

"Look, that's sensitive material. I do know that it's supposed to remain in private hands. I don't want its contents becoming public knowledge." I struggle to find the right words without giving too much away.

"I assure you that I'll treat this with the utmost discretion."

He's being serious now, but I'm just not ready to give in. Maybe I could phone campus security ... and tell them what? That some professor of linguistics has stolen my ancient vampire manuscript that I can't admit even exists? I don't think so.

Damn. Frustration builds in me. Here I am, just starting my career as a vampire hunter like my mother and I've already screwed things up.

"It's just that this is such a valuable manuscript," I say, my voice breaking. "I don't know if I can trust you with it."

His face softens for a moment, and he tilts his head to the side again as if he's feeling real sympathy for me.

"Oh, Eve. So emotional over an ancient manuscript? You're making me feel like an old monster. But I just can't let you take this back."

He shrugs and raises his eyebrows like he's helpless. He puts the manuscript down on the coffee table and steps towards the door as if he wants me to leave. I eye the manuscript, wondering if I can snatch it and run. I'm a very fast runner, but who knows how fast he might be?

"I wouldn't even think of it," he says.

Damn – am I that transparent? Yes, of course I am. I can't lie. I can't cheat without giving myself away. My mother always said I wear my heart on my sleeve.

I finally give in and push past him, my face hot, determined to just leave without another word and grab my coat from the coat tree but he beats me to the door and closes it with one hand, blocking my exit.

Oh, double damn... This is creep territory. Now, my frustration is replaced by fear.

"You're not going to let me leave?"

He smiles sadly. "Not until I make you forget all about our little meeting. I just can't have you walking around knowing this manuscript exists."

"What?" A sick feeling comes over me. What does he mean, make me forget?

He steps closer to me, and now that I see him up close, his lips have a slight bluish tint to them. I didn't notice it before because I was trying not to stare at him. He smiles, baring his teeth and his canines are just a little bit longer and sharper than all the others.

Oh, crap...

He touches my cheek for a moment with the back of his fingers and this wave of emotion goes through me. I close my eyes, dropping my backpack and coat, leaning against the wall for support. It's like he's searching my memories for in the brief seconds he touches me, I am back to that day – the day my mother died and all I can see is her face, the blood frothing at her mouth. When I'm able to open my eyes again, his face is just inches from mine, but it's blurry for my eyes are filled with tears.

"Poor Eve," he says, his voice soft, his gaze moving over my face. "Your first instincts are usually right and you should learn to trust them. I am a vampire, and you should have run when you had the chance. I'm not going to let you have this manuscript. I'm not going to translate it for you, either. I'm going to make you forget about it. Forget about me."

CHAPTER 2

"REGRET for the things we did can be tempered by time; it is regret for the things we did not do that is inconsolable."

Sydney Smith

"You're not Professor Cormier, are you?"

"No, luckily," the vampire says, a lopsided grin on his face. "He's a bit stuffy, lacks imagination but is very easy to compel."

He steps even closer, his arm on the wall beside my head.

"I've been looking for this manuscript for a decade, Eve, so I'm so glad you posted that message to the forum. You see, it's about my brother and me. It was written after we were both turned in 1224."

"You're one of the de Cernay twins," I say, blurting it out like they're a pair of rock stars and I'm a fan. "How did you find me so quickly?"

"I have a service that scans the web specifically for requests to translate 13th century French documents. Don't blame yourself, sweet Eve," he says and wipes tears off my cheek, slipping his finger into his mouth, his eyes closing like the taste pleases him. He keeps saying my name and I wonder if he isn't trying to mesmerize me — I think vampires can do that.

I'm standing there, pinned against the wall, barely able to breathe because he's so close and he's a vampire and could kill me in a second if he wants to and he's tasting my tears like some connoisseur of human bodily fluids.

"Please don't hurt me."

"Oh, I'm not going to hurt you, Eve. What do you think I am? A monster?"

Yes. I do think you're a monster — the most beautiful monster I've ever imagined. I'm breathless as he stares into my eyes, brushing the hair back from my cheek. He runs a finger over my bottom lip and leans closer and I fear he's going to kiss me.

"I know who you are as well," he says almost whispering. "I know what you are even though you don't. The last thing I want is to have you find out my secrets, and they're contained within that manuscript, just in case you decide to come after me one day with all your dreams of vengeance and your freakish vampire hunter skills."

I hold my breath, waiting for what he's going to do. I can't move, and I wish I'd had more time to read my mother's files. I don't know much about vampires, except the usual folklore. Can he make me forget about him and the manuscript?

"How do you know who I am?" I manage to whisper, barely able to speak from whatever it is he's doing to me.

"Let's just say vampires have a special touch."

Then he touches my cheek, holding his fingers there and a wave of elation flows through me, washing away the last remnants of sadness from the memory he made me relive. I can't help but close my eyes until it passes. When I can think clearly again, I open my eyes and I believe him when he says he's going to make me forget. I don't want that to happen.

"Which one are you?" I say, hoping to keep him talking so that he's not biting my neck or making me forget. "If you're going to wipe my memory, at least tell me now."

"Curiosity killed the cat," he says and smiles, then runs his fingers along my chin, stroking my skin. "But I'm Michel, the former priest, the once-Bishop of Carcassonne, at least for a few days before it was taken from me by death."

He pronounces it Mee-*shell*, not *Mi*-kul like Americans do. When I hear that he was the priest, I can't help but raise my eyebrows.

"Oh, you're surprised that I was the priest? The chaste one? Well, my chastity was taken from me the day I became a vampire." He says it with such emotion that I know he's been hurt very deeply.

"Please don't make me forget," I whisper.

"I have no choice," he says and he truly looks like he feels regret, his brow furrowed. "You're very sweet, and very lovely and I admit it is tempting to induct you into our secret world. You're so tempting. You have such unique coloring. Fair hair like silk, and I love your lips," he says and runs his finger over my top lip now and I close my eyes for it's like something passes between us whenever he touches my skin – some kind of strange connection I've never felt before.

"I love your eyes," he continues. "Such a unique shade of hazel. So many flecks of different color – gold, green, brown, even violet. And your freckles," he says and smiles. "They make you look like..." He pauses. "*Vous avez l'air d'un brat.* You look like a brat. I love brats, Eve."

He pauses for a moment, watching me.

"But most of all, Eve, I love your dimples," he says and strokes my cheek. "You're not smiling now, but you did earlier and when I saw them, I had the most inexplicable desire to grab you and kiss them, dipping my tongue into each one."

When I open my eyes, he's no longer smiling. He looks at me for a moment as if deciding, blinking rapidly. Finally, he exhales, his eyes closed for a moment.

"I'll give you the Cliff Notes version," he says and plays with a lock of my hair, passing it under his nose and breathing in. "Long story short, identical twin brothers, both priests. When the Church turned against our family for tolerating Catharism, my brother Julien left the Church, forsaking his vows, remaining loyal to our father while I remained loyal to the Holy Father." He pauses for a moment, looking down as if remembering hurts.

As he tells this story, he pulls back from me and I can finally breathe almost normally.

"Julien wrote the manuscript," he says and then looks in my eyes. "He's always been far too open about everything, impetuous, indiscreet. On the other hand, I'm a paragon of reticence and discretion. Big fight ensued, a house divided, et cetera, et cetera. Very boring."

I pull away just a bit as well and I can see the manuscript out of the corner of my eye. I briefly consider grabbing it and running, but one thing I do know about vampires is that they're preternaturally fast. So am I and I wonder if I could beat him in a race to the front entry...

"I joined the crusade and my brother fought against it," he says, staring at the wall thoughtfully, running a finger along the grain in the wood panel. "Then one week, when we were winning, and I had just taken over the Bishophood of Carcassonne, a monster claimed us both, turning us into vampires and we've been fighting each other ever since, still on opposite sides of the cause. We may be identical in looks, but not in character or temperament. He's adapted to this existence. He wants to keep being a vampire." He turns to me, his eyes dark. "I'm the one trying to kill us all off."

I swear I can see pain in his eyes even now, after eight centuries.

"You want to kill off all vampires?"

"Every single one of us."

"Then you're on my side," I say and shake my head. "We should fight together. Don't make me forget."

"I'm on no one's side but God's," he says and looks away again. "If I do this, perhaps I'll get back my immortal soul and then I can die in peace."

He wants to die...

"I want to take up my mother's fight," I say. "Please let me remember. You have the manuscript. I want you to succeed."

He shakes his head quickly. "Pleading won't work on me, Eve. I'm committed to my path and it doesn't involve pretty pre-med students, however much I'd love to corrupt you."

He presses against me and if I wanted to run, I should have done it while he was still a few inches away. As soon as I feel his body against mine I lose all strength to resist. When he touches my cheek again, my eyes close briefly from this rush of euphoria and every sensible thought flees.

"So lovely," he says, his voice a whisper. "And since you're going to forget this, perhaps just one kiss. You're so like Sleeping Beauty in your innocence. I'd love to awaken you."

"Don't," I say, struggling to emerge from the drugged-like state he's put me in.

"You won't remember me," he says and strokes my cheek, "but you'll remember my kiss. I can't erase physical memories – just the knowledge of how they came about so this kiss will play in your dreams, in your fantasies. Every human you kiss from now on will always seem somehow inadequate. You'll always wish you could meet someone who would kiss you like this, but you won't, will you?"

And then he takes my face in his hands and his lips press against mine. They're cool and pleasant and even though I intend to fight him and try to pull away, I can't. In a moment, his lips warm against mine, and his breathing becomes more intense, one hand dropping to my shoulder, then down to my hip, pulling me against his body. His lips part and mine do as well without me even being aware of it. His tongue touches mine, cool and wet, and a jolt of desire rushes through my body.

Then, something bizarre happens. It's as if the wall between us – the wall that separates two people – disappears. I feel his senses, the press of my lips against his, the scent of my hair in his nose, the pounding of my heart in his ears, the warmth of my body against his coldness, the soft mounds of my breasts against his chest. I feel myself as he feels me and his desire for me is so much more intense than anything I've ever felt before.

On top of it all, I feel his bloodlust – his desire for my blood and it almost chokes me with its intensity. My knees weaken, my legs like jelly.

He breaks the kiss, our lips parting, and I'm panting, my heart racing. He smiles as if he enjoys how much he's affected me.

"Now, *cheri*," he says, and takes my face firmly in his hands, his voice husky. "It's time to forget." He stares into my eyes. "You're going to leave the building and once you step outside, you'll look around and wonder why you're here. Then you'll remember that the idiot who told you he'd meet you failed to show up."

He pauses, shaking his head as if he regrets this.

"You'll go home and delete my email. Then you'll forget the email and my name. You'll forget you ever saw the manuscript and you'll rip up and burn any other documents you still have that mention it or me or my brother."

Please," I think. "*Don't make me forget…*"

"You'll decide to continue your studies in music instead of medicine and put all your mother's files into storage and forget where you stored them. Soon, you'll forget about vampires entirely. If you ever see me again, you won't think twice about me and move on as if I'm invisible."

I'm leaning against the wall, him pressed up against me, and I'm listening to him but nothing happens.

"Do you understand, Eve?"

I try to brand his name and face on my memory, the kiss, trying to remember the first lines of the story – the image of the full moon stained red from the smoke, the crusades splitting up the brothers, and a vampire taking their lives. Perhaps I could go to the language lab and use a computer, send myself an email describing all this before the memory wipe takes effect…

"I said, do you understand?"

I struggle to speak, barely able to even whisper.

"Don't do this, Michel."

He frowns and adjusts his hand on my face.

"Forget me, Eve. Forget the manuscript, forget my name and face. Forget that vampires exist. Do you understand?"

"I don't want to forget." I say, my voice breaking. I take hold of his hands, trying to pry them away. "This is my fight as well. Your brother gave that manuscript to my mother for a reason. I don't want to forget this. I want retribution for her killer."

"This is very strange." He steps back and releases me, rubbing his forehead as if he's confused. "I can affect your emotions but I can't compel you."

He stands for a moment and examines me, his hands on his hips. Then, he opens the door.

"Go out of the building. Perhaps it will take effect then."

I shake my head. "I won't leave if it means I'll forget."

"Eve," he says, and I can hear the frustration in his voice. "You have to forget. You don't want the life you think you're committing to. It killed your mother. It's killed everyone like you. Now go. If I must carry you out and throw you onto the street myself, I will."

I cross my arms. "Fine."

"You are a brat. Perhaps I should spank you before I take you outside."

"I'll fight you," I say, standing firm.

"Don't tempt me."

He doesn't smile. Instead, he grabs my coat and backpack and takes my hand, pulling me along with him out of the office, down the hall to the stairs. He doesn't even look at me while we descend as if he's angry.

Then he drags me to the front door of the building. Outside, the street is deserted and he opens the door, throwing my coat and backpack on the landing and pushes me down the steps. I make it down the first two and despite the fact I've taken years of dance and martial arts and should have better balance, I trip and fall on the last step, going down on my hands and knees, scraping my palms on the rough cement.

"Shit!" I struggle to stand, looking at my injured hands. They're scuffed and scraped. Thin lines of blood seep out of the deeper cuts. I cradle them against my body, breathing in deeply from the pain. There's just been so much emotional shit happen to me tonight, I can't fight tears and once more, my eyes brim.

I turn around and face the door, staring through it but see only darkness. I hold up my palms to show him, because I'm sure he's standing there in the shadows of the entry watching to see if I do forget him. Well. Sorry, you prick. I remember you.

"You are a bastard," I say, hoping to hurt him. I wipe my eyes on the backs of my hands and bend down to pick up my coat, shrugging it on with difficulty because of my injuries, then I use my thumb to hook the strap of my backpack because I can't bend my hands.

I'm miserable as I walk down the street to the bus stop, wondering when I'll start forgetting, vowing to start my own journal online just in case he comes after me one day and makes me forget. I want a record of everything. My mother kept meticulous notes, and I realize now how important it would be to have a journal and to update it regularly.

While I'm struggling to regain control over my emotions, he walks up wearing a long black coat that resembles a cassock, a messenger bag over his shoulder.

"Sorry to have to tell you this," I say. "But your little trick with the Vulcan mind meld didn't work. I remember everything."

"No, it's me who's sorry." He takes my hands and examines them, clucking his tongue in disapproval. He looks in my eyes. "What kind of a prick would do this to you?"

He bends his head to my palm and then he licks the cuts. I gasp and try to pull away, but I can't. He's so strong, his grip like iron. There's a brief bright sting from the wetness, but then his tongue soothes it and the pain is almost gone. He moves to the other palm and repeats this, his tongue following the cuts, dipping between my fingers. I'm horrified that a vampire is licking my cuts, tasting my blood. Will he now go all batshit and start biting my neck?

When he finally lifts his head, his face has changed. His eyes have become red rimmed, bloodshot, his pupils huge, his teeth sharp and long, his lips stained with my blood.

"Oh, Eve, now look what you've made me do..."

～

CHAPTER 3

"Is it better to out-monster the monster or be quietly devoured?"
Nietzsche

"Come."
He takes my arm, pulling me away from the bus stop. When I try to fight back, he stops, his perfectly-square jaw tensing.
"What are you doing?" I say, standing my ground.
"I'm not letting you go home on the bus with injured hands." Then he takes my wrist and for some reason my ability to resist flags and he leads me towards a darkened parking lot, my body compliant even if my mind still rebels.
Oh, *hell*. Is he taking me there so he can finish what he started? Fear surges through me, choking me.
"Don't be afraid," he says and stops again. "I don't kill humans anymore. I kill vampires."
He seems calmer, his eyes no longer red, his teeth have receded in length and even in the low light, I can see that his pupils are now almost normal.
"Then how do you survive?"
"We don't have to kill humans to survive. Merely drink human

blood. There are always donors and pets, and when I kill a vampire and drink his or her blood, it is like feeding off ten humans."

"You drink vampire blood? You have human pets?"

"No, I don't have pets. I detest the very idea. I subsist off donor blood. But some people like being our pets, Eve."

"I don't believe that," I say, but the thought of being his pet appeals to me in some way I can't explain.

He turns and smiles at me. "Even you might enjoy it..."

My cheeks burn. How did he do that? "So you can read my mind on top of everything else?"

He doesn't answer as we walk towards a lone car parked near the rear door to the linguistics building. It's a Mercedes hybrid, sleek and jet-black. He opens the door.

"In you go."

I sit inside and he has the nerve to fasten my seatbelt, apparently enjoying the opportunity to get all cozy with me, then he takes my hands again and examines them as if checking to see how they are.

I can't help but notice how attractive he is.

Then he makes a funny noise in his throat, like exasperation or a grunt of enjoyment, I can't tell which. He leans close to me, smirking, his face just a few inches from mine, and adjusts the strap across my chest.

"Eve, I'm flattered you're attracted to me, but really, I fastened your seatbelt because your hands aren't very useful right now."

Of course.

I feel another blush rising. How does he do that? I glance at my hands and he's touching my wrist. It must be skin on skin contact so I quickly pull my hand away. He remains there, leaning over my seat, his gaze moving over my face.

"You have to learn to build up mental walls."

He stands back up and closes the door. When he gets in on the driver's side, I turn to him.

"How do I do that? Build up mental walls?"

"Oh, no," he says and shakes his head. "If you think I'm going to tell you, you're extremely naïve."

So he wants to be able to invade my mind? "It's not fair. No one should be able to do that."

"Life's not fair, Eve. I'm proof of that. Besides drinking blood, it's our ability to affect your minds and read your memories that vampires crave. It keeps us from losing our humanity."

I look at him closely. "You really resent being made a vampire."

"Duh," he says and starts the car. For a moment, I'm at a loss. Duh? Is that some archaic French curse?

"Did you just say 'duh'?"

He smiles and looks at me with that grin on his face.

"I may be eight hundred years old but I do try to keep up with the times."

"Well, let me enlighten you, Michel," I say, pronouncing his name in an exaggerated manner – Mee shell. "Duh is so nineties."

"Oh, Eve, Eve, *Eve*." He smiles as he shifts into gear. "I can see we're going to have a lot of fun, you and I. But let me get one thing perfectly straight. If I'm going to do this – if I'm going to let you in – you have to learn obedience."

Obedience? As in obey him? "What do you mean, let me in?"

"If I'm going to train you as my..." he pauses. "As my Adept, you have to learn to obey."

I'm a modern woman. I'm a daughter of several generations of feminists. I must be my own woman but with vampires, it's impossible to avoid. Unless you're like me and immune to compulsion.

"Train me? What do you mean, obey?"

He makes a funny throat noise again.

We drive on for a moment in silence. "Obey as in you take orders from me." He looks over at me once we're on the road and up to speed. "You're a hunter, you know, despite the pretty face. I just need to bring out those gifts that are hidden away."

"What gifts?"

He shifts down as we come to a light.

"You never noticed how fast you can run? How well you can see at night? Those are all traits of hunters. But you," he says and shakes his head. "You're special. You're what we call Adept. This ability to connect minds? That's unique."

"I never knew about the mind thing," I say, frowning. "How come I never felt it before?"

"This connection is unique between vampires and Adepts. It's touch telepathy. All vampires have it, but it's one way. We use it to read our prey's minds, to control your brain chemicals, make you struggle less when we feed. We use it to make you obey and forget things – or at least, most of you. For some reason, you're immune to compulsion and having your memory erased."

"My mother never told me about any psychic abilities."

"She didn't want this life for you," he says as we drive off once the light changes. "She and your father wanted you in the arts. Dance or music."

"You knew my mother?"

"Only through Julien." We drive on in silence for a moment, and he's frowning as if in thought. Finally, he turns to me.

"Eve, Adepts were meant to be trained from an early age. Your parents wanted to train you as a musician or dancer instead, which I'm sure violated the terms of their contract."

"Contract?"

He turns and glances at me, frowning.

"One thing at a time. Let's get you home and get your hands fixed. Now, please, no more questions. I have to think things through."

I want to ask what he means about my parent's contract and what things he has to think through but I keep quiet, watching the scenery pass by. I do see well at night and when I glance at him in the darkened car interior, I can see him as if it was the middle of a cloudy day, his skin gray like in a black and white image. I was always a fast runner but my parents said no to track because I had to dance and practice piano instead. They finally took me out of regular school in fourth grade and homeschooled me, giving me dance and music lessons and hiring private tutors.

We drive up to my apartment building. "How did you know where I live?"

He looks at me and taps his temple.

"Think of using telepathy as a short-cut. We don't always have to use words. Neurons and neurochemicals are so much faster. And, of course, if you were my blood slave, we could even communicate at a distance."

Blood slave? Oh, that doesn't sound good.

"What's a blood slave? Do you mean telepathy at a distance?"

"Yes," he says. "There'd be no need to touch. Blood slaves are addicted to vampire blood. Vampire blood causes high levels of neurotransmitters to circulate in your brain and gives a heroin-like high. People try to steal it, sell it on the black market because of its drug-like effects and temporary healing properties. If you drink too much, you get addicted, like any other drug. Whatever you do, don't ever let a vampire feed you his blood in large quantity." Then he turns to me and smiles that lopsided smile. "Unless the idea of being a slave appeals to you, that is… And, if I read you correctly, it does."

I make a face at him and turn away. He can touch me and find out things? Personal things, private things? And until I figure out how to block him, he can do it at will. All he has to do is touch me skin on skin.

He opens my door after we park on the street and stands too close to me, like he enjoys making me feel uncomfortable. I sidle by him and start up the stairs to my building, opening the door. He follows me in and I stop and frown.

"How can you come in? I haven't invited you."

"I've been in Boston for a long time, Eve. I've been invited in this building before."

He follows me up the stairs to the third floor where my apartment is but I stop at the door, my key in hand.

"Here," he says and reaches for my keys. "Let me."

"I don't think so," I say. "This is where you leave."

"I don't think so," he says.

"You're not coming into my apartment."

"I am. Let's go, Eve. I need to fix your palms and we need to talk."

I stand my ground. He's not coming in. "I can fix my own palms, thanks. You can send me an email and tell me whatever it is you think I need to know. I'm not letting you into my apartment because then you'll be able to enter any time you want."

"Eve, we need to talk. Open the door. I'm coming in."

"You have no right to order me around."

"I'm coming in."

"Why are you so domineering?"

"Why are you so emotional?" he says and steps closer to me, touching my cheek. Instantly, I calm down from whatever brain chemicals he's making me release. "Don't get me wrong," he says softly. "I love that in you. It makes it so easy for me to read you without even having to touch you. Of course, I do so like to touch you." He smiles.

"If I'm emotional, it's because this matters."

"I know," he says all full of sympathy, tilting his head in that characteristic way. "I don't trust people who control their emotions too well. You can't lie and I value that. You might as well just stop lying to me and then this will all be so much easier. Now, open the door. Invite me in."

"I don't want you to come in."

"I know you don't, Eve," he says softly. "All of this must be very upsetting to you. I didn't want this either. I tried to erase your memories so you could go on and just live your life without becoming involved in our world. But now that you are involved, you have to trust me."

"I can't just trust you," I say, frustrated. "Trust is built and based on evidence of trustworthiness."

"You really have no choice. Either you let yourself trust me, surrender to it, or you fight me every step of the way. And believe me, this is a fight you will not win."

"Surrender to it?" I say, barely able to keep my voice under control. "You mean surrender to you. I've never been one to just give over to anything."

"I can sense that," he says and sighs. "It will just make things more difficult and painful. So much easier for us both if you just comply."

We stand there at an impasse.

"I'm not letting you in willingly."

"So be it," he says and grabs my wrist. "I'm committed to my cause, Eve. Nothing – no paltry resistance on the part of a pretty Adept is going to sway me from it. I'll do whatever I have to – whatever it takes – even if I hate myself for it. Even if you hate me for it. Now open the door and let me in. I can't compel you but I can hurt you."

I close my eyes as pain burns through me like a knife searing in my gut. I gasp at its intensity and bend over at the waist. It's so sharp it brings tears to my eyes. Then it's gone as quickly as it starts.

"You...*monster*..."

"Yes, I am a monster," he says and shakes me, his expression dark. "Don't forget it." After a moment, his face softens. "Eve, I don't want to hurt you," he says, his voice quiet. "Quite the opposite. But you must know with complete certainty that I will do anything and everything to succeed, including hurting you if it's the only way to get compliance."

I turn away from him, my face all hot from the pain, my eyes all teared-up for the umpteenth time this evening. I open the door and step inside but I don't invite him in.

He just stands there for a moment, waiting. Then he closes his eyes and I swear I can see him fuming.

"Don't make me force you. I'm very old and very powerful and very angry right now."

I give in. "Please, come in."

I hear his sigh of relief and then he steps over the threshold.

"You live alone?" he asks, glancing around.

I want to say that I have a boyfriend living with me who plays linebacker on the football team, or a big Rottweiler, but he'll know both are a lie. He's touched me quite a bit tonight and probably already knows I'm a single cat lady in waiting.

"Yes. I have two cats, but otherwise I live by myself. I also have two real Samurai swords on the wall in my bedroom."

Damn. I didn't really say that, did I?

He smiles and then laughs out loud, his too-blue eyes filled with amusement. My face burns and so I go to my closet and remove my coat and hang it up, depositing my umbrella inside.

He comes over to me and takes my hands in his. I try to avoid him, but he's far too strong. He turns my palms face up and inspects each palm.

"They're already healing," he says. "It's that good old Adamantine magic we have in our saliva and all bodily fluids."

"Adamantine?"

"An undying eternal property. The principle that keeps us immortal. Your mother should have something about it in her files."

"So you really didn't need to come in and fix my palms."

"No," he says lightly. "I lied. People who can't lie aren't very good at detecting deception. They're two sides of the same coin. But we do need to talk."

"Make yourself at home." I wave to the apartment and exhale with frustration. "Since you can now, whenever you want, no matter what I want."

"Thank you."

He's so damn pleased with himself, like he's just won an important battle. He starts walking around my tiny flat, inspecting things like he's searching for something. At my old upright piano against the wall, he sorts through my sheet music, selecting Chopin's Ballade No. 1, tilting his head to one side. I don't play it very well because it's so damn hard.

"You were a prodigy."

"Supposedly, but you take any three-year-old and drill them like they're an army recruit and make it so that every ounce of love they get is premised on performance and you'll produce a little piano playing machine, too."

"*Dieu,*" he says and glances at me. "God, you sound bitter. I'd think you'd be pleased that your parents invested so much time honing your talent."

I shrug. I guess I am bitter. All that practice and performance for nothing. All those years wasted taking ballet and music when I could have just been a normal kid and had normal experiences.

"I studied for eight years. Besides dance, practicing piano was my whole life. I used to envy other kids who weren't forced to play or perform. After a certain age, I was pulled out of school and tutored because my father wanted me to be a professional like him and my mother wanted me to be a dancer the way she always dreamed of being."

"Yes, parents can be such beasts at times," he says. "I hope you'll play for me one day." He looks up from the keys and smiles at me, just a quick smile. "Music is one of my great passions."

The way he says it – passions – makes me feel suddenly uncomfortable for I can't help but think of him being passionate. He looks like someone who could get all passionate – like an obsessive musician or artist – and that's dangerous ground for me.

"Is playing part of my job description?" I say, trying to be a smartass.

"No, of course not. Music is my greatest love. It makes existence bearable."

His words have a strange effect on me. Music makes his existence bearable? I'm a bit unnerved by that and I don't know what to say for a moment.

"I'm out of practice. I've been pretty busy with finals and haven't played for quite a while."

He frowns. "You shouldn't let your skills rust, Eve. When you have a beautiful gem, you should make sure to keep it polished. Such a waste otherwise. And so sad that all you have is this old piece of junk on which to play."

"It's all that could fit in my apartment." I turn away and make a face, unsure how to respond. Is he chastising me for not playing enough? Where does he get off?

He stands in the middle of my piles of paper from my mother's files, which are spread out on the hardwood floor.

"You need a filing cabinet."

I start picking up the piles, placing them on my desk at the side of the room.

"They're my mother's files. The university just released them from the archives."

When I'm done, I sit on the couch while he wanders around my apartment, my knees weak from everything that's happened since this afternoon.

He moves to my desk eyeing the pile of books and papers, pushing them around, stooping to my wastebasket – the letter ... I've been writing a letter to include in a birthday card to my best friend Cecile, who's off in Philadelphia to do her MD. I've handwritten them and crunched up one after another draft, unhappy with the results.

"Those are my private things," I say, alarmed.

"I know."

"Leave them alone." I try to sound forceful, which is ridiculous, given who and what he is, but I don't want him to read anything too personal. He rustles through the letters in my wastebasket and pulls out the one on top.

"Don't," I say, dreading the thought that he'll read my uncensored remarks. "That's private."

"Dear sweet Eve," he says with his soft almost-imperceptible French accent, "I've already been in your mind. This," he says and holds up the letter, "this is nothing in comparison."

He reads it, and I close my eyes, grimacing in embarrassment at what I've written. I go to him and snatch it out of his hands and go back to the couch, reading it over to see which version he's read.

Dear Ceci,

Happy Birthday, girl! I miss you so much and wish you were here or I was there so we could go out and dress all up and pretend we're the geek versions of Carrie and Charlotte and drink those crazy cocktails you love so much!

What's new with me? I finally have my mother's research – after three years of fighting. Looks like some interesting stuff in her archives. Should keep me busy all summer.

In answer to your question, I really hate blind dates, so thanks but no thanks. You know I have a weakness for men in uniforms but I'm afraid of flying so dating an airline pilot? Not such a good idea ...

Don't worry about me living by myself now that you're in Philly. I really don't mind being alone. Much. Not really much at all. Hardly. Barely lonely. Really... I'm sleeping well enough. Besides, it's time for nightmares to stop. I'm a big girl now so no more being afraid of the dark. After I check all the closets at night and triple lock the door and windows, I'm fine... Honest, I will get rid of my old Barney doll – some year! He's twenty now and time for the back of my closet. Where he can protect me from the monsters...

Yes, I have been seeing my counselor about the cutting. She says I have to keep my mind busy so hopefully I'll find something in my mother's files to occupy my summer. It's just that I'm so bored sometimes I cut myself just to know that I'm alive. She says the cutting stops the memories. She wants to do this whole regression stuff but it scares me. Some things are better left forgotten.

Really, Ceci. Don't worry. I know you're afraid I'll end up a crazy cat lady dying alone in my apartment, no one noticing until the meowing of my cats drives the neighbors crazy and the police break down the door to find my rotting bloated corpse . . . But I'm sure things will eventually get better for me. I'm so happy the university finally released mom's files. It makes me feel closer to her to carry on her work.

Happy twenty-second birthday and I will come to Philly and see you soon,
Love, Eve

Oh, damn.

Then, I feel him on the couch next to me, and I try to cover my face, but he takes one arm and pushes up my sleeve. He sees the scars running up the inside of my forearm – some old, silvery ghosts of past pain, some new and still angry and red, barely scabbed over. Razor blades are my weapon of choice.

I freeze, my body tensing. He runs his fingers over the scars.

"I didn't see these," he says quietly and looks in my eyes. "Eve..."

He takes the letter from me and pushes me down on the couch, lying on top of me. He holds the letter in one hand, and with the other, he turns my chin so I have to watch him reading it, his blue eyes so intense.

After reading for a moment, he stops and shakes his head.

"You're so bored sometimes you cut yourself just to know that you're alive?"

I close my eyes, but he shakes my chin and I open them again, my vision suddenly blurry. And then he leans down and kisses me. Softly, the kiss chaste, and I feel him trying to enter my mind, as if he's hoping to find out why I'm a cutter but there's nothing to find except a big black hole of fear. When he pulls away, he examines my face, touches my cheek with a finger, running the tip through my tears once more, licking his finger and closing his eyes.

"I can't see why you need pain when I read you," he says. "It must be very deep."

I turn my face away. I don't know why I need the pain. It must be because of my mother.

Finally, he gets up and takes the letter back to my desk, smoothing it out, leaving it on top of the pile rather than in my wastebasket. I sit up and feel as if I need a drink of something strong for his touch and the feel of his body lying on top of me have made me uncomfortably aroused. He's still standing there, staring at my things and I'm sitting here, wondering what it would be like to have sex with a vampire.

There – I'm now officially a traitor and all it took was one meeting.

"Your flat is very small."

"I'm a student," I say defensively.

He ambles over to my bedroom door, which is ajar, and looks through the crack. I hear him inhale as if he's trying to smell my bedroom, which I find just a bit creepy…

Hey—quit looking at my private life. Which is, of course, a ridiculous thing to think. Who knows what secrets he's mined from my memories while touching me?

After returning to the living room, he sits on the chair across from me, crossing his legs and stretching out his arms on the back.

"What's your scent?"

Huh? None of your business. He asks such personal questions and once again, I feel that he's intruding.

"Why do you ask?"

"I like it."

"It's 'Noir' by this little French perfumer I visited on a field trip to Paris."

He smiles. "I like the note of citrus in it. And jasmine I think. Very nice."

"Are we going to talk about my perfume and piano practice habits?"

He ignores my attempt to be rude and leans forward, his face earnest now.

"There's a whole process to you becoming my Adept, Eve, and working for the Council. You have to pass a few tests, interviews, that sort of thing."

His Adept?

"Is there some kind of vampire hunter job?"

"Yes. I can set the process in motion," he says and nods, looking at me with that intense gaze. "Plead your case. You were supposed to have been better-trained by now, but obviously, things didn't go as planned with your family. Your foster parents started training you in martial arts and science but you're not ready. I can train you. Are you willing to undergo the tests?"

"Will it mean I can take over my mother's work?"

He nods, his head tilted to the side.

"What about the manuscript? Are you going to let me read it?"

He sighs. "What is it about the manuscript that intrigues you so much?"

"Your brother gave it to my mother for a reason. I have to know why. Maybe it has something to do with her death."

He lifts the messenger bag from the floor and opens it, withdrawing the manuscript.

"You really want to read it?" he says, taking it out of the envelope and laying it on my coffee table. "It's very explicit. Too explicit and personal."

I nod, unable to get Sir Julien's words out of my head from even the short passage I did read.

"Is the manuscript that violent?" I frown. "I know all about violence." I say quietly. "And pain."

"Yes, I think you do. But this," he says and holds the manuscript up. "This is both very violent and very personal," he says quietly. "And sexual but not in a good way." He looks away from me. "You can understand why I don't want it translated."

I squirm a bit. Now I'm dying to read the manuscript.

"It's that bad?"

"I'd burn it now, happily, if I wasn't curious myself. I have to read it at least once before I do."

"You're going to burn it? But you can't! It's not yours to burn. Your brother gave it to my mother and now it's mine."

"Eve," he says and his voice is frustrated. "This documents my debasement and destruction. It's nothing more than a chronicle of my pain and despair. I consider it part of the world of vampires and Ancients and want it and them destroyed."

Ancients?

I don't say anything, for I don't want to appear ignorant. I'll have to read more in my mother's files to find out what that means.

His debasement and despair? Now I'm desperate to read that manuscript. The thought of him being debased, his chastity taken from him as he described it is horrifying. He's so beautiful.

"But just to build trust between us, Eve, to lay a foundation, I will read you some of it. Not tonight, and not the parts about myself, for they would only pollute your memories, but those Julien wrote about his own experience. He wanted those to be known – he wants to be known. So be it."

My jaw drops at this offer. "When?"

"Oh, Eve," he says and shakes his head. "So eager to read about our fall? To know our pain?"

"It's about vampires," I say, but I know, deep down inside, that it's more than just curiosity about vampires. "My mother's life was dedicated to killing you off. I want to know why your brother gave it to her."

"Who can understand Julien's motives?" he says and packages the manuscript up. Then he stands. "I'll read it to you another night. Now, I have to go. I'll arrange the whole interview process to test you and see if you can be an Adept for the Council. I'll send you an email or call you with the details."

He takes one last look around my apartment and then at me, his head tilting to the side.

"You won't be safe any longer, now that you've re-emerged. I'll be putting a security detail on you 24/7 but they should be invisible to you. You may not be cut out for this work. These trials will let us know either way."

Then he's gone and I'm alone in my apartment, but the world has changed and I wonder what I've gotten myself into.

CHAPTER 4

"WHETHER WE FALL BY AMBITION, blood or lust, like diamonds, we are cut by our own dust."

Webster

Several days later and an hour after dusk, I get out of a cab half a block down the street from the address Michel included in his email with details on my first interview. I glance around but so far since that first night, I haven't been able to spot the security detail Michel claimed he'd put in place, but it makes me feel strangely safer knowing people are watching me.

I spent the last few days in the library and at home going through my mother's files, box by box. The university released almost twenty cardboard file boxes and they're piled up in a corner of my tiny flat. I'm searching through each one methodically, indexing them in an Excel file so I can keep track of everything. So far, I've only gone through five. These boxes are mostly histories and articles on the vampire species. There's lots to read and absorb, and slowly, a picture is emerging in my mind about vampires – their secret world that most people have no idea exists. But with another fifteen boxes to get through, I know there's so much more to learn.

I have an hour to kill before the interview and stop at a little diner on the way to grab something to eat. It's one of those fifties replicas, with posters of James Dean on the wall and faux leather seats. There's even old tableside jukeboxes, with music from the fifties and sixties.

I sit at an empty booth and examine the menu – old favorites. Cheeseburgers, fries, hot turkey sandwiches, meatloaf, liver and onions. Not much for a vegetarian. There's an all-day breakfast so I order a veggie omelet and some tea.

I'm sitting deciding what to play when someone stands beside my booth. I startle out of my reverie of music choices and gasp. It's Michel – except it's not Michel unless he's just had his hair cut and has a scar that's very rapidly healed, for one follows the side of his head next to his hairline from his brow to below his ear. He looks very dashing, dressed in a black leather trench, a black fedora and black and white patterned scarf around his neck. Underneath, he's wearing a black sweater and faded jeans, big black military boots of some kind. He smiles at me.

"Hello."

I put my hand over my eyes for a moment. When my heart's slowed just a bit, I look up at him.

"You must be Julien."

"The very one. Let the bells ring out and the banners fly. Feast your eyes on me." He grins that characteristic de Cernay grin and holds his hand out to shake.

I glance at his hand. It's bare and I don't want to shake, but I do to be polite and of course, he leans down and kisses my knuckles. "Eve," he says.

"Julien."

If he's reading me, I don't feel it. I quickly end the shake.

"I hear you found my manuscript," he says. "Quite the read."

"I don't have the manuscript, if that's why you're here. Michel took it from me."

He frowns and shakes his head, then sits down across from me.

"Michel is such a prude to deny you some good smut."

"It's smut?"

"Just kidding. To him it would be." He leans over. "He's got a terrible soft spot for you, Eve. He wouldn't want you to think less of him." Julien shakes his head, still grinning. "You know – devout priest debauched, turned into a vampire's plaything. Only a prude would deny the reader the pleasure of reading it and I thought he got rid of all his prudery long ago."

"He doesn't even know me."

"He doesn't even know you? Are you kidding? He's known you since you were ten and your mother returned to Boston."

"He never said anything. He said he didn't really know my mother."

"Well," Julien says, pursing his lips, his hands clasped on the table top. "Know could mean many things." He grins suggestively at me.

"I thought you were the one who knew her."

He nods. "You know, you were supposed to be for me."

"What do you mean?"

"Your mother – she wanted me to have you as my Adept." His expression is serious now. "She trusted me to train you. She just wanted you to have a choice and decide yourself whether to join the Council once you were eighteen rather than being forced into this life. She was going to have me train you in martial arts and forensics so you could be a Blood Witness – if you wanted. Then, she was murdered and everything came crashing down."

"Blood Witness?"

"You know – like a human psychic sleuth. You have the ability to connect with vampires telepathically and read memory traces in the objects killers touch. The SCU will use you to police the Treaty, investigate cases. Didn't Michel explain? Didn't he show you?"

My face heats at the memory of just how he showed me.

"Oh," he says, smiling slowly. "I see he did show you. Oh, Michel, Michel..." He shakes his head, still grinning suggestively. "That surprises me. But a Blood Witness?" he says and settles back. "It's like any other crime scene investigator, except your job will be to touch vampires who are suspected of killing a human outside of the treaty to see their last kills. You can see if they were sanctioned or not. Gather evidence to use against them and read violent memory traces in physical objects they touch."

"I can do that?"

"Yes, but you've been kept out of this world and are untrained. Your skills have to be developed. Training should have started when you went through puberty, but we lost you..."

"You said the SCU. What is it?"

"The SCU is Special Cases Unit of the Council of Clairveaux. It's a special police unit that investigates vampire killings to ensure they are sanctioned. Blood Witnesses work with ordinary police investigators to gather evidence. A Blood Witness's testimony is used as evidence in a trial. You can also use telepathy to search for evidence at crime scenes, but I suppose if you work out, Michel will be explaining it all."

"Are there others like me?"

"Exactly like you? Not very many, no. There are some humans with touch telepathy but not with your special gifts. You're like gold."

"Special gifts?"

"Now that would be giving too much away. Besides, that will be determined tonight at the interview."

I frown at his unwillingness to tell me more. "My mother never said anything to me about you."

He shrugs one shoulder. "She was waiting until you were older. Didn't want to start you too young. Wanted to give you a chance to shine in the arts."

"You gave her the manuscript so she could understand you and Michel."

He nods and his gaze moves over my face. "Michel must love torturing himself," he says. "To take you on."

"Why?"

"Because you look a lot like her."

"Who?"

"Oh, that's right. You haven't read about her. Danielle." He gives a low whistle. "You look a lot like her. No wonder my brother's smitten."

"I don't know about that," I say and avert my eyes, my cheeks hot. "We just met."

"Oh, yes you do know about it. Just remember, he's still a priest in his mind, if not in office. He has ethics so despite how attracted he is to you, he won't act on them. I on the other hand, have only appetites."

His admission makes me strangely warm. He has appetites. Michel has ethics. But for someone with such ethics, Michel sure seemed ready to betray them, kissing me twice. Making me feel his desire when he did. The two are so different – like night and day.

Julien motions to the waitress, who comes by and takes his order for a double chocolate milkshake.

He stands after she leaves, and takes off his hat and coat. In the very short moment while he's busy hanging it on the coat hook, I examine his body. He's well-built although not overly buff like a bodybuilder, but there's a sense of strength and hardness to his body beneath his clothes. Narrow hips and tight ass fitting very nicely in his low slung faded jeans and thick black belt. Wider shoulders almost straining at his black t-shirt. He sits down again. From beneath the scarf he keeps on hangs a wooden crucifix on a long black leather rope.

"God, I hated the fifties," he says and glances around. "Everyone was so uptight. There was the whole nuclear holocaust thing starting. McCarthyism took over, making everyone paranoid. I'm more of a sixties and seventies man myself. You know – hippies, pot, free love. But then again, I did love the nineties – the seventeen-nineties, that is. Mozart, Beethoven. Hell, I loved the whole eighteenth century, for that matter. The Age of Enlightenment. Vienna. Paris. Rome. Florence. The French Revolution was great for vampires."

I shake my head and just stare at him in amazement. "It must be wonderful to live so long, see so much."

He tilts his head to one side for a moment, looking at me. "There are some perks to being damned."

"Damned?"

"You know. Undead. Fallen. Vampire…"

"Don't tell me you ascribe to the cursed by God thing?"

"Oh, we're cursed all right," he says. "And who else but God would do it?"

I shake my head. "I'm an atheist. I don't believe in curses." The waitress brings my tea and I stir in some sugar.

"Ah but God believes in you, Eve, no matter what you believe."

"You were a priest as well?"

He leans back, clasping his hands, his fingers entwined. "Yes. Until the Church went against my father."

"Michel said you left the Church?"

He nods and looks around as if he doesn't like this line of questioning.

"So, what are the other perks?" I ask, curious.

"Strength, I suppose. Senses are superior. Speed helps when someone's chasing you with a stake." He takes in a breath and leans forward, his grin starting. "Un-believable stamina, not to mention knowledge gleaned through hundreds of years of practice." He wags his eyebrows suggestively.

I feel my cheeks heat at that and glance away, unable to hide my own grin.

"God, you're sweet looking, Eve," he says. "And that blush." He mock-frowns and puts his hand over his heart as if in pain.

The waitress returns with our food and Julien takes a big sip of his shake.

"A vampire drinking a milkshake in a fifties diner," I say, while I cut up my omelet. "Who would have ever thought?"

"Come on, Eve. We're just humans who have a really hard time dying. We do everything the same as you. Eat, sleep. Fuck." He grins. "So," he says, leaning forward. "Tell me about what happened since I last saw you."

"We've met before?"

"Not formally. Your mother kept you away from me," he says, grinning, and I wonder if he takes anything seriously. "Didn't want to scare you, but I think you saw me once at your house when you got up late at night and I was walking to the bathroom. You screamed, if I recall, because you saw me in the dark. Your mother had to assure you that I wasn't a monster. Or," he says and makes a face, "at least, not one who was going to hurt you."

The waitress arrives to ask us how everything is and he thanks her, touching her hand, smiling like he's some kind of celebrity. She's all giggly and leaves, whispering to the other waitress when she goes behind the counter.

"You were saying?" I don't know why his paying attention to the waitress bothers me, but it does.

"Oh, yes," he says, turning back to me. "Your mother wanted to wait until you were a bit older before you met an actual vampire. But I was around, in the background, watching. I met with her quite a lot to discuss the Council. She was having a hard time deciding which side to take and I was trying to influence her as was Michel. Did she support the treaty? Did she support eradication of us all? It was difficult for her because she actually liked some of us."

"What do you support?"

"The Treaty, of course. Anything else would be suicide."

"Michel wants to eradicate all vampires."

"You don't have to tell me that," he says, and for once he's serious. "That's why we're not the best buds any longer. I happen to like existence." He takes a sip of his milkshake. "I like it a lot. Let me tell you something I've learned in the long years of my life. Existence is far preferable to death. Mortality sucks. Dying sucks."

"You say your 'life', but you're a vampire. You're dead."

"I'm not really dead," he says. "I'm undead. Undying. There's a difference."

"What do you know about my mother's death?"

He exhales heavily, as if he doesn't want to discuss it.

"Not much. She was working late at the office. You were reading in another room when she was attacked. You found her and remained with her for hours until a janitor found you with her body. You were in shock. They took you to the hospital and you were almost catatonic. Your father fell apart in the weeks that followed, and he stopped caring for you. You were supposed to go into a Council-sponsored foster family when your father cracked up and was put in the asylum but somehow, both you and your file were lost and that was it. We lost track of you. It's all there in the files at the SCU."

"What was in the manuscript that you wanted my mother to read? Was there some clue about vampires and how to destroy them all?"

"I don't know why your mother wanted it so badly. I think she wanted to understand what we faced when we became vampires. What it was like. She was surprised that not all of us were monsters."

"So it's not important to her research?"

"She seemed to think so – that there might be hints somewhere that she could use. I'm not up on the science side of things but I do know they were looking at gene therapy to alter vampire DNA. Also human. There's also lots of good info at the SCU, if you do become a Blood Witness and of course, your mother's files."

I finish my omelet and check my watch.

"Speaking of which, I have to go. I have to meet Michel at the SCU." I motion to the waitress for the check.

"Let me get this," Julien says. "I think I'll stay and listen to some early Motown."

"Thanks," I say and place a ten-dollar bill on the table. "But I'm able to pay for myself."

"Eve," he says and pushes the money away. "Really. I may not look it but I'm a viscount with a huge inheritance. Let me get this."

I relent and take the money back. "Very well."

He stands and watches while I get my things together then extends his hand once more. I take it and he leans down once more and kisses it.

"It was really nice to meet you, and see that you're doing well. Good luck tonight," he says. "I hope you won't need it."

I force a smile. I don't know if I'm doing well. I seem to have found myself right in the middle of a very dangerous turn of events. Finally, he lets go of my hand.

"Good night," I say.

When I close the door to the diner, he's still standing there, looking beautiful, watching me through the window.

~

45

CHAPTER 5

"Love is the only sane and satisfactory answer to the problem of human existence."

Eric Fromm

I open my umbrella against a sudden spring deluge. Darkness does nothing to improve the neighborhood's ambience and despite the security detail, I glance nervously behind me, still spooked by the darkness. Shadows fall long across the sidewalks and spill out from alleyways when I arrive at the Foster Building. I feel like prey aware of my vulnerability, but not knowing where the predator hides, in wait for a chance to pounce but I know it's there – somewhere.

I climb the steps to the old brownstone huddled between an empty lot and an abandoned brewery. There's no intercom. The door is unlocked and I enter and walk to the elevator to take it to the second floor. As the old doors close and the elevator jerks into service, I shake out my umbrella and wipe a few stray drops of rain from my cheeks. Whatever's waiting for me on the other side of the elevator doors, I hope I can handle it.

The elevator opens and admits me to a small hallway. There's a door across from me and I knock.

"Come," a voice says from the other side.

I enter and find myself in a dojo – a small room with mats on the floor used for martial arts training. At the front of the room, a man and woman sit and so I go to them, my backpack in one hand, my umbrella in the other. The man looks like some kind of cop with a shirt and tie and half-eye glasses and the woman is very hard looking, with short grey hair and tortoise shell glasses perched on the end of her nose.

"Hello. I'm Eve Hayden. I'm here for the interview."

Then motion out of the corner of my eye distracts me and I turn to see Michel, dressed in black SWAT-like uniform, short Wakizashi swords at the ready.

Holy hell. I wasn't expecting this.

I glance at the two people and see they're waiting, watching expectantly to see what I do. I glance around the dojo, and on a table at the side of the room are several wooden weapons.

"I hope you can fight," Michel says quietly. "If you can't, you're of no use to us."

He lunges at me, challenging me. What the hell? Does he expect me to fight him? With what? Wooden practice swords?

I hesitate for a second then drop my bag and umbrella, running away from Michel as he comes at me. I reach the table on which the wooden swords rest and grab them. I face him, and something strange happens to me. I can't understand it, but everything seems to slow down, like everyone but me is stuck in molasses. It's like I'm in a different time dimension from them and I can see Michel's intentions in the tiniest movements of his muscles, the smallest change in direction in his line of sight, and the way he tenses.

I throw myself at him, my wooden blades slamming him on the side of his head and he's like a statue. I dive and roll, then rebalance, my wooden swords poised. Time returns to normal and I watch him respond, stumbling and then righting himself.

"Commendable," he manages, raising his swords once more.

He challenges me and the time thing happens again. I lunge at him, aiming my swords at his to disarm him. His response is too slow and my blades strike a direct blow, knocking a sword out of his hand and it goes flying. Now he has only one sword.

I can fight.

I land, use my momentum to pivot, plant my feet, blades up and at the ready, and then I feint to the left. Michel responds but I jump at him from the right, knocking away his other sword and then, with my wooden swords crossed, I catch him against the neck before he can respond. The force of my weight knocks him backwards and he stumbles. Together, we fall back on the mat.

If my blades were real, he'd be without a throat. Only after we come to a stop with my wooden blades still at his neck does time return to normal for me. Michel raises his arm behind my back, but it's more of an embrace than a threat.

"Beautiful." There's real pleasure – and some admiration – in his blue eyes.

I'm lying on top of him, my face just inches away from his and he's so beautiful with those perfect blue eyes and dark lashes, the full lips, and I have the most irrational urge to just lean down and kiss him.

For a moment, I'm tempted and he looks in my eyes, lips parted as if waiting. I move closer, my heart racing, and Michel's eyes close, but then the man from the table pulls me off him and the moment passes. I adjust my clothes, which are all out of shape from the struggle. I'm barely out of breath.

"What do you think?" the man says, his hands on his hips as he examines me. "How'd she do?"

"Perfect," Michel says as he stands, and he sounds truly impressed.

"What the hell is going on?" I say, glancing between them. "I thought I was here for an interview."

"This was the first test," Michel says. "We had to see if you could fight and beat me. Beat a vampire."

I can beat a vampire… The thought does something strange to me, a thrill goes through me, but I remember what my mother said to me when I'd have nightmares as a child. She said she was faster than the monsters and could kill them.

Now, I know what she meant.

"What happened to me? It was like time slowed down for everyone except me."

"You can see a few seconds ahead of current time when you feel threatened. You have what's called 'fight sight'. The only way a vampire can overcome you is before you feel threatened."

"There are other tests?"

"Yes." Michel picks up his swords and puts them on the table and then takes the wooden practice swords from me.

"That was the most important one, but yes, there are others."

He comes back to my side. In his hand is a dagger, which he places in my hand, closing my fingers around it.

"When you hold this, what do you see?"

I frown and try to pull my hands away, but he holds them firmly.

"Just let your mind blank for a moment. Remember the connection I showed you the other night. Think of how it felt. Open yourself to the knife. Let the images come to you. Don't be afraid."

I relent and focus on the dagger, its steel blade shining in the overhead light. I remember when Michel touched me the night we met and that strange connection that formed between us. I glance down at my hands on the blade and try to imagine forming that kind of connection with it.

The ivory hilt has strange symbols etched that resemble letters from the Russian Cyrillic alphabet. I turn it over in my hand and close my eyes, trying to blank my mind as Michel instructs. Then I feel as if the ground beneath my feet heaves and my stomach lurches with it. The world around me disappears and I'm in a room somewhere, the walls dirty, pockmarked, the furniture worn. On a table, plates and cups are stacked, half-empty bottles line up beside them, and in the center is an ashtray overflowing with cigarette butts. Everything is covered in flecks of crimson.

I turn in the vision and see a man leaning back in his chair, a bloody gash from one side of his neck to the other, the blood flowing down his chest, bubbles of blood frothing out of his mouth. The scent of blood is thick, turning my stomach and I glance down and see blood covering my hands and arms, and in my hand is the bloody dagger.

I'm trying to cut off the man's head.

I cry out, dropping the blade. As soon as I do, the vision dissipates and I'm back at the dojo. Michel reaches out to steady me as vertigo strikes, holding me up as my bearings return, taking one of my hands in his.

"Tell me what you saw."

I look in his eyes. "I saw," I say struggling to speak over my dizziness. "I saw a man with his throat slit. I was covered in blood. The dagger was in my hand..."

"Yes," he says. "It was used in a recent murder. I brought it along to show you what your gift is. This is why you're so valuable."

I close my eyes for a moment and try to calm myself. When I feel somewhat better, I try to pull my hand out of his but he resists me.

"How are you feeling?"

"I'm fine," I say and finally, Michel lets go of my hand. "I feel a bit dizzy, that's all."

He nods. "It affects people differently." He bends down and picks up the dagger, returning it to the table.

"What happened? How did I do that?"

"You have touch telepathy, like I already said. But more than that, you can feel memory traces of violence in the objects you touch. When humans commit violent acts, their extreme emotions leave traces in the material they touch – weapons, everyday objects that have been touched soon afterwards. This exists at the quantum level and persists over time, depending on the material. In some materials, it persists longer, in others much shorter. After a while, the traces lose their power and vanish so it has to be relatively recent violence."

"How long does it last?"

"Depends on the person who left the trace, depends on the intensity of the event, depends on the material. Could be a few hours, a few days, or even weeks."

"I've never felt it before."

"You've led a very sheltered life. You've been kept from violence on purpose because your parents wanted to mute your gift, keep it from being used. If you had grown up in a violent environment, you would have felt it and it would have really bothered you. Since you weren't, you have to learn to use it, learn to focus it like any skill. The more you do this, the better you will get."

I try to understand what just happened and glance around, hoping to shut the awful image off in my mind's eye.

"Agent O'Neil will take you upstairs to sign some papers and let you know when the next test will take place. Go." He nods toward Agent O'Neil.

O'Neil leads me to the door to the stairwell and to the third floor. I glance back at Michel as I leave the dojo.

He's smiling to himself.

~

AGENT O'NEIL – Ed, he says I should call him – sends me home after I sign a few papers, including a contract to work with the SCU.

Ed introduces me to his partner Dr. Terri Starr and we shake hands. She says they knew my mother and that they're happy that I've resurfaced and am old enough to take on this role. They've been looking for almost a decade for me – since she died and I was taken into state custody and the file was lost – or stolen, they're not sure which.

Then I leave, going back down the elevator and out the empty entryway to the street. I'm surprised – and a little saddened – that Michel doesn't come up to the third floor and say anything to me before I leave.

I beat him – the memory of the very short battle and the moment after when I almost kissed him lingers on my mind. It all happened so fast. It was like something took over and I knew how to defend myself and how to attack. In the excitement of the moment, my emotions almost got away from me.

~

I take a taxi back to my neighborhood and get out a block away so I can stop by my coffee shop and get a cup of decaf chai tea latte before returning to my apartment. As I'm standing in line, I feel someone brush against me and I shrink away, trying to be polite. The person persists in standing too close to me. I turn and it's Julien with that smirk on his face.

"Oh, Julien," I say, covering my throat. "I didn't see you there."

"Don't worry," he says, gesturing to my hand on my neck. "I'm not going to bite you. At least, not unless you want me to."

He lets that statement stand for a moment, and I don't know what to say in response but I don't uncover my neck. His expression becomes serious now.

"One thing you have to learn about people like me and Michel," he says and steps closer to me. "We're stealthy. Even more than the usual security detail. We can sneak up on you when you're not paying attention and if that happens, you're toast if we have bad intent. Keep aware at all times, Eve. I know Michel has a detail on you, but they're just ordinary Adepts and no match for older vampires like me. You still must be on guard now. I managed to slip past all three and into the café. If I had been here with the intention to harm you, I could just take your hand, take over your ability to respond and have you out of here, out the back door and into a van waiting to take you away. Your security detail would be out of luck. Remember that."

"Why am I so at risk now?"

"You did well at the SCU," he says, his voice dropping lower as if to stop others from hearing what he says. "You've just moved up from 'interesting but unproven' to 'invaluable and coveted'. Things will never be the same for you again."

"In what way?"

He shakes his head. "It's not for me to tell you this. You're not mine."

"What do you mean by that? I'm no one's."

He smiles briefly. "You better search through your mother's files and find something on what an Adept is. And read up a bit more on how it is between humans and vampires."

"Why don't you tell me?"

Then I place my order and I turn away from him. When I turn back, he's staring at me intently, his brow furrowed.

"Well?"

"Come and sit with me for a bit. We can talk."

I nod and move over to wait for my latte. He orders an espresso and comes to stand beside me. Once more, he stands too close to me.

Our drinks are ready and he takes his and walks over to a semi-circular booth – the only place open. He gestures to it, all gentlemanly, and waits for me to take a seat. Then, he slides in beside me, once more far too close.

I try to sidle away a bit but he just moves a bit closer, as if he thinks I'm giving him more room.

I frown and turn to my latte, stirring some sugar into it.

"So, you were telling me about why I'm at risk now."

He takes a sip of his espresso and glances at me.

"You sure don't know much."

"No one's told me much. Why don't you tell me?"

He exhales, stretching out his arm on the back of the bench behind me. He turns to face me, his face conspiratorial. He nods to me as if he wants me to move closer.

"Every single one of us would kill to have someone like you. Will kill to get and keep you."

"Why? Am I strategic?"

"Every vampire wants someone like you because you can connect with us. Share emotions, sensations. Thoughts. Come on, Eve. Don't give me that. Haven't you thought about how touch telepathy would be very… enhancing to certain very intimate experiences?"

My cheeks heat at the innuendo. God, he's a cad.

"So you're saying it's purely sexual?"

"Oh, so you have thought about it." He grins, and his eyes widen as if in delight.

"You're rude."

He laughs at that. "No, I'm not. I'm just honest."

"Well, if you're so honest, tell me why things will never be the same again for me."

"I'm honest. I won't lie to you, Eve. But I won't always tell you things. It's not my place."

"Whose place is it?"

"Michel's, of course, if he's going to claim you. Although by all rights, you should be mine…"

"Claim me?"

"Yes," he says and takes another sip, all the while staring at me, amusement clear in his bright blue eyes. "You know. Stake his claim. Take possession."

"I'm not a gold mine."

"Oh, yes you are. The mother lode."

"I'm not a possession."

He turns away and finishes his espresso. "Like I say, you better catch up on your reading. There's a lot you don't know about how things are done with us."

"With who?"

"Between vampires and humans."

"I've read about the Treaty of Clairveaux. I know you can't kill us anymore."

He nods. "Yes, but there's a lot more we can do than just kill you and the treaty says nothing about that. In fact, it gives us license to do everything but. Eve, I hate to be the one to tell you…" And then he hesitates, looking at me, frowning a bit.

"Yes?" I say, impatient to hear what he can tell me.

"I shouldn't. Michel should be the one."

"Can you at least tell me what an Adept is?"

He sighs. "An Adept is a human who shares a vampire's ability to enter into another's mind and body, sense their emotions, their sensations, their thoughts. It's very rare and so it's very coveted. Your mother was Adept. Usually, it doesn't pass from one generation to another but in your case, it was given a bit of help. There's a lot about you that is unique."

"If she was Adept, who claimed her?"

"Like I said, that's not for me to say. Ask Michel. Read the files at the SCU when you get a chance. For example," he says and eyes from under a frown. "You can't be compelled."

He takes my hand and turns to me abruptly, staring in my eyes, moving closer, so close that his mouth is just a few inches from mine. "Kiss me, Eve."

I frown and try to pull away. "Not on your life." I try to jerk my hand out of his grasp, but he's too strong. "You can't compel me so don't even try."

"No, I can't, but I can do this." He must release a brain hormone that makes me unable to resist him and he leans in closer, his head tilting, his lips almost touching mine. A little jolt of something goes through me. Fear? Or attraction?

"Don't." I'm barely able to speak above the pounding of blood in my ears.

He pauses there for a moment, and I can hear his breathing, feel it on my lips, and it's fast. Almost as fast as my own.

Then he pulls back and releases my hand. "Nope," he says, his voice all matter of fact. "Can't compel you. I thought that Michel was just fooling me." He shrugs. "There's more than one way to skin a cat."

"What do you mean?" I say, confused. "And by the way, that's a terrible metaphor."

He grins. "Sorry. I forgot you're one of those cat people."

"How do you know…"

Then I remember that he's touched me quite a bit. He's probably sensed I have two cats.

He rubs his fingers over my hand, which is resting on the tabletop. "I just have to touch you to know anything I want to about you, Eve. Keep that in mind."

I pull my hand away. "Do you like making me feel uncomfortable?"

He turns and moves a bit closer. "Do I make you uncomfortable?" he says, all faux innocent. "I apologize, Eve. My intent is not to make you feel … uncomfortable."

God, being with him is like being with a naughty trickster. I can imagine him as the evil man with the curling moustache who's trying to take advantage of the innocent young woman in those old silent films, tying the damsel in distress on the train tracks...

"Look," he says and now his face is serious. Contemplative. Almost regretful. "I feel bad, that's all. You were off the radar. Safe. Blissfully unaware. Now, here you are, right smack in the middle of things that are so much more dangerous than you can possibly imagine." He stares at me, the grin gone, the blue eyes now serious. "I'm sorry, Eve."

The abrupt change from leering cad to thoughtful man makes my head spin.

"Sorry for what?"

"For everything. Everything that happened. Everything that's going to happen." He shakes his head. "But the cat's out of the bag, so to speak and in keeping with the cat theme. There's nothing to do now but hang on tight." He takes my hand and turns it over, then presses his lips on my outstretched palm. "If you need me for anything, if you ever feel in danger, you just have to call me. I knew your mother. We were friends. She trusted me to look after you. I feel a certain degree of responsibility for you even if you aren't mine. I will come to you at any time if you need me."

Then he lets go of my palm and finishes the last drops of espresso in his cup. He doesn't look at me, just stands and buttons his coat. "Gotta go. Being so close to you makes me realize it's time for a bite to eat," he says, grinning. "I'd ask you to join me for a meal, but I don't know if food would satisfy me now."

Now the cad is back and the brief glimpse of a decent man disappears.

I turn my face away from him. "Goodbye, Julien."

"Good night, Eve."

Then he's gone and I sit alone in the booth.

I'M BACK in my apartment a few moments later, glad to be home, my nerves all on edge. I have a bath to warm up, and then return to my mother's files and start sorting through them, hoping to find something about the SCU and the tests to be an Adept but can't find anything in the first new box I open. It's then I hear a knock at my door.

I go and check the peephole. It's Michel.

I unlock the door and peer at him. He has a big smile on his face.

"Hello," I say, unable to not smile back.

"I just wanted to come over, see how you're doing. I brought this," he says and holds up the manuscript. "I thought I'd read a bit for you."

I'm in my nightgown and socks, but I want to hear him read the manuscript so I open the door. He comes in and I can feel his gaze move over my body. My nightgown is to the knee and flimsy and I have no underwear on.

"You'll have to excuse me," I say. "I just got out of the bath."

He makes that throat sound and steps inside and takes off his boots and coat. I take his coat and hang it in my closet and motion to the tiny living room.

"I'll be right back," I say. "Make yourself at home."

I go to the armoire in my bedroom and take out the matching robe that goes with my nightgown and slip on some panties. Then I return to see he's standing in the living room, glancing around.

"Can I get you anything to drink? What would you like?" I point to the kitchen but stop speaking when I see his expression. He's smirking, a very wicked smirk, and I know what he's thinking. I can't repress a smile.

"Ah, those dimples," he says and reaches out to touch my cheek. "Remind me to make you smile more often. But now that I've tasted you, Eve, you must know I'll want you."

I frown and fear races through me.

"Don't be afraid," he says. "I'll want you but I won't drink your blood. I have donors."

He must do something to calm me, for I relax at his touch and then he drops his hand. I go to the kitchen to get a glass of water for myself for the night's events make me feel as if I've run a marathon. He's serious once more when I get back. I sit across from him, the glass of water in my hand, butterflies in my stomach.

"First," he says. "I want to say how pleased I was by your performance tonight. If there was any doubt about your worth to us before, there can be none now. You're very gifted. I'll need to train you, of course, but once you are fully trained, you'll be so very important to us."

I can't help but respond to his words. I'm pleased that I did well. It makes me feel warm inside.

Then he leans over and takes my hand from across the coffee table.

"Just know that I never wanted this for you. I did everything I could to prevent it."

I nod. He did try to keep me out.

"Michel, tell me how it is between vampires and humans. I know there's the treaty. But beyond that."

He considers for a moment and inhales deeply as if steeling himself.

"The Treaty prevents vampires from killing humans for their blood. But it says nothing about the relationship between us. Eve, between humans there exist laws and rights and responsibilities. You are equal before the law. There are laws to protect you from each other. There are no such laws that govern relations between vampires and humans. There are no rights. There are no protections save one – the prohibition against murder." He glances away as if it's hard for him to admit this. "In our dealings with humans, for the most part, you are our servants, our slaves. At the most, you are our subordinates. Never our equals."

I frown. "Why? Who would agree to that?"

"The Council. They knew that vampires would never consent to a treaty if it meant that we would be expected to treat humans as our equals. We're not. We are stronger, faster, more able. Our senses are sharper. Our minds faster. We can compel you. We can control you. We are your masters. Only humans like you – those who can't be compelled, are immune to compulsion. You're the wildcards. The problems."

"So you treat humans like servants and slaves?"

He nods. "That is the way it's done. You will find very few vampires with any power who treat humans as equals."

I don't say anything for a moment, the knowledge not sitting well in my gut. Slaves? Servants? Subordinates?

"What about you?"

He hesitates. "When I am with other vampires, I fit in. When I am on my own? I don't tend to interact with humans. In my dealings with humans through the SCU, I rely on rank to determine how I treat a human. Most are automatically my subordinates."

I make a face. I don't like that. Not one bit.

"I'm sorry to be the one to tell you this, Eve but it's the truth. My kind view you as food. As toys. As amusements. As tools."

"I don't know what to say."

"When you're with me, when we are around other vampires, its essential that you adopt the proper decorum. You have to act subordinate or else you'll be at risk, at least until you learn to fight and avoid being ambushed."

I sigh and point to the manuscript, for as curious as I am about the relationship between vampires and humans, I'm even more curious about it. "Are you going to read?"

He opens it to the first page, running his finger under the text. He reads for a moment and then inhales heavily as if the words are painful.

"*Une pleine lune se lève, tachée de rouge des feux dans la place du village...*" he says, reading first in French, his voice hesitant, already filled with emotion. He sounds so cultured with his soft French accent. It contradicts the content of the words he reads.

"A full moon rises, stained red from fires in the village square where five heretics burn at the stake. The Crusades broke my family, estranged me from my brother and now have killed me. I died, not on the battlefield as befitting a knight protecting my father's estate, but in a bed in an abandoned castle at the hands of an ancient vampire who bewitched me."

He pauses for a moment, and I realize that this is very painful for him, and part of me feels incredible guilt that I'm intruding on his privacy.

But I don't stop him from reading.

~

A MEDIC STANDS impassively at my feet. He checked me over moments ago, his face grim.

"This one," the medic says and points down at me. A woman on a horse comes into focus. She's blurry, but I can tell she's beautiful with the palest skin and ruby lips. She'll be the last thing I see in this world. God has taken pity on a dying knight to give him this last vision of beauty.

She slips off the horse and kneels down beside me.

"Will he die?"

"Yes," the medic says. "That's what you wanted, my Lady? The ones not yet dead, but who will not survive?"

"Yes," she says. "Only those. I relieve them of their pain as they lie dying. It is the oath of my holy order. The ones who are dead are already with the Lord. The ones who will survive do not need me."

The truth spoken so clearly brings tears to my eyes despite my resolve to die with honor. The medic makes the sign of the cross and helps her roll me over onto my side and the pain takes my breath away. I groan and grit my teeth, squeezing my eyes shut.

Please God stop...

"This is one of the Comte's loyal vassals," she says as she rolls me onto my back once more. "Bring him to my tent."

"If he's the Comte's, shouldn't he be taken to the city?" the medic asks, wiping his hands on his tunic.

"No." Her voice is firm. She takes the medic's chin in her hand, staring into his eyes. "Take him to my tent." The medic stares back, open-mouthed, as if bewitched.

"I'll take him to your tent," he says, his voice flat.

She turns away, re-mounting her horse, and rides off.

The two ragged young men set to work, unrolling a pallet, struggling to lift me onto it and every movement brings another wave of pain. All I want is for them to end my life quickly but that prayer goes unanswered like all the others.

~

I WAKE, lying on a table, my teeth chattering.

"Why aren't you dead, beautiful Sir Knight?" she whispers. "Your wounds would kill any man."

I hiss in pain as she removes my chainmail hauberk and undershirt. Finally, she lays her hand over my brow, and in a moment, a sense of bliss spreads through me.

"Beautiful Julien," the blonde woman whispers, her face close to mine, her lips beside my ear, brushing my cheek. "Yes, I know who you are, Sir Knight. I've been watching you for a while. Should I be merciful and let you die or should I heal you and take you for my own? Do you want to die?"

"No," I gasp, for I don't believe in heaven.

She leans down and kisses my lips. "Then I'll heal you." She bites her own wrist, drawing blood with sharp white teeth, and places the wound over my mouth.

"Drink," she says, holding it against my lips, pinching my nose, forcing me to swallow or suffocate. I struggle, horrified at what she does, but she's so strong. "Drink and receive eternal life."

I swallow – my body forces me and after the first mouthful, an incredible need fills me and I must drink. I grab her wrist, and suck, for the blood is so sweet. And then darkness closes in once more.

An incredible headache pounds in my temples when I next awaken. The bright sun beaming in from the window beside the bed makes my eyes burn and so I throw a hand over my face and take an accounting of my body. I'm naked beneath a thick coverlet and my body feels as if I've just come back from battle.

Which, of course, I have – outside Carcassonne. I remember now.

How have I come to this place? And more importantly, where am I? The rooms are unfamiliar.

Cradling my aching head, I sit up on one elbow and glance around. A fire blazes in the hearth, and beside it sits a woman with very pale skin and, due to some trick of lighting, with eyes that seemed to glow red in the firelight. A very beautiful woman with waist-length flaxen hair. She wears a thin nightdress and I can see the hint of a rosy nipple through the muslin.

"I remember you, but my apologies, my Lady. I can't place your name."

"You don't know me, but I know you, Sir Julien de Cernay, Knight Defender of the Comte de Toulouse," she says and crosses the floor to stand in the shadows at the foot of the bed. "Bastard son of Vicomte de Clarmont, identical twin of Michel, the very new Bishop of Carcassonne. You're finally awake. How do you feel?"

"Like shit," I say and grimace at the loudness of my own voice. "Michel's a Bishop now? What of my father?"

"Dead."

I frown. He was a brutal father, but still my only one and a wave of sadness fills me. She watches me carefully as if gauging my response.

"Carcassonne is now in French hands," she says and continues her story. "Michel was given the Bishophood for his loyalty to the Church, while your father lost his life for going against it."

Michel the Bishop. He has everything he wants now – our father dead and the Bishophood. Betraying our family was good for him.

"What happened to me? The last thing I remember was the battle. How did I come to this place? Who are you?" I try to sit up fully, but when I do, my head pounds. "Do you have some wine? I'm very thirsty."

"My name is Marguerite," she says and smiles beguilingly. "Wine won't slake the thirst you have, my love."

My love ... So that's how it is between us. I wish I could remember...

Marguerite. Her age is hard to guess for she appears rather fragile with paler-than-pale skin. She leans against the post at the corner of the bed and the neck of her gown falls open to the waist, revealing delicious curves...

~

MICHEL STOPS reading for a moment and I'm pulled out of the story.

"What's the matter?"

"It's very explicit. Are you certain you want me to continue?"

I nod, embarrassed that I'm such a voyeur for their pain.

"Very well," he says, as if he's reluctant. He reads for a moment and then clears his throat.

~

"STRANGELY, my flesh doesn't respond to the sight of her naked breast. Yes, I admire its heavy fullness, but whether it's my headache or thirst – I can't tell which – I don't feel the familiar ache in my groin that I expect when a beautiful half- naked woman stands at the foot of my bed.

"I need something strong," I say. "I feel like the dead."

She laughs, a light sound like crystal being struck.

"You're more right than you think."

"How did I get here? I have no memory..."

"I'm not surprised," she says and comes closer to me, but stops at the edge of the beam of sunlight that streams into the room and falls over me "I found you near death on the battlefield and brought you to my tent. I," she says and hesitates. "I healed you, beautiful Sir Knight. I brought you here. I saved your life."

"Thank you, of course," I say, squinting against the light. I hold up a hand and shade my eyes. "Do you think you could close the drapes? The light is murder on my eyes."

She goes to a small table by the hearth and rings a bell to summon the servants. When she turns back to me, she examines me like I'm a new toy or prized possession. I don't remember her, but I must have been with her. I'm naked. She's practically naked. My body feels – well, it feels as if I've bedded a dozen women and been beaten by each one of their husbands.

In comes a servant girl, her head bowed as she stands in front of Marguerite.

"My Lady?"

"Close the drapes. And bring in the girl. Quickly."

The servant bows and then closes the drapes so that the room is now dim, lit only by several candles and the light from a flickering hearth. I exhale in relief. My eyes felt somewhat better but my head still aches and my throat feels as if it's lined with sand. My belly growls with a hunger that seems to fill my veins, and my upper jaw throbs as if I've had my teeth kicked in. I run my tongue over my teeth. Two protrude, unfamiliar in their prominence, sharper than I remember.

The servant returns and following her is a young woman dressed in a thin nightdress with its neck open. She's lovely, with long dark hair and wide green eyes. Marguerite smiles and takes her hand, pulling her over to the bedside.

"She's a gift for you, Julien. Do you like her?" Marguerite pulls back the girl's long hair, drawing down the gown's shoulder to expose her neck. "You need her to complete the ritual."

Ritual? Does she expect me to bed the girl? I rub my forehead and grimace in pain from the ache in my teeth. There's no way I can – not the way I feel.

What's wrong with me?

Marguerite pushes the girl onto the bed beside me, so that she half-lies half-sits on me, her hands on either side of my hips. Marguerite crawls onto the bed as well, and once more pulls back the girl's long hair, exposing the creamy smooth skin of her neck.

"Take her, Julien," Marguerite says. "You need her."

"Take her?" I say, confused. "I'm in no condition..."

"Of course you are. You have a need and so you take." The girl's nearness seems to intensify all my senses and the ache in my veins grows stronger, my teeth hurting, my vision focusing in on the girl's neck. I can hear her heart-beat from where I sit, feel her warmth radiating from her body and most of all, I can smell her blood. It stirs something in me that I've never felt before.

"Bite her, Julien," Marguerite says. "The skin on her neck just under her ear. You know it's what you need. Do it now, and you'll feel better. If you don't, you'll die."

"What?"

Marguerite creeps closer to me on the bed, and pulls the girl into my arms. The girl complies as if she's drugged, tilting her head to reveal more of her neck. I can't help but inhale sharply. Now I feel a need for blood. My heart pounds, and the ache in my teeth grows unbearable. I run my tongue over my teeth and the canines have become longer, sharper as if I'm some predator ready for the kill.

"Bite her," Marguerite says, her voice soft but compelling. "Drink her blood. It's what you need. If you don't do this, you'll die forever."

"Is this some kind of devilry?" I say, staring into Marguerite's eyes. She shakes her head.

"Only that which will make you immortal." She pushes my head down towards the girl's neck. "Take her."

I'm unable to resist the pull of the girl's blood. I bend down, my mouth hovering over the girl's skin just below her ear. I press my mouth against her and feel the thrum of her heartbeat against my lips. My desire almost overwhelms me, my lust building – bloodlust – an overwhelming need.

"God help me." I take the girl more firmly into my arms and bite down and the sensation is so powerful. When my teeth break her skin, cutting into her flesh, releasing a pulse of blood into my mouth, I shudder from the pleasure of it.

"That's it," Marguerite coos, and her voice sounds as if from a great distance. "Drink, beautiful Julien, and live forever."

∼

MICHEL READS SILENTLY, and I blink as if awakening from a dream.

"There's much more explicit material coming," he says and glances up at me. "Should I continue?"

"How bad?"

"Bad enough."

I hesitate. "Read. I'll just blush."

"Yes, you will." He smiles softly and looks back at the manuscript, tracing ahead on the text with one hand, touching his lips with the other. "You do it very well."

He pauses and then starts reading again.

~

"I PULL my mouth away from the girl's neck and the girl is limp in my arms, her skin pale, twin gashes where I bit her oozing blood, the skin around the wounds bruised from me sucking. The fog of pain and lust that shrouds my mind lifts. I no longer feel that pull, that need, and the pain is all gone. I feel – alive. I feel completely energized, my hearing acute, my vision sharp.

I see things – details of everyday objects – that I've never noticed before. The minute threads in the girl's gown, the fine down of hair on her cheek, tiny blood vessels in her skin. I hear noises I've missed –the crackle of the fire in the hearth, the wind underneath the windowpane behind the curtain, a branch tapping against the leaded glass window. Every thing, every sense, comes into sharp focus.

The girl's heart beats very fast, far too fast, and I know then that I drank too much. She exhales suddenly and her heart stops.

I killed her.

"No." I shake her but it's no use. "No, don't die." She's dead, her eyes staring blankly ahead, her head and limbs flopping. Marguerite's smiling as if supremely pleased with me. "I killed her!"

"Shh," Marguerite says and strokes my brow. "Beautiful Julien. You drank what you needed, no more. She was mortal. Mortals are meant to die."

She pulls the girl out of my arms and lets her fall to the floor with a thump. Then she crawls into my lap, her legs on either side of my hips, her hands stroking my face. She kisses me, licking my bloody lips. It's then I see her sharp teeth – just like mine.

"You're now immortal," she says. "I gave you the gift of eternity. These mortals – they exist for your pleasure. Look at them as if they were your servants, your toys, your food. You are a hunter, now. The supreme hunter. They are your prey."

"They're humans," I say in protest.

"And you're no longer human. You're superior. You can run faster, you're stronger, your sight and hearing and touch and smell and taste – every sense is heightened. Every emotion magnified."

Even now, so soon after my metamorphosis, I know I'm no longer the same. I'm no longer one of them.

"What am I?"

"You," she says and kisses me again, deeply. "You are vampyr."

MICHEL CLOSES the manuscript and my cheeks are hot from the description of Julien as he kills his first human.

"The rest is not for you to hear," he says quietly as he flips through the pages. "It concerns my own debasement." We sit in silence for a moment and I can tell he's uncomfortable.

"Is yours worse than Julien's?"

"Much worse. Sacrilegious would be one way to describe it," he says, his voice quiet. "I was still a believer, and a priest."

Of course, I want more than anything to read it, but I feel very sorry for him and for Julien after hearing about Julien's turning. They didn't ask for this existence. It was forced on them.

"Now, I must leave," he says, not meeting my eyes. He returns the manuscript to its envelope and gets up, shrugging on his coat. He walks to the door and I follow, feeling very awkward.

"I'm sorry," I say, after opening the door for him, not able to think of what else to say.

"For what?"

"That you both were made into vampires against your will."

He turns to me and smiles softly, reaching out to touch my cheek with the backs of his fingers.

"Sweet Eve," he says. "Little ballerina and child prodigy. Sad for a vampire even though one took your mother from you and left you alone?"

"You were human once."

"I was."

A flood of warmth goes through me from his touch, taking away the sadness I feel from the story I've just heard. I feel so sorry for him and for Julien. It's then, of course, that I think of meeting Julien earlier before the test and then afterwards.

Michel frowns, for he's found my memories. He drops the manuscript and takes my head in his hands, staring in my eyes.

"You met with Julien, twice?"

"He found me. He followed me after the test."

He shakes his head and I feel him probing my memories, and as he does, I relive them. Michel goes over each word, each gesture.

"Stay away from him, Eve. You're not for him."

I pull away and he lets me go.

"He said my mother wanted him to have me as his Adept. That he was supposed to train me."

"We don't always get what we want." He frowns at me, then he takes in a deep breath and exhales. "Eve, I don't want to forbid you. But if you're going to be my Adept, you have to just accept my will. Don't see Julien. He'll only try to make things more difficult." He bends down to pick up the manuscript, but his face is dark now, his brow furrowed.

I don't say anything. I want to be Michel's Adept, I think. I'm not sure what I feel.

"Good night," he says and strokes my cheek.

Then he's gone.

CHAPTER 6

William Shakespeare

After Michel leaves, I return to my mother's file boxes and take one that's still unopened and sift through its contents.

About an hour in, I come across a file with a thick document inside. I look at the cover and then my heart jumps. It's a full line-by-line translation, the original French above and English below. It must have been misfiled when my mother's work was packed up after she died.

I sit on the sofa with it in my hands, filled with guilt at reading it, but there is no way in hell I can put it down. I realize that this is a betrayal of Michel's trust. I know he wouldn't want me to read it. It's painful for him to even remember.

I turn to the page where Michel left off and I can't not read it. I rationalize that he can read me anytime he wants simply by touching my skin.

Turnabout is fair play.

~

BASILICA OF ST. Nazaire and St. Cerse, Carcassonne, France, 1224

Je me tiens dans l'ombre et je regarde mon frère prier.

I stand in the shadows and watch my brother pray. The sanctuary is filled with the scent of incense and the candles on the altar burn down low, wax pooling on the base and dripping down the sides. With the walled city of Carcassonne now abandoned, the Basilica is under French rule and Michel has been appointed Bishop by the Pope's envoy to claim it for his own. He's been here for hours, praying, his hands clasped in front of his forehead, kneeling on the hard stone floor of the Basilica before a statue of the Madonna holding a dead Christ.

He's whispering his desperate prayer, but even at this distance I can hear every word and it breaks my heart. I thought he hated me.

"Blessed Virgin, let him live," Michel says, his voice breaking. "Please, Blessed Virgin, hear my prayer. Intercede on my behalf. Let him have survived and escaped to some place where he is even now recuperating from his wounds..."

Marguerite pushes past me, unwilling to wait any longer. We've been together only one short week but already, I feel enslaved. She looks beautiful as usual, her fair hair piled high on her head and adorned with pearls, tendrils falling out and cascading around her shoulders. Her skin is pale and her lips a deep red – crimson – stained with fresh blood.

"Who let you in?" Michel demands when he sees her.

"Your servant, I believe," she says and motions behind her, where I stand with his servant in my arms, having just finished drinking his blood. Michel frowns and watches as I drop him to the stone floor and wipe my mouth on a sleeve before stepping over the body like it's nothing more than a sack of grain. I draw back my hood and reveal myself.

"Julien!" Michel rises from his knees, hobbling over to me, almost falling several times and I know he's been kneeling for hours, his knees bloody. He clasps his arms around me, drawing me into an embrace, his joy at my presence making my heart squeeze.

"I thought you were dead," he says, kissing both of my cheeks.

"I am."

"What?" Michel examines me – my face is now as pale like Marguerite's – deathly pale. My cheeks are cold. "Julien!" He reaches down and takes my hands – they, too, are like ice. "You're so cold..."

"Cold as the grave, perhaps?" I can't resist saying it, unable to keep a dark note of humor out of my voice.

Michel frowns and reaches out to touch my face. His fingers come back stained blood red. Flecks of it are on my chin and white collar. Michel looks at the servant – the man's throat is bloody – the red gash visible from where we stand.

"What did you do to him?" He bends down at the man's side, reaching for his wrist to feel a pulse, but there is none. He's dead. Michel glances up at me. "You killed him."

"Mortals are meant to die."

"Have you joined this Cathar heresy?" he says, his voice soft, filled with horror. "Has the witch possessed you?"

I smile, purposely revealing my sharp teeth. "This has nothing to do with the Cathars or witches."

"What evil is this? What have you become ensnared in?" He turns to Marguerite, who's lifted herself onto the altar, pushing the reliquary and chalices out of the way. She releases the tie on her cloak to reveal a very low bodice, displaying her ample bosom. She smiles, her own lips stained with blood.

"Get off!" Michel says, trying to shove her off the altar. "Don't pollute the altar with your baseness."

She laughs. "Silly Michel. It's just a slab of marble." She grabs him with her legs and pulls him into her embrace and she's so strong – monstrously strong – he won't be able to fight her. "There's nothing holy about it, Michel, except in your mind."

"Let go of me," Michel says, his voice low. He tries to twist out of her grasp but he's trapped. When she grabs his face and kisses him, he jerks his head away. "I'm a priest."

"You're a man," she says and runs her fingers through his hair. "A beautiful hot-blooded man who's wasting all that beauty and passion on a preacher who died over twelve centuries ago, who is now nothing more than a ghost. I want your passion and your blood." She turns to me. "Shall I take it?"

Michel glances to where I stand but I'm helpless to defend him.

"You'll do as you wish, Marguerite," I say, for I'm unable to deny her anything.

"Yes, I will, won't I?" She turns back to Michel and runs a finger over his mouth. He tries to pull back from her touch, but he's immobilized by her powers, frozen in place. "I wish..." she says slowly. "I wish to drink your beautiful priest-brother's blood, Julien, until he's almost dead, and then, I think I'll turn him into an immortal. I'll do it right here on the altar. How gloriously blasphemous would that be?"

"Very gloriously blasphemous, Marguerite," I reply.

"And you'll watch, won't you, Julien?" she says, her hands running down Michel's cheeks to his shoulders.

"I am your servant, Marguerite," I say. "I do your bidding."

"Please," Michel says, a look of abject horror on his face. "Please don't... Mother of God, I beseech you..."

"Your holy Mother won't help you now, Michel," she says. I close my eyes against my brother's pain, and at that moment I hate her more than anything.

"Witch," Michel whispers. "Demon."

"No, Michel," she says. "Not a witch or a demon. Now, up you get onto the altar. Lie down, your arms spread. Think of your Lord with his own arms on the cross, dying to save the world from its sins. You'll die, sweet priest, to help me sin even more."

"Please, have mercy..."

"I have no mercy," she says. "No god or virgin showed me any. Why should I show it to you?"

Then I feel her eyes on me.

"Julien, you must watch," she says, and I'm unable to deny her. I turn back and watch as Michel climbs onto the altar, lying there with his arms spread beneath the Basilica's flying buttresses.

She climbs on top of him, leans down and turns his neck to the side.

"Sweet, sweet Michel. How good it will be to corrupt you." She bites down on his neck and I know how she feels at that moment – the blood lust, the desire, the warm rush of blood into her mouth...

Michel cries out, his body arching from the pain and horror.

"You see," she says, her mouth bloody, her teeth sharp. "There was no bolt of lightning to kill us both for this sacrilege. There was no avenging angel come to rescue you. Free your mind, Michel. There is no God but there are gods. Us." Then, she bites her wrist and presses it against his mouth. "Drink."

Michel does, for he's so weak, like me before him, he can't stop himself.

LATER, Michel lies on the bed in our residence, his surplice bloodied. On either side of him are two young women, a redhead and a brunette. He wakes with a gasp, pushing their hands away as they try to undress him, pulling away the woman who has her hands in his breeches.

"I'm a priest," he says in horror, but they only giggle at him.

"You're not a priest any longer," the brunette says. "You're dead. But you're not all dead." She turns to Marguerite. "He's quite alive down there."

"Stop!" he shouts, and pushes her away forcefully.

Beside me, Marguerite claps.

"So chaste in mind, lovely Michel, if not in body," she says, glee in her voice. "So noble, so dedicated to your vows. How impressed would your Pope be if he could see your resistance? Do you not know that through the years, priests, bishops and even popes have married or had concubines?"

"We're all sinners," Michel says. "We struggle each day with our base desires."

"You're a fool. God made you a man with desires. Why would He then deny them? Even many of the Apostles were married. You're aroused by what these women are doing to you. Why fight? You're not a priest any longer. Not now."

"Why are you doing this to me?" He turns to me. "Julien, why are you letting her?"

Marguerite goes to the side of the bed.

"Don't blame your sweet brother," she says. "He has no free will when he's with me just as you'll have none. I'm doing this to you in part because I want you for myself. Imagine – beautiful identical twin vampires to stay with me forever. My Sire abandoned me and what choice do I have? Now, I'll have a man of God and a strong knight to protect me. God's had you long enough, beautiful priest and He's wasting you." She sits on the edge of the bed.

"Do you enjoy seeing me shamed?" Michel says, his voice breaking. "Seeing me break my vows?"

She smiles sweetly. "Why, yes, I do. I love seeing your shame, Michel. I know it hides your lust and it's that lust that I want."

Michel grimaces and grips his head, squeezing his eyes shut and I know he's starting to feel the need. A need he doesn't yet understand but which will consume his life from this day forward.

"What's wrong with me?" he says.

"You're dead, as the girl said." Marguerite leans closer to him. "You need only drink blood to complete the transformation. I've brought these girls for you. Pick one and drink her blood. Become immortal."

"If I were dead, I'd be with God in Heaven," he says, shaking his head.

"Forget your god and forget heaven." She waves a hand. "It's a lie told by old men to keep you in their thrall. I'm offering you real immortality. Stop being obedient to some distant and tyrannical god and become one instead. It is we who are the gods. We are the ones who choose those who live and those who die."

"You corrupted Julien as well?"

"Yes." She nods. "I'm turning you for him, sweet Michel, although he doesn't want it. Julien loves you so much despite your betrayal of your family that he begged me not to turn you, to leave you to your god. But I want you and one day he'll thank me. Now, drink their blood," she says and motions to the girls. "Live forever with Julien at your side."

"No," he says. "I won't. I'd rather burn in Hell than be a monster."

She shrugs. "So be it. You'll suffer a long and slow death if you don't soon drink. Your body will start to wither, your breath sucked out of you. Pain will be all you know. The process will take several days, perhaps a week but you will be dead, and there will be no heaven for you. Just a bed of worms." She rises and motions to the two girls to follow. "Call me when you change your mind."

IN THE END, it's his love for me that convinces Michel to relent. He was prepared to die, to endure the pain but I kneel at his bedside for days on end, my hands clasped around his, weeping like a boy for him not to leave me.

"Forgive me," I say, choking with emotion. "I tried to stop her. She has such power over me. I tried, Michel. I really tried but God has forsaken us both."

Michel finally reaches out a hand to me, stroking my head as if in a blessing.

"I won't forsake you," he whispers.

By then, he's too weak to take a mortal himself, and so I drain one of the girls and capture her blood in a chalice – one from the altar at the Basilica.

Just one more sacrilege to accompany the rest.

He drinks and becomes immortal.

I CLOSE the manuscript and cover my eyes for a moment, overcome by what I've read. It's almost midnight and I'm tired, my mind horrified. I can't help but feel grief for Michel – for both these brothers turned by a vampire against their will. No wonder he didn't want to read this to me – it shows him being murdered on the altar in his church, then assaulted by those women and that despite his horror, he responded to them.

The love the brothers feel for each other despite their break comes through loud and clear and now I'm curious about their fate over the years. The manuscript is thick and I can't wait to read more but I'm tired. I put it away and stand at the window for a moment, remembering Michel, thinking about everything that's happened since that fateful message I posted.

I remind myself that I'm hoping to become a vampire hunter and my role is to find them and condemn those who reject the treaty, not know them – figuratively and for real – out of morbid curiosity.

And of course, the ultimate goal of my work will be to find a cure and end vampirism once and for all.

I go to bed haunted by the images of Michel's death and rebirth, tossing and turning for hours before finally falling asleep when the sun starts to rise.

CHAPTER 7

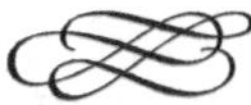

"THOSE WHO RESTRAIN DESIRE, do so because theirs is weak enough to be restrained."

William Blake

Just after dusk, I take the bus back to the SCU for another interview. I'm hoping I don't have to fight again and that all I have to do is answer questions. I'm also dreading seeing Michel. How can I look him in the face after reading his story, knowing how much it would horrify him for me to know?

I get off at the stop and walk the block from the stop to the old building. When I get to the abandoned brewery beside it, a figure steps out from the alley onto the pavement.

It's Julien.

I put a hand over my heart because he startled me.

"Are you stalking me or something?" I ask when he starts walking beside me.

"No," he says, a touch of affront in his voice. "Just thought I'd come down and see how things go. I work for the SCU. I'm interested in what happens with you, considering my history."

I frown and keep walking, not sure what I think about his interest.

We stop outside the steps leading up to the front door of the SCU and he just stands there with his hands in his pockets, looking at me. I try to avoid his eyes, which are like Michel's – so clear blue, fringed with thick dark lashes and framed by arched brows.

"Are you coming in?"

"Nah," he says, shrugging. "Just part of the security team. Keeping an eye on any movement in the vicinity."

"I don't see anyone else."

"That's good. If you could see them, I'd fire their asses. They're supposed to be undetectable."

"Michel said he had a detail on me. Are you part of it?"

"Are you kidding? No way he'd agree to let me near you."

I frown at that. "Why not?"

"He'd be afraid I'd get a little too close to you. I have my own detail on you."

"You two brothers," I say and shake my head. "Why do you each think I'm your possession? This is the 21st Century. I'm a modern woman in a democracy. Slavery ended a long time ago."

"Not between vampires and humans."

"You should be ashamed, then. What's wrong with vampires that they still want slaves?"

"It's our power. We're stronger. We're faster. We're more strategic. We can't help but dominate humans. It takes a lot of self-control not to. Most of us just barely keep our basic natures in check to abide by the terms of the treaty."

I turn and start up the steps. "You're just humans with mutations. Not some kind of separate species. We should share the same rights." I turn around to face him and he just cracks that half-grin like he thinks I'm cute. "Don't smile at me like I'm a child."

"Eve," he says softly and climbs the steps so that his face is on level with mine. "To me, you are an embryo. I'm eight hundred years old."

"Then you should leave me alone."

He smiles briefly. "I know. You have to understand something about us. We can't resist you, Michel and I. Twins have a special relationship. We have a shared past. We have many things in common. You're one of them."

"I don't even know either of you."

He exhales. "No you don't, but we know you. I have a feeling that you will be getting to know us both very well."

I glare at him and turn away to enter the building. As I stand at the elevator, I turn back briefly to see him still standing there on the steps, watching me.

I ENTER the boardroom where Michel and the others have gathered for my next test and take a seat across from their table. Michel's gaze is fixed on me – I can feel it from where I sit and I avoid him, looking everywhere but in his direction. I'm determined to get through this without looking him directly in the eye because I fear I'll blush or give away the fact that I know what happened to him.

He shouldn't feel shame about it. He's innocent of everything, but he's a priest, one born in an era very different from ours, and no doubt his experience has formed the man he's become. I've taken classes in psychology and know how traumas affect people. Hell, I have my own deep dark secrets that my mind won't let me remember.

"How are you, Eve?" he says to me while Ed and Terri confer over a file in the corner of the room.

Now I can't avoid looking at him. When I do, I try to keep my face impassive but as usual I'm struck by his beauty – like Julien, he has black hair against such pale skin, his blue eyes fringed with thick black lashes under expressive brows, his soft mouth and square jaw. My heart beats a little faster, remembering our kiss. My cheeks heat under his gaze but I force myself not to look away.

"I'm fine, Michel," I say, keeping my voice light as if nothing has changed. And it's then that vivid images of him being killed on the altar in the Basilica fill my mind's eye. I try to blot the image out of my mind, but of course, my mind won't let me consciously forget any of these images. Instead, it keeps forcing me back to them.

I smile at him, purposely, trying to appear calm and cool.

He smiles back at me, pressing his index finger into his cheek and then points at me accusingly, a grin on his face. Then I get it – my dimples. He's reminding me of what he said about my dimples... It's so intimate and sweet, my breath hitches. I feel all mushy inside and my heart breaks just a little for him.

He and Julien are nothing like the monsters of my imagination. I thought taking on my mother's work would see me finding a way to kill vampires and now, what's foremost on my mind is whether I'll have sex with one of them.

Terri takes her seat and Ed closes a file and comes around the table, leaning against it, his arms folded.

"You met Dr. Theresa Starr. She's the lead profiler for the SCU."

"Call me Terri," she says and smiles.

"And of course you already know Agent de Cernay," he says, pointing to Michel. "He's our advisor from the Council and operations lead on the River Man case."

I raise my eyebrows at mention of the River Man serial case. It's been the talk of the city. I make eye contact with Ed and Terri, but I've already played eye games with Michel and so I don't with him.

Finally, Ed hands me a case file and I turn my attention from them to the papers inside.

"Take a look," Ed says. "I know you're not trained in forensics or police procedure, but just look through and tell us what you make of it. We want to see your analytic skills. Your ability to encounter new information and synthesize it – make inductive leaps. You have ten minutes."

The thick file contains a series of grisly autopsy photos in vivid color. The crime scene photographs reveal fully-dressed bodies with their gloved hands shackled in front of them, their decapitated heads in their embrace. Half submerged in water, the limbs are tangled in seaweed and ropes attached to old dock pilings.

All six victims were similarly murdered. I read over the autopsy reports – there's no evidence of drugs or alcohol. No defensive wounds. No sign of trauma. No ligature marks indicating they've been restrained before being killed. They were just all drained of blood and then bound and decapitated post-mortem and then dumped into the rivers. I read over the reports made by the people who found the bodies, by the police officers who attended the scene, and the detective notes.

"So," O'Neil says, checking his watch. He removes his glasses and slips them into his pocket. He folds his arms. "What are your first thoughts after reading over the file?"

I flip through the file.

"I'm only pre-med, but it's pretty clear that they were all killed by a vampire and had their head cut off after. There's no lividity so their blood was drained before death. There's no bruising from the decapitation. Because there are no wounds or marks on their wrists or ankles, it seems they weren't assaulted first or restrained. They must have either known the vampire and submitted willingly or have been compelled. The one thing I don't get is the brain scans on the victims. They all had strange neurological findings."

"How so?"

"They have growth in certain areas that suggest prolonged drug use. Or use of SSRIs, MDMA or other drugs that increase serotonin and dopamine. But the ME's reports say no traces of any of the meds. Were they blood slaves?"

The three of them exchange glances and I wonder if I'm on track or completely off track.

"Why do you ask?"

"Their brain scans look like addicts, but they had no evidence of long-term drug use."

Ed nods. "Anything else?"

"They were all dumped in similar locations in a limited geographical area – all in shallow water in the waterfront district, weighted so the current didn't take them. The bodies were all called in to 9-1-1. So it seems the killer wanted them to be found, and soon," I say.

Ed returns to his seat and scribbles something down on his notepad. He looks up at me.

"Anything else? Take your time."

I flip through the file once more, peering at the autopsy photographs, then back to the coroner's reports.

"Given the 9-1-1 calls directing police to the dumpsite, and the fact that they were all decapitated, it sounds as if these are executions meant to send a message."

I glance at Ed but his face is poker straight, as is Terri's. Only Michel is smiling as he looks down at his own file. That must be good. He wouldn't be smiling if I was doing a bad job…

"Anything else?"

I shrug. "That's all I have," I say and close the file. "These victims didn't put up a fight. There are no restraint wounds." I look up at them. "They were drained, and then decapitated and bound post-mortem like animals for slaughter."

"Did you note anything unusual about the autopsy photos?" Michel reaches into his briefcase and pull out a small magnifying glass, handing it to me. "Take another look."

"Give me a moment," I say and bend over, passing the lens across the photographs. I wipe the surface of one where I see a small mark like a brand beneath the ear. A Lorraine Cross.

Then I examine another victim's neck.

"The scarring," I say, looking up to see if I've got it right. "It's a brand of some kind. Looks like a crusader cross."

Michel doesn't even bother to suppress a smile – just looks up at me, beaming. I feel a rush of elation at his expression and can't help but smile back, feeling a little giddy.

"Well done," Ed says and leans back. "What do you think a tattoo like that means?"

I shrug. "A cult of some kind?"

He nods. "Good job. Now, just a few words about our work. We track vampires, and do whatever we can to keep any information about them from the public. You'll be what we call a 'blood witness'. You'll help search for evidence on cases where a vampire might have been involved in an illegal kill, and if we get a suspect, you'll read them, use your telepathy to search their memory for kills. You'll be working nights from now on, and Michel will be your partner."

I nod, trying to keep my expression professional, but of course, the notion of being Michel's partner makes my heart beat a little faster. He'd called me his 'Adept' and I wonder if there's a disconnect between what Ed thinks and what Michel thinks about my relationship to him.

"During the summer, you'll work for us. In the fall, you'll study once more, and work only part-time. You can use our resources to help find who killed your mother. In fact, we're hoping you succeed because her case is still cold."

Terri takes up the narrative. "Now, just a few things to get straight about the SCU," she says. "We rely on the utmost secrecy and work off the books. We're both clandestine and black. Our cases, if revealed, would cause widespread panic and threaten the very fragile truce between vampires and mortals. Now, to the difficult part," Terri says. She turns to Michel and nods. "Agent de Cernay has to read you, make sure that you're not working with or under the influence of any rogue element."

"What?"

"As representative of the Council, he has to certify that you're not in league with the enemy. Just let him read you, briefly and then he'll show you how to witness."

Uh oh. He's going to read me?

All I can think of is that he'll know I have a translated copy of the manuscript and he'll freak on me.

"He's already read me," I say, hoping to prevent this. "He knows I'm not involved with anyone."

"I know, Eve, but this is a formality. It won't take long. Just relax and follow his instructions."

Michel pushes his chair back and panic rises in me as he leans over me, his hands on the armrests of my chair.

"Do you have to do this?" I say and cringe, pulling away from him.

"Relax Eve," he says softly. "You have nothing to fear from this or from me."

With his face just inches from mine, I can smell his scent again – sandalwood. It reminds me of him being so close in his office, of the feel of his body against mine when he lay on top of me on my couch, of his kiss and already, my body warms from the thought. He takes one of my hands in his and of course, a thrill runs through me at his touch – a thrill of fear and of desire. I try to blank my mind, closing my eyes, pressing my lips together.

"This won't take a minute," he says, his voice a little breathless, as if he's already felt my attraction for him. "Look at me, Eve." I open my eyes. "First, I'll check to see if you're compromised. Then you can read me, see my last illegal kill because that's what you'll do when you witness. Try to concentrate."

Of course all I can think of is how beautiful his eyes are. I try to focus on the color – they're so blue – pure blue. Soft blue. I think to myself that he shouldn't be so beautiful, that a vampire should look feral, evil, dangerous. I think of anything but what I don't want to think about. But that just brings up exactly what I don't want to think about and my heart aches for him. I try to blot out the images that pop into my mind's eye but fail – I see him on the altar with the vampire above him, then him back in the castle, the women trying to undress him.

His grip tightens on my hand and he blinks rapidly. When he inhales sharply, I know then that he knows. He releases my hand and stands up, his body stiff, his hands fisted.

"Excuse me," he says and walks to the door.

"What's the matter?" Ed says but Michel ignores him and leaves the room, closing the door behind him.

Oh, damn…

"Let me," Terri says and stands, removing her glasses and following Michel out the door, leaving me alone with Ed. He turns to me.

"What happened?"

I cover my eyes for a moment, horrified that this happened. I had no idea that he'd be expected to use his telepathy on me and would find out I'd read the manuscript.

"Eve, what happened?" he says again. I take my hands away and bite my cheek to keep control over my emotions.

"I don't know."

Ed frowns and leaves the room as well. I sit alone in the boardroom, facing an empty table.

Oh, no, oh no, oh no…

IN ABOUT TEN MINUTES, Terri returns to the room alone. I've managed to get a grip on my emotions, and I've tried to think of how to respond to their questions. The manuscript was mine. I had every right to read it. But I know it's a betrayal of Michel's trust and here I was going on to him about how he had to prove he was trustworthy and yet I'm the one who betrayed his.

"Michel's not feeling well so we have to postpone this part of the interview. You should go home now, Eve. We'll contact you when the interview's rescheduled."

"OK," I say and gather my things up. "Tell Michel I'm sorry."

"For what?" she says, frowning. "He's just ill."

I nod, trying to recover. "That's what I mean. I'm sorry he's not feeling well. Tell him I hope he feels better."

She nods as if she understands and smiles politely.

I gather up my coat and backpack and leave.

When I hit the street, I stand for a moment on the corner and try to catch my breath. Michel knows I have the translation. He'll be by to take it from me.

I walk to the bus stop and check my cell to see when the next bus is due. Just then, a car drives up and the passenger window rolls down.

It's Julien.

"Get in. Let me take you home."

"I can take the bus," I say, not sure I want to be alone with him.

"I insist. Consider this part of the security arrangements you're going to have to get used to from now on."

I glance around the darkened streets. Even with streetlights and a few businesses that are still open, it's pretty creepy in this neighborhood. I'll be home in under ten minutes if Julien drives me. If I take the bus, it will be at least thirty minutes.

I get in, buckling up. The car is an old GTO, royal blue, with a leather interior. The radio is tuned to some jazz station. There's a police scanner and computer system hooked up as if Julien monitors the police calls.

"That was short. Tell me what happened."

I don't say anything. Julien takes my hand for a moment. I try to pull it back, but he persists, his grip strong. I feel him at the edges of my mind, and wish I could learn how to block him and Michel out. That way, this mess with the translation wouldn't have happened.

"Eve, I know what happened. Tell me."

"If you already know, why do I have to tell you?"

"I want your side of the story."

I exhale and he finally releases my hand. We drive off, the car's engine rumbling.

"I found a translation in another file box. I read the part about Michel being made into a vampire."

"Ohh," Julien says and nods. "That explains it." He's silent for a moment, watching the streets, checking the rear-view mirror. "That would upset him. Poor Michel. He's very sensitive about his fall from grace."

"He shouldn't be. It wasn't his fault."

Julien shrugs. "I know that and you know that, but to Michel, it feels like God's punishment."

"That's crazy. It was Marguerite being a nasty vampire. It wasn't Michel's fault."

He turns and watches me for a moment. I glance away from his too piercing gaze.

"You're very forgiving."

"Why do you say that?" I say, frowning. "He's done nothing that I have to forgive."

"Eve," Julien says. "We've all done things for which we need to be forgiven. Michel just has a lot more guilt than most. More of a need to atone. Keep that in mind…"

"What does that mean?"

"Take it whatever way you want, but if you want to understand Michel, remember that he feels a lot of guilt for things that have happened, even if they weren't his fault. And they weren't his fault, but he bears the guilt regardless."

We drive through the streets towards my apartment block and I'm happy once we arrive. I hop out and am upset when I hear him turn off his engine.

He gets out and follows me to the door to my building. "Let me come up," he says, taking my arm. "I'd like to see your place."

"I don't think so, Julien."

"Why not? Fix me a cup of that chai tea you like so much."

"Julien!" I say, angered that he knows things about me. "This is complicated enough without you trying to get involved in my life."

"In case you were under some misunderstanding, I'm already involved in your life."

"Well, no more than you already are, then."

I put my key in the lock and open the door. Julien stays on the step as if he can't cross the threshold. At least I can keep him out. I let the door close and smile at him through the glass.

"Sorry. Can't let you in."

"That's OK," he says and shrugs. "I'll just compel someone from the building to let me in. Eve, you can't keep me out. You might as well let me in. We need to talk."

"We've already talked enough." I turn and start up the stairs to my apartment. I glance back and see him bending down to check the names on the buzzer outside the door.

"I can answer your questions, Eve," he shouts at me through the mail slot. "Michel won't because he has a conflict of interest, but I will.

Ask me anything and I'll tell you what I know. No funny business. I promise."

I stop at the top of the landing. I can see his feet on the step outside the door.

"Go away, Julien," I say. I climb the other flight of stairs to my apartment.

~

CHAPTER 8

"It's not a death that man should fear, but he should fear not ever
beginning to live."

Marcus Aurelius.

I hide the manuscript under a pile of dishtowels in my linen closet,
determined not to read on until I know how Michel responds. I think
of ways to make a copy and keep it so I can continue reading in case
he comes for it, but am at a loss. He can always just touch me and
discover where I hide any copy I might make. I can't deceive him as
long as I have no ability to put up mental walls against his telepathy.

I could send a copy to someone I know and get them to put it
somewhere safe, but he'd be able to compel anyone and force them to
tell him where it was...

There's just no way out of this except to give him the copy.

I've been home for less than an hour and have just had a warm
bath and am in my nightgown and fuzzy socks when I hear a knock at
my door. I've been searching my mother's work trying to find some-

thing on how to block others from reading my mind, but so far, no luck. I put down one of her files and tiptoe to the door and peer through the peephole.

Of course, it's Michel, staring straight at me, his beautiful blue eyes just inches from the door.

I panic, my heart starting to speed up at the thought he's here to take the translation from me to prevent me reading any further. He was so upset back at the SCU. I tiptoe back to my bedroom. I'm not sure if Michel can enter my apartment in some strange vampire way or whether he has to enter the normal human way but whatever the case, I want to hide. I suspect he left the conference room earlier because he was angry. I've been waiting for him to come and demand the translation. I don't want to give it to him.

I take one of the swords off my wall and hide in the corner of my armoire, pulling the door shut behind me, holding the sword straight up in front of my face. Maybe he'll get sick of waiting outside and leave. I'm determined to wait here all night if I have to. Unless he can resolve into a fog and creep in under the door, he'll have to break it down to get in and then at least I'll hear him coming.

Besides, he'll have to go before dawn...

Then I hear a key in the lock and the latch clicks open. Damn. Where'd he get a key?

"Thank you," I hear Michel say in a soft voice. "Now, give me the duplicate and forget that you gave this one to me. Tomorrow, you'll go and make another one. Do you understand?"

I hear the building Super reply, kindly old Mr. Williams, his voice monotone.

"I understand."

Oh, hell. Now Michel has a duplicate key to my apartment? At least that tells me he can't actually become a fog and vaporize into my place through an open window...

The door closes, and I sit in the darkness of my closet, the sword grasped between my hands, anxiety building inside me. He'll find me by smell alone. Vampires are like bloodhounds, able to track humans long distances by scent – especially one whose blood they've tasted. Which just happens to apply to me and Michel.

I grip the sword more tightly. Can I attack him? If he threatens me, I will. I know I can kill him if I get a chance.

I hear his boots on my hardwood floor as he paces around my apartment, hear the rustling of papers, the opening and closing of drawers.

"Where's the translation?" he says, and his voice is so angered.

I don't say anything, my heart thumping in my chest. I can't help it – fear engulfs me and my throat chokes up. Tears bite at the corners of my eyes.

Then he enters the bedroom and stands across from the armoire. I can see him through the gap between the two doors and he's wearing his cassock coat and his hair is mussed, and he's breathing fast, his jaw clenched.

A long moment of silence passes.

Finally, I hear a heavy sigh from him – it sounds of exasperation. It's not the sound a vampire hell-bent on torturing and killing me would make. I wipe my nose, which is running due to my tears.

Stupid stupid... I should never have read that manuscript.

"Are you that afraid of me?" he says in a voice edged with frustration.

Finally, he sits on the bed across from me and watches the armoire, his elbows resting on his knees. It's as if he's staring right at me. He can't see me, can he?

"I'll wait all night, Eve. I'm a very patient man."

"Wait for what?" I say and I think how stupid it must sound for me to be speaking to him through the closed doors of the armoire.

Oh, damn... this is a nightmare.

"For you to bring me the translation."

I should do what he says, because this stand-off is stupid and I know it.

"How do I know that you won't go all vampire on me and kill me once I give it to you?"

"What?" he says and I can see him shaking his head, his frown resolving into a look of disbelief. "Why on Earth would you think I'd want to kill you? Jesus, Eve. Are you that unaware?"

"I don't know what you'd want, Michel," I say, feeling a bit foolish now. "I don't even know you."

"Eve, right now, I'm more in danger from you than you are from me. In case you forgot, you can beat me. If you had real weapons when we fought, if you'd have had a stake, you could have killed me."

"You can kill me as well," I say and sniff. "All you have to do is get close enough to mesmerize me."

He smiles at that and rubs his eyes.

"Well, then I think we're evenly matched. I promise not to mesmerize you," he says, a grin on his face, "if you promise not to try to decapitate me with that Samurai sword."

"How did you know I have a sword?"

"There's one missing from your wall."

I scrunch up my face. Of course. He knows about the swords because I told him, pointedly.

"The manuscript's in the linen closet in the bathroom," I say. "It's under some tea towels."

He nods but doesn't get up.

"Thank you," he says and waits, watching. "Are you coming out now?"

I don't say anything for a while. I can't face him.

"No," I say, wiping my eyes. "Just go get it and leave."

He runs a hand through his hair and makes a face of some kind. I can't quite see it because he moves briefly out of my field of vision.

"But I want to talk to you," he says.

"I'm listening," I say after a moment.

"*Sacristy…*" he says, hitting his forehead with his fist. "Eve, I want to kiss you."

Oh, God…

That admission sends a rush of warmth through my body, right to the deepest part of me. I close my eyes and try to breathe, my face hot. Here I thought he was going to kill me or torture me. Now, he wants to kiss me?

"You can't," I say, barely able to speak over my breathlessness, my heart fluttering.

"Why not?" he says, his own voice soft.

"Because my nose is all red from crying."

And then he's at the armoire opening the door, and he reaches for me, taking the sword out of my hands, throwing it onto the floor so that it skitters across the hardwood. He takes my arms and pulls me up, restraining my hands behind me, holding them firmly so that I can't resist. With the other hand, he wipes tears off my face with gentle fingers, his expression all concerned, his brow creased.

"Eve…" He doesn't kiss me. Just looks at me, his gaze moving over my face. "I don't want you to be afraid of me." And then he leans down and kisses me. Softly. When he pulls away, he examines my face, touches my cheek with a finger, running the tip through my tears.

He seemed so angry when he came into my room, but now, he seems sad. I do fear him, despite the knowledge that I could kill him. The thing is, I feel far too much desire for him, far too much empathy for him, far too much admiration for him after reading the manuscript.

I want him – so much. I don't think I've ever felt this way for any man and I barely know him. I've never felt this much desire, this much lust, this much human sympathy, and it chokes me. But he's far too old and experienced and powerful and I feel like a small child compared to him. Like he could just overwhelm me and I'd lose myself, drown under his power like a swimmer caught in a riptide.

"What do you want?" I say, so confused by him and his actions.

He shakes his head. "You."

And then he kisses me hard, his eyes closed, and a wave of desire floods through me, making me dizzy and I realize it's that connection thing again. I'm feeling both our desire. My legs tremble, threatening to give out so that he has to hold me up. He picks me up and carries me to the side of the bed, laying me down across it, leaning over me, pinning my hands above my head, and I feel as if I'll pass out from the intensity of the emotions that rush through me.

He rests on his elbows, his body between my thighs, his hips pressing into me, his face directly above mine. I can barely breathe as I wait for what he'll do. He does nothing – just looks at me, fingers brushing hair off my cheek, then tracing my mouth. I close my eyes, unable to keep looking into his too-blue ones, and just lie there, not sure what I think should happen despite what my body and heart tell me I want to happen.

My body aches for him and I want him now.

He exhales heavily, making a sound in his throat, and leans his forehead against mine.

"This could get very complicated."

Then, much to my shock and confusion, he releases my hands and rises up, standing at the side of the bed.

"I have to think," he says finally. Then he leaves the bedroom.

I sit up on the bed and watch him through the open door, my heart only now starting to slow. I feel humiliated by how much I wanted him and how it was only his self-control that kept me from letting him take whatever he wanted.

He goes into the bathroom and I hear him open the linen closet door and then shut it. He's found the manuscript. He returns to the bedroom and stands beside me, flipping through the pages as if he's looking for specific parts. He finds something and then rips the pages out, one after the other, placing them on my nightstand. He moves on further and repeats this process, selecting pages and tearing them out of the manuscript.

"There," he says, handing the manuscript back to me, and it feels much lighter – half of its original size. He gathers up the loose pages and folds them, then tucks them into the inside pocket of his coat. "I think that's all of it. You can read the rest if you wish."

He holds out his hand to me and I just look at it. What does he want to do – shake my hand?

"Take my hand," he says.

"Why?"

"Being here in the bedroom is just too damn distracting. I thought I'd offer my hand just in case your legs are still too weak."

"I can stand," I say, my face hot from our contact and he looks so damn calm and cool. "So that's it?" I say, my pride stinging that it was so easy for him to control my body.

"What do you mean?"

"You kiss me like that and we're back to business?" I shake my head, avoiding his eyes because I'm so damn embarrassed.

He pulls me into his arms and sighs once more, pressing me against the wall, one knee between my thighs.

"Oh, Eve..." he says and tilts my chin up so I'm forced to look in his eyes. "It took every ounce of strength to resist you." He says nothing for a moment, and I feel all choked up. "I apologize," he says. "I rashly encouraged you but this can't happen between us."

"Why?" I ask, trying to look away but he prevents me.

"Eve, I'm not sure I'm ready for this," he says.

"For what?"

"For *us*."

"Well, that's a first," I say, my voice wavering. "Usually, I meet a guy and he's all over me and it's me who can't commit. Who takes so long to warm up."

"I'm warm, Eve," he says softly, his forehead against mine. "I'm more than warm. I'm incendiary. But there are things I need to be sure of. Things I have to do before this can happen..."

I close my eyes, because the feel of his body against me has just reignited my desire once more.

"Don't do that if you're not going to," I say and stop, unable to say the words.

"If I'm not going to what?" he says, his mouth quirked into that damn lopsided grin.

"You know."

He leans closer, his lips beside my ear, brushing the skin on my cheek. "If I'm not going to be your lover?" he whispers and his words alone nearly make me faint. "I can't do it. I'd have too much power over your body and mind. It wouldn't be fair." He takes in a deep breath. "I forget how inexperienced you are." He strokes my cheek with the back of his fingers. "I have to be very careful. Vampires have a lot of power over mortals. We can read your minds and it's hard to resist you."

"Tell me how to put up mental blocks," I say.

He shakes his head. "No."

"Why not?" I say, frustrated. "So you can just hop into my mind anytime you want?"

"Yes."

I turn my head away in frustration, but he takes my chin and turns it back. He's smiling, and his smile turns into a full-out grin, and it's contagious because he's so beautiful in his paleness and black-lashed blue-eyed way, and he's being so honest. I can't help but smile back, my eyes tearing up a bit when I do.

"Oh, Eve..." he says and closes his eyes briefly before bending down and kissing my cheek, his tongue touching my skin and I know he's after my dimples and it makes me both smile even harder and imagine where else he might put his tongue one day – when he's ready for this – for us.

Whatever that means.

He presses his cheek against mine, exhaling into my ear.

"I have to go – now – or I'm afraid I'll never leave."

He takes my hand, leading me to the door. When we reach it, he folds me into his arms and strokes my cheek.

"So lovely," he says and I feel my cheeks warm under his so-intense gaze. "You have to know that I want you so much, Eve. But there are things taking place and before I ..." he says and hesitates. "I want to make sure of them first. I can't say anything more. You'll have to trust me that I'm not doing this to play with you. I never intended for this to happen. I let things get out of my control tonight because you read about my past and your too-warm heart and body got the better of me."

"None of what happened to you was your fault," I say, tenderness for him filling me when I remember what happened to him.

He shakes his head quickly.

"I'll be in better control of myself from now on."

"Do you have to control everything?"

"Oh, yes. I exist for one purpose and that's to achieve my endgame. To attain it will require my utmost focus and self-control. I have to keep everything under control."

"Even me?"

"Especially you. You more than anything."

I frown, not knowing what that means or if I even like the idea. Or if I really like it.

He breathes in deeply and makes that throat noise.

"Please don't tempt me." He kisses me, his kiss chaste and then I think how different he is from Julien and my mind goes back to the image of Julien standing on the front step just a short while earlier.

He frowns and cups my cheek with his hand.

"You were with him again?"

"He followed me," I say, trying to find some excuse. "He said he has a security detail on me of his own. I didn't let him into my apartment."

He shakes his head and then he relives everything that happened between Julien and me.

"He's not going to give up. Eve," he says and holds my gaze, his brow furrowed. "You have to stay away from him. He'll try to get in between us. Try to take you from me."

I frown and two emotions battle inside of me. I like the way he sees me as his, despite protesting earlier to Julien about the twins and their possessiveness. At the same time, I don't like it – in my mind. I'm an adult. Not a child. I'm not a possession.

I'm so confused.

He bends down once more and kisses me, harshly, his tongue finding mine, and a surge of his desire fills me and it's mixed with frustration and some fear. I can't help but respond, my body warming in response to his touch.

"Just please, stay away from him." He strokes my cheek with his thumb.

Then he's gone. I'm standing alone at my door, my body still so in need of release even if my mind is now so confused over these brothers. I go right to my bed and snuggle under my covers.

I wonder whether one day we'll be lovers. I want it to be so, whenever he's ready. Whatever the hell that means…

CHAPTER 9

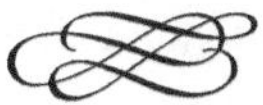

"IF I KNOW what love is, it is because of you."

Herman Hesse

I wake in the middle of the night and can't fall back to sleep. My sleep is still all out of whack and so I get up and make a pot of decaf blackberry tea and take the manuscript – or what's left of it – and sit wrapped in a blanket on my couch.

I wonder what Michel's torn out of this document – what was it that he felt was so bad he didn't want me to read it? Was it worse than the chapter I did read?

I turn the pages to where I left off last night. Michel had just consented to be turned and drank the blood he needed to become a vampire – with Julien's help.

The next page starts a new chapter. The picture at the top of the page is an image made of the original and is of a black-cowled Death rising up out of the midst of a fiery pit. Beside Death, angels weep, their tears dripping down their faces. The title of the page is *Lacrimosa – Day of Tears*.

The words at the top of the page are of those from the funeral mass, part of the *Dies Irae*, first in Latin and then translated to English:

Lacrimosa dies illa (Ah! That day of tears and mourning!)

Sounds like the content will be intense. I sip my tea and hope what's in this section isn't too graphic, but read on anyway.

"The subjugation of Michel," reads the translation, *"provides Marguerite with endless amusement."*

Michel's subjugation...

I feel like a filthy voyeur taking pleasure in reading the intimate and tragic details of his life and death – and resurrection. Still I read on, surprised that Michel's left this part in.

~

"BY TURNING Michel so soon after my father's death, she denied him the right to attend our father's funeral mass and so he is forced to return to the Basilica that evening where he kneels alone with his grief at the front of the sanctuary while monks chant Agnus Dei – Lamb of God.

Agnus Dei, qui tollis peccata mundi, miserere nobis. Lamb of God, you who take away the sins of the world, have mercy upon us.

I fear there is no mercy for either of us. I refuse to kneel beside him as he wishes me to, having forsaken the Church when it sided with the King of France against my father.

But standing here in the shadows, listening to the chanting, I feel such a great loss. It's not my father I miss – he was an old drunkard who beat Michel and me mercilessly, treating both of us as a burden to be borne rather than sons to father. I miss the Church – I miss Mass and the connection I felt to a God I now have trouble believing in. Strangely, Michel mourns our father, whom he betrayed for his beloved Church. Perhaps neither of us perceived what we were losing when we chose sides.

Now, we've lost it all.

Michel cannot take up his position as Bishop of Carcassonne, and has had to relinquish his vows, so the Bishophood has passed to another loyal servant. I had to compel the Deacon to allow us into the Basilica and the monks to chant so that Michel could say his goodbyes to our father's corpse as it lies in the sanctuary. It was the least I could do for him considering the hell Marguerite has put him through.

Despite it all, he wears his vestments, perhaps to keep alive his belief that in spite of the humiliation Marguerite subjects him to, he is still a priest, beloved of God, called to the Church, and that his suffering on this earth will ensure he is welcomed into Heaven.

But he is as undead and damned as the rest of us.

After my father is buried, we say our goodbyes to Carcassonne and our father's residence and leave, following the Crusaders as they make their way across the Languedoc in search of heretics to burn and estates to rob.

IT IS two years before we return to the region, but to a vampire, two years is like a week to a mortal. Two years of traveling across France finds us in a small village outside of Toulouse where the fighting is fresh and there's ripe picking among the fallen and few to ask questions when bodies turn up drained of their blood. Battlefields are notorious and the weapons leave terrific wounds that bleed freely. Exsanguinated corpses are all too common.

Marguerite is still the same, and she has finally won. Michel is now her servant in body and I fear, soul. He no longer fights her.

It isn't just his enslavement that she takes delight in, but the complete control she exerts over his life and how much she disrupted it. Here we are, knight and priest, her servants, waiting on her every word. I wonder if all Sires are this imperious. If I were to make a vampire, I wouldn't treat her this way. I would share with her the wonders of immortality, but Marguerite seems only to delight in having power over us, in killing mortals as if they were stock animals.

For the past two years, she has delighted in controlling Michel and seeing him humiliated. Our only consolation was that we had each other, and indeed, our mutual tragedy has drawn us together more closely than since we were young boys and I took on the role as his protector from our father.

The inquisition is in Toulouse to investigate claims of Waldensian witchery, and so the three of us have to be very careful not to raise suspicions. We have enough wealth from our dead father's inheritance to live in elegance. Money for bribes is plentiful and so we relax and enjoy ourselves as much as is possible.

We take rooms in an inn nestled on the side of the mountains. Night fell several hours earlier, and I've fed and now stand in front of a basin of water, cleaning off the blood from the kill.

I watch Michel with Marguerite. He's sitting on the divan in front of the fire, having freshly bathed and wrapped in a sheet, his chest bare. She sits facing him, equally unclothed, enjoying his attentions as he feeds her sweet dates brought all the way from the Holy Land.

He plucks one after another from a small container and feeds her, kissing her after each morsel, smiling, enjoying himself. I'm not jealous – it's the most peaceful I've seen my brother for a very long time – even before he was turned. I feel no real love for Marguerite. She's beautiful, and she's smart in a feral way, but she's brutal and manipulative. I never know what she's planning next. Whatever it is, she tries to make Michel and I rivals for her affection, but neither of us play into her plans, much to her chagrin.

"These are so good, Michel," Marguerite says. "How sweet of you to get them for me. How thoughtful. Your brother doesn't seem to think of me the way you do."

I turn to face her, drying my hands on a towel.

"Rest assured, dear Marguerite, that I think of you constantly. You've made it impossible for me to do otherwise."

"Ignore my brother," Michel says and turns her face back to him. "Thoughts can be hidden, if one is strong enough. Only actions matter." He kisses her. "As for these, I purchased them from a vendor in the night market who had just returned from Jerusalem. I'm told they are the very best of their kind. You seem hungry and I'm only too pleased to feed your appetites. All of them." He smiles, and it's a wicked smile I've never seen on his face before.

"These are just so sweet. You are so sweet, I can't resist," Marguerite says as she chews on a date.

"You taught me not to resist," Michel replies and kisses Marguerite again. "To love obedience to you in all things."

"And I'm so glad you no longer resist."

"Oh, I no longer resist any of my inclinations," Michel says, his voice low, husky. "Whether for sex or blood – or vengeance."

She pulls back at that and looks at Michel quizzically. Even I turn to regard my brother. What does he mean by that? Vengeance against whom?

"What do you mean, vengeance?" she says, a frown on her pretty brow.

But Michel ignores her. Instead, he pulls Marguerite into his arms and kisses her, a hand tangling in her long fair hair, his kiss silencing her questions. She lets him kiss her and slips her arms around his neck.

For my part, I pour a glass of wine and decide to go out onto the terrace while they play with each other so I can watch the stars. I'm in no mood to watch them and I'm surprised and a bit saddened that he seems so ready to accept her control, but his happiness is all that matters and Michel truly does finally seem to have accepted his lot. She has finally broken him and it has taken only two years.

I lean on the terrace rail, looking out across the valley below. A full moon hangs in the sky and thin wisps of cloud obscure the stars. I turn around and lean against the balcony rail, staring straight up in the other direction, hoping to catch sight of a few stars but the moon's too bright.

When I look back inside the room, I see Michel laying with Marguerite and so I turn back to the stars. It's nothing I haven't seen hundreds of times before. Instead of watching them, I watch the moon rise over the valley.

When I next turn back to the room, Marguerite appears to be

asleep, for her eyes are closed. Michel stands and pulls on a pair of breeches. He turns and sees me on the terrace.

"Come," he says and pulls on the cassock of his vestments. "We don't have long. The potion will last less than an hour."

"Potion? What are you doing?" A jolt of fear races through me.

"Getting my revenge," Michel says without emotion. "I met a woman in town who claimed to have a potion that could make a witch powerless. Of course, I didn't believe it, but I thought I'd try anyway. I tried it, and Marguerite didn't even notice. Poor dear thought she'd simply drank too much wine. I decided to use it again. This time, I'm prepared."

"What are you planning?" I dress while Michel pulls his white surplice and alb over his head and slips on his boots. He straightens his vestments and runs a hand over his head to smooth his hair.

"The witch will burn, tonight. While you kept her busy last evening, I met with the Inquisitor and arranged for the local sheriff to come and take her away to the square. They're only too happy to have a witch burning as a lesson for the town." He slips on some gloves and then goes to a leather bag by the door. Inside is a long length of chain. It's shiny, and I know it's silver.

"Put your gloves on and help me," he says. "This will disable her. I'll have to gag her or she'll try to compel the humans who come too close to her."

I do as I'm told, my mind numb, slipping on my own gloves, and then help Michel tie up her hands and feet with the silver chains. Her skin burns, smoke rising from where the silver touches her bare skin. Whatever the magic is, it's powerful enough to prevent her from waking.

"You know this is going to displease her Sire," I say. "From what she's said, Soren's an Ancient. Very old and very powerful."

Michel shrugs as if he doesn't care. "I've never seen him, so he must not care too much for her. I'm leaving for London once this is done," he says. "Come with me and we'll start new lives there."

"You mean to go through with this? Destroying Marguerite? Has all this been an act?"

"I learned to act when I was very young, Julien," he says. "I acted obedient to father to avoid his kicks and blows, and then to the Church to avoid the same. I even appeared obedient to God since it was He who chose this fate for me. It helped me to appear obedient to Marguerite, but I never intended to be her slave forever."

"You surprise me." I watch dumbfounded as he places a balled-up piece of muslin into Marguerite's mouth and ties a strip of cloth around her head to keep it in place.

He stands up from his task. "I surprise myself, but a man reaches a point where he can no longer comply with his own debasement. Even a vampire."

A knock sounds at the door. Michel motions to me, and so I go to the door, admitting two men and the local Sheriff. A priest follows them in. He bows to Michel and the two speak in quiet voices as the guards pick up Marguerite and carry her, chains and all, out of the room.

"Won't she be questioned?" I pull Michel aside, unsure what I feel about this. "Do they not need a confession?"

He smiles. "That's been taken care of. A confession was written and signed, witnessed by me, trusted priest, loyal to the Holy Church. Money goes a long way to speeding up these things. We're so fortunate we have a great deal of it."

I'm stunned. "You bribed the *Inquisitor?*"

"I lost my illusions, brother, the night I lost my life." Michel motions to the door. "Let's go. I want to make sure this happens quickly, before I lose my resolve. She's a beautiful thing, and it wasn't her fault she was turned so young and with such little moral development. But she's still a monster and even if we leave her, she will only create more vampires to fill her needs."

When I hesitate, not sure if I can support this, he puts his hands on my shoulders.

"Come," he says, his voice solemn. "Be free of her. If we don't do this now, we'll never escape her compulsion. I must be free to do God's work."

"I thought you said God abandoned you."

"God may have abandoned me, but that doesn't mean I need abandon Him. To the village square. There's a witch to burn."

"She's not a witch," I say in weak protest.

"If anyone is a witch, Marguerite is," Michel says. "She killed us both, Julien. She turned us both into monsters. She's bewitched me so that I am her slave."

"You enjoy her. I know you do."

Michel shakes his head and when he speaks, his voice is close to breaking.

"Can you even begin to imagine how that makes me feel?"

I shrug. I distanced myself from the Church after I left, but I now realize Michel hasn't, despite pretending to do so.

"How many humans has she killed?" he says. "Thousands? She'll never leave us. She must die. Surely you can see that?"

"And how many humans have you killed since you were turned?" I say, trying my best to argue her case, but in truth, I can't see any other way out. Both of us are compelled to serve her. Both of us unable to refuse her demands. "Are you going to kill yourself as well?"

Michel closes the door behind us as we leave the rooms.

"Not until I can find a way to kill us all."

A SMALL CROWD gathers in the village square. In the center, workmen raise a post and stack wood around it. The guards tie Marguerite to the post and then the priest joins Michel and together, the two say prayers in Latin and circle the pyre, anointing it with holy water while the guards pour pitch on it.

Finally, one of the guards lights the bed of wood and sticks with a torch. Marguerite appears still drugged, her head bowed forward, her long fair hair obscuring her pretty face. I hope that she doesn't regain consciousness for it will be a horrible death if she does.

"She was far kinder in the manner of death she chose for us," I say to Michel, unable to keep reproach from my voice, hating myself for not fighting harder to save her.

"What?" he says, almost sneering. "She denied you a knight's noble death, taking you off the battlefield, stealing your soul. She corrupted me, killing me on the altar in God's own house while she debauched me. She's tortured me. She wasn't kind, Julien. Not at all. If you think so, then you truly are besotted. When she's dead and we're both free of her compulsion, you'll see. You'll feel differently."

The flames leap around Marguerite, growing in intensity, and then I see her awaken, her head straightening. She glances around in a panic, her eyes wide. She screams but the sound is muffled due to the gag, and my heart squeezes at the thought of her suffering.

Yes, I've hated her at times, angry that she turned us both, angry that she used us, that she played with us, that she manipulated us using her greater powers, but she was only a young girl of eighteen when she was turned against her will and has apparently been abandoned by her Sire. She survived using her wits, and now she'll die because of her need for attention and affection, her willingness to believe she could corrupt a priest and make him into her slave.

"For God's sake, won't you do something?"

"Do what?" Michel's arms are folded as if he's watching an amusing performance rather than the death of someone he's fucked a thousand times, but his face is tense, his jaw clenched.

"Ease her suffering – kill her quickly!"

"She deserves to suffer."

Michel seems immune to her pain, and so I find a long pole with a sharpened end stacked against the wall next to the blacksmith's shed and run to the pyre. I kick some burning embers aside and step onto the pyre, ignoring the flames licking at my breeches, and thrust the wooden point into Marguerite's heart so that she dies quickly, instead of slowly from fire.

I fall back off the pyre and roll on the dirt to extinguish the flames on my clothing. I go to where Michel stands mesmerized by the fire, his shoulders shaking. Is he laughing?

I turn his face to me. There are tears in his eyes.

"You have to understand," he says, his voice breaking. "She destroyed me." He shakes his head. "I'll never be the same."

Then he covers his eyes with his hands and I take him into my arms.

IN A FEW HOURS, there's nothing left of Marguerite except a charred corpse and a gold chain with an ornate cross that she enjoyed wearing out of some sense of irony. I gather up her ashes, placing them and the remnants of her bones into a pail, picking the crucifix out from among the bones and teeth mixed with cinders and ash, wiping off the blackened soot. Besides her charred bones, the only thing left of her is a tiny crucifix – a symbol she loved to hate.

I take her remains and go to where Michel sits in the dirt, his head in his hands.

"I'll place her ashes in our family crypt. She deserves that much." Then I hand him the crucifix. "Here." I say, holding it out. "It was hers. Take some solace that once she wore it with true belief. Before she was killed and turned against her will by her own Sire. "

Michel looks up. His tear-streaked face is stained with soot from the fire. He accepts the thin gold chain and cross.

"When I find him," he says and places the chain around his neck, kissing the crucifix. "I'll kill him as well."

I PUT the manuscript down and go back to bed, but sleep eludes me for a long time.

When I wake later in the afternoon, I check my email and there's one from Agent O'Neil, inviting me back to the SCU for the interview we had to cancel yesterday. There's also one from Michel, which I open and read, eager to see what he's written.

Eve,

Please excuse my indiscretion last night.

I realize you are unused to being in the company of vampires – indeed, there's no reason for you to feel anything but hatred for my kind. You must understand that I mean you no harm, either physically or emotionally. Had I been able to erase your memories of me and of the manuscript, none of this would have happened and you would be living your life as you've always lived it but ignorant of our world.

But I'm weak. I'm also unable to change what happened between us and therefore, we must move forward. When I realized you were an Adept that night in the office, and that I couldn't just wipe your memory of me, I knew that we'd have to use you no matter what I feel. Your kind is far too valuable to let waste away in some hallowed hall of academe and if I didn't claim you, someone else less moral would. This battle is too important and personal sacrifices must be made.

As for my behavior, all I can say is that I am used to exerting total control over mortals. I couldn't with you, and more important, I've failed in the simple task of controlling my own emotions. I assure you that it won't happen again and that from this day forward, our relationship will be conducted with the utmost respect and professionalism.

Yours,

M.

What? Professionalism? Respect?

I don't want professionalism. I don't want him to respect me if it means nothing more will happen between us.

And then, once again, reality rears its ugly head and I'm filled with guilt. Vampires killed my mother. They're my enemy. I should be thinking of ways to eradicate them, not how I can become Michel's lover.

So it feels as if Michel thought better of 'us' and is trying to bow out gracefully from whatever 'us' might mean. The thought that I won't ever actually get to experience him makes me sad, disappointment flooding through me.

I was looking forward to going back to the SCU so I could see where this goes, but now, I feel like crawling back into bed and hiding from the world. Instead, I shower and get ready, fix something leftover in my freezer for a breakfast of supper, and have to drop by the university once more to finish up some paperwork for my next semester.

On a whim, I drop into the Linguistics Department and go to Room 304. The door is ajar and inside sits an older man with frizzy grey hair and thin metal eyeglass frames.

I stand at the doorway.

"Professor Cormier?"

He glances up.

"Yes," he says, rising and coming to the door to meet me.

"Do you know a Professor Michel de Cernay, by any chance?"

He frowns. "Doesn't ring a bell. Sorry."

"Thank you," I say and leave.

Michel must have compelled his way into the office so he'd have a place to meet me. I realize that he's the consummate actor, the consummate liar, as he said in the manuscript. As I go down the stairs where I fell and over to the bus stop where he came to me, I remember my scraped palms. They're almost perfectly healed, due to the healing properties in Michel's saliva.

Michel wants us to remain professional. I try to console myself that this is what my mother would want. Not to be some vampire's trifle but it does nothing to soothe my disappointment.

CHAPTER 10

William Blake

I arrive back at the SCU at about 7:00, and enter the boardroom where Ed, Terri and Michel sit. I avoid Michel's eyes and wait for the interview to begin.

"My apologies, Eve, for the disruption yesterday," Michel says and I'm forced to look at him. "I wasn't myself."

"I understand," I say. But I don't and already, my cheeks heat.

He avoids my eyes and I can tell that what I suspected about his letter being the brush-off is true. A sense of renewed sadness fills me. I feel close to him despite only knowing him for a few short days because of everything that's happened – our psychic contact, the manuscript. The desire I felt didn't help, either.

It hurts to think he's shutting 'us' down before we even happened. He said I had no idea. Now, I'll never know, but this is like Pandora's Box – once opened, you can't put that question back in.

I swallow hard and try to wipe my own mind of these thoughts, for he's going to have to 'read' me and there's no point in trying to deny how I feel. He'll know as soon as he touches me. But I do try to be a grown-up and take in a deep cleansing breath.

He comes over to me and once again leans down over me as I sit in the chair.

"Now, I'll just do a quick read and then I want you to try to read me."

He takes my hand in his and despite everything, my heart skips a beat from his touch. After a moment, I feel him at the edges of my consciousness, warm and strong. Then something floods through me and I know he's using his powers to take away my sadness and it's a relief not to care any more.

I do care, but now it's in an abstract, intellectual way, not a deep emotion.

He looks up at Ed and Terri. "She's clear," he says. "I've checked back on her recent associates and none of them are connected in any way to Blackstone."

Ed nods and writes something down in his files.

Blackstone?

"Now, Eve. I want you to try to search my mind for my last unauthorized kill. As an Adept, your mind is primed to detect violence and although you've had a very peaceful life, it's there, if you can learn to tap into it. So just let your mind free when you connect with me. Let it go where it will. You'll find it."

I blink and try to do as I'm told, but what he's said makes me frown. My mind is primed to detect violence?

"How do I know when I've found your last legal kill?"

"You just have to let your mind go like you did in the dojo."

"Can't you just block me?"

"Not everything. Your gift is that you can sense violent memories, either in objects or in us – see our kills. I can try to block other memories, but not of my kills or anything associated with them."

"Some gift," I say and close my eyes. I blank my mind for a moment, focusing on my breathing, and when he enters my mind, I almost gasp from the connection that forms. It feels so intense and disorienting... I'm aware of his senses, as he leans over me, touching my hand. I can tell he doesn't want to look at me, but can't help watch my face, his eyes moving over my mouth with a sense of longing, going to my cheeks and remembering my dimples. His sense of regret that he can't – that he shouldn't – have me.

"Concentrate," he says. "Focus."

Then I seem to fall into a memory, like I've tripped over the entrance to a deep well. When the memory comes into focus, it's late evening, moonlight, a woman with garish makeup and a low-cut bodice, and beneath it is a long skirt. She stands in a dark alley as if looking to turn a trick. Another century. London. 1896. I'm in his point of view, and I feel his feelings, think his thoughts as he experienced them.

That night, he's hot for human blood, and there's still a part of him that's reluctant to reveal how base that lust was and still is. He still lusts after humans, our bodies and our blood, and even now, getting one is almost all he can think of like some junkie for a hit.

But that night, he sees the whore standing there, her ample bosom and flesh suggesting she's full of blood. With only a tiny hint of remorse, he slips to her side and pulls her into the doorway in a dim alley before she can even protest. He's so fast, unnaturally fast, and in the dark she can't see him.

His blood lust builds, his heart pounding, and the woman bared her neck, willing Michel to touch her. His eyes are so acute he can see the tiny capillaries in her fair skin. When he touches her, he feels her pulse like it's his own. But more than this, he searches her memories and relives them as he prepares to bite her and the memories are almost as important as the blood. He bites down, draining her blood, taking it in, lost in the sensations.

I feel everything he does – the woman's blood draining out of her and into him, warming him, the pleasure in the sensations so intense. He's reliving some memory from her past when she was happiest, in the arms of her first lover. I see and feel the moment just before the woman dies, her body going limp in Michel's arms. Then, just before the woman's heart stops, he drops her to the ground and is gone, no more than a shadow in the darkness, his bloodlust slaked but a renewed sense of self-revulsion building in his consciousness.

"That's enough," Michel says and I ignore him, not wanting to break the connection. I keep it between us, unwilling to stop and just like he says, he's unable to prevent me from staying. Despite what I've just witnessed, despite what I've just felt, every fiber in me screams out for him to let me continue. I want to prolong that moment of connection for as long as possible. I try to find more and he feels so much affection and desire for me but also guilt and fear and then he physically pulls back, blinking, stepping away and our connection breaks because we're no longer touching. He leans against the table and runs a hand through his hair, breathing hard.

Nothing I've ever experienced can match the need vampires feel for human blood, for that connection with the human is overwhelming. How they manage it and function, I have no idea.

I cover my face with my hands, trying to get hold of my emotions. Finally, I breathe normally and sit back up, avoiding Michel's eyes, my cheeks hot from the intimate moment we shared.

"I saw you kill a woman." I swallow as I remember the scene. "I felt it. London. 1896."

"She was the last human I killed illegally," he says, his voice soft. "Now, like all other vampires who are part of the treaty, I subsist off donors."

Terri pours me a glass of ice water from the pitcher. "You passed the test." She offers me the glass and I spill a bit in my eagerness to drink. Ed turns to me.

"Welcome to the Special Cases Unit of the Council of Clairveaux, Boston Division. You're hired," he says. "Not that there was ever any doubt once you beat poor Michel." Ed grins at me. "I think his pride is still smarting."

"Not at all," Michel says, not meeting my eyes. "If she couldn't beat me, she couldn't work as a witness." Then he does meet my eyes. "We need you, Eve. You must be able to protect yourself from my kind.

You're very valuable. Vampires will kill each other to get you on their side."

That's what Julien said. "Why?"

"You can kill us. Some want to use your kind as assassins against their enemies."

Terri speaks up. "Michel can fill you in on the politics of this unit and why it started some other time. For the next six months, you'll train to be a blood witness. You'll help on special cases – those that involve vampires killing outside the law. You'll gather evidence to help us find those they work for. When we get a suspect, you'll read them – see their kills. Judge if they were sanctioned or illegal."

I shake my head. "I thought I was going to do research."

"You will, but you need to train as a blood witness, because you're very rare. When we get one, we don't let go."

"I know it's a lot to take in," Ed says. "Come with me. I'll show you your new office." He leads me to a room at the back of the building. "The cubicle in the corner," he says and points to a small alcove by the window. I check it out. A small desk and filing cabinet. A laptop computer. A partition that separates me from the rest of the room. At least I have a window.

"The case files for each murder are there as well as background information on the SCU are in the filing cabinet," he says. "Everything you need to get up to speed. I trust your university courses have made you a quick study." He buttons his jacket. "We'd usually just let you do some reading on your first day, but we have a new murder to investigate."

I raise my eyebrows. This is a surprise and I turn to see Michel standing in the office, leaning against the wall. He's put on his cassock-coat and has his hands in his pockets. He looks like a blue-eyed long-haired very pale Neo and I can't shake the sense that I've truly swallowed the red pill and there's no going back.

O'Neil hands me the River Man case file. I opened it up once more, my hands shaking just a bit. I flip the pages, the crime scene photographs, autopsy diagrams, the witness testimony.

"Get your coat," Ed says and pulls on his trench. "We're going to the crime scene."

~

IN THE SEDAN, O'Neil reminds me to keep quiet around the Boston PD detectives and uniforms who are there on the scene. No mention of any special skills or of vampires.

"Hopefully, the killer left a bit of himself behind so you can get a better sense of him and what drives him."

"What should I look for?"

"Anything," he says, shrugging. "Could be a cigarette butt, a coffee cup. Who can tell? They often leave some trace. Trick is finding it."

"Do I touch the body?"

Ed shakes his head. "You're there to look for physical evidence before Crime Scene Unit messes things up. Besides, dead bodies don't hold memories for very long due to decay. As soon as a person dies, their cells start to die and the neurons lose their structure at a quantum level. Solid objects retain theirs and so they're more useful to a telepath. In general, the lack of forensic evidence at the dump sites indicates that the victims were killed elsewhere and their bodies decapitated before being transported but even an extremely well-disciplined killer will touch objects and often leave something behind. As long as the kill was recent, anything a killer touches will hold traces of their memories of it."

We drive along the streets to the docks. The floodlights of the forensic unit are visible from a block away and my pulse increases at the prospect of a real crime scene. Ed parks the sedan and the four of us walk the rest of the way. We stand on the periphery while Ed ducks under the police tape that cordons off the crime scene. He shows the detective in charge his credentials and speaks to the man in hushed voices, gesturing towards us.

Mist rises off the Charles River, blocking the view of the Charlestown Bridge. The late May night is unusually cold. I shiver and it isn't just the fact that a real vampire stands beside me – one who shared a very intimate, almost sexual experience with me not so long ago.

I try to block the memory from my mind.

The waterfront bordering the dock area has become an industrial graveyard. In the harsh floodlights surrounding the dump site, the moss-covered ruins of the old piers rot in the tides and old float barges and crumbling docks decay along the shore.

Michel stands beside me, his long hair tucked behind his ears as he reads messages on his cell.

I pull my collar up against the breeze off the water. "God, it's so cold."

"Really?" he says without looking up. "I wouldn't know."

I glance at him and he turns to me. Sure enough, there's that lopsided smile on his lips. I can't help but smile back. He looks at me and makes that throat sound, his smile fading, his eyes on my cheeks and I know he's doing it – making me smile on purpose so he can indulge himself and it sends a little jolt of something through me.

He turns back to his phone.

What is this? Torture? I thought he was going to be completely professional.

As I gaze across the river, I try to imagine what it would be like to work with him on a daily basis and not go there – to 'us'. I can't imagine it. It will be hell.

"I don't know if I can do this," I say softly. "Staying just professionals."

He stops typing for a moment.

"There are many things we don't choose in life," he says and glances at me, his bright blue eyes intense under the floodlights from the forensic unit. "The thing is, we need you. Personal desires must be denied."

I say nothing in reply for what he said makes sense, as much as I hate it. I'm numb, uncertain how to feel. Instead, I watch the detectives from Homicide examine the body.

While we're waiting, I see another figure arrive on scene. Another detective? Then I see his skin and I know it's Julien. He's wearing the same leather trench with a scarf tied around his neck and faded jeans.

"Julien," Michel says. "What are you doing here?" Michel glances at me as if he already knows.

"Ed called me. Said another Adept had been killed. I thought I'd drop by, see what you're up to." Julien turns to me and stuffs his hands in his pockets, giving me that lopsided grin. "Of course, I already know what you're up to."

"Leave Eve alone," Michel says, his voice dark.

"I'll do what I want. If Eve wants to talk to me, that's up to her. Eve has a lot of questions about her mother. It looks as if you're not much into answering them."

"You won't be answering them either," Michel says, putting his phone away. "Eve only has to know so much. To tell her more would put her in danger."

Julien laughs at that. "You mean put your little suicide mission in danger."

Michel takes my arm and pulls me towards Ed, who's waiting at the shore.

"Ignore him," Michel says. "He just likes to stir things up."

We join Ed and stare down at the corpse, which has been photographed and removed from the water. Julien joins us as well and stands off to the side. The body's laid out on a plastic sheet in wait for the coroner to come and do his work, the severed head at an odd angle to the neck.

"Check around, see if anything catches your eye."

"What should I look for?"

"Forensics hasn't swept the scene yet so whatever looks out of place. Most Adepts I've worked with before just feel around, hoping something they touch grabs their mind."

"What about my prints?"

"Forget about it. We have jurisdiction and your work is more valuable than their pitiful tests."

I take a flashlight from Ed and walk along the shore, hoping something draws my attention. I look for something the killer might have dropped or touched but nothing pulls me closer. Pebbles and seaweed litter the mud between the stumps of wood that used to be part of a dock – nothing more. I bend down and run my hands over the dirt bordering the area where the body was found. A piece of green beach glass glints in the flashlight's beam and so I pick it up.

For an instant, my world collapses away and I'm him. The killer -- whoever he is -- sat here. A strange sense of being out of time washes over me as I slip into his perspective and I feel an incredible dread. I try to focus, opening myself to the experience. I don't get much from it at first, except the knowledge that the killer touched the pebble.

Then, I sense him. The killer was here scoping the place out a few nights earlier, staring out across the river, deciding where he'd dump the body. He picked up the glass and rubbed it between his thumb and fingers the way I do now, turning it over, admiring it. Then he dropped it. He had more important things to occupy him than an old bit of beach glass. Like when Evan . . . . I try to focus, squeezing my eyes shut. When Evan Cooper would die.

"Evan Cooper," I say, clearing my throat, struggling to resurface long enough to communicate. For an instant, I see the victim as the killer saw him, stepping out the back door of a dry cleaners into the alley for a quick smoke break. In the vision, I look down from a window across the street. "He saw Cooper from a building across from the alley behind the dry cleaners." My voice is gravely. "Second floor window."

Ed nods and gets on his cell, speaking into it in a soft voice.

I return to the pebble. The killer has an emotional distance from the victim, a studied sense of purpose rather than one filled with passion and bloodlust Michel had when I was in his mind and he drained the woman. The killer doesn't hate Cooper, either the man himself or what he represents. The killer feels more like an executioner than a vampire searching for a blood feed. The killer has a sense of mission. Even a sense of religious fervor.

I drop the glass as quickly as possible, for the longer I spend in his perspective, the dizzier I become. While Ed and the detective speak in quiet voices, I take in several deep breaths, trying to combat this vertigo.

A light rain starts to fall, just a mist at first, the air cool on my cheeks. Michel comes to my side as I lean against the remains of the dock.

"Are you all right?"

I nod, embarrassed to show weakness. I'll have to get used to being in the mind of a killer and so I go back to the glass and touch it once more. Maybe if I fight the vertigo, something else will come to me – some detail that will lead us to the killer.

I search through the sensations and impressions of the killer as he surveys his victim. Nothing comes to me at first. Then, a hint, just a fleeting image of a river in the middle of a desert. Tall reeds line the riverbank. A sense that he's protecting someone fills me, but who that someone is remains hidden. As I turn the shard over, I know that the manner of death is important. Decapitation is significant in some way.

"He killed in this way and dumped him here to send a message." I swallow hard, fighting the nausea that rises in me at the continued connection to the killer.

O'Neil nods. "What does decapitation and dumping the body along the shore mean?"

I shake my head. "No idea. I saw a river at nighttime," I say, remembering a momentary image of a river. "With tall reeds along the shore. But it was only very brief."

"Nothing else?"

I shake my head, getting nothing more from the glass. It's as silent as the now non-existent breeze.

~

ONCE WE'RE FINISHED at the dump site, we walk back to the sedan and Julien joins us.

"So, Eve, why don't you and I have a cup of coffee, talk about things," Julien says to me. "I'm sure you have more questions."

"What things?" I say, but I think I know what he means.

"Oh, your mother, being a blood witness," he says, smiling as if everything amuses him, as if he takes nothing seriously. "Training. The whole killing all vampires thing my brother's on."

I look at Michel and he shakes his head quickly.

I take in a breath. "I'd like that."

Julien smiles broadly, glancing briefly at Michel as if he's scored some kind of point.

"Great," he says. "How about tomorrow night? The coffee shop?"

"Sure."

"Great espresso."

"Eve will be working tomorrow night," Michel says, his voice low.

"We can meet before. Say, just after sundown?" Julien smiles.

I smile back. "Sure. I'll be waiting."

"Ooh, those dimples," he says and clucks his tongue. He just stares at me for a long moment, taking in a deep breath. "I'll come up and get you," Julien says. "What's your apartment number again? 3C?"

Michel takes my arm. "You can meet her at the coffee shop," he says, pulling me along with him.

Julien holds his hands up in mock surrender.

"Ok, ok," he says, laughing. "I won't go in her apartment. Unless she invites me up, that is."

I glance back at him as Michel opens the car door for me.

"Until tomorrow night, then," Julien says, grinning.

I get in the sedan and Michel gets in beside me, sitting closer to me than necessary as if he's trying to show Julien I'm his. He starts to do up my seatbelt, but I take it out of his hand.

"I'm not a child."

"Compared to us, you are. Don't forget it. Just because you can kill us, don't think you can manipulate us."

"Oh, I'd never think that," I say, emotion welling up inside me. Does he really think I'm a child? I clip my seatbelt in place and turn my face away.

"I'm sorry, Eve," Michel says after a moment. I turn back and he's rubbing his forehead. "He has that effect on me."

"Was he always that cheeky?"

"No," he says and shakes his head. "But when you're a vampire, everything about you is strengthened. You feel everything with ten times the intensity. Whatever cheek he had before is just that much stronger."

"And you? What did becoming a vampire do for you? What did it intensify?"

"Julien would tell you I've become boring, but I have fervor, Eve," he says, staring at me, his face close to mine. He touches my cheek with the backs of his fingers. "I'm fervent. More than ever."

"About religion?" I say, hoping not. I don't want him to be a priest.

"About everything."

I hope so.

"You don't want me to meet with him?"

"No," he says. "I'm asking you to reconsider. I don't know what his motives are, but I can guess. He wants you for himself and will try to mess things up. But I can't force you not to."

I turn away and look out the window at the passing scenery. I don't know if I'll meet Julien. Part of me wants to. Part of me wants to please Michel.

From the front seat, Ed tells us we're going to the building I described in my vision, check out the second floor to see if the killer left some trace there.

We arrive at the building across from the dry cleaners where Evan Cooper worked. Ed uses his key kit to break into the warehouse because it's empty and there's no security to admit us. Michel and I can see clearly even in the darkness but Ed doesn't have our advantage and follows us up with a flashlight. There are rows of empty offices overlooking the alley and we each go in and check. I enter a couple and then find one that has footsteps in the dust that are clearly visible in the light flooding in from the moon.

I go to the window and can see the alley clearly, including the back of the dry cleaners where Evan Cooper must have been standing, having his cigarette. It's exactly as I saw it in my vision. I glance around the empty room and see a piece of paper folded up on the windowsill and pick it up. Immediately, I get a strong sense of familiarity – the killer held this and so I open it. In the darkness, I can just make out a careful script.

Hello, Beautiful Eve.

Love,

Me

I get very little from the piece of paper except that the killer was amused with himself when he wrote this and he knew we'd eventually find it. I hold it out when Michel comes in the room and he takes it, looking at me.

"What's this?"

"Just read it."

He does and glances up at me, shaking his head.

"*Sacristy,*" he says, his breathing shaky. "Whoever it is knows you're working for us and that's only a very limited number of people."

I feel as if my blood turns to ice. Michel, Terri, Ed, Julien... some techies at the SCU. Cecile – I emailed her to let her know I had this job, but there's no way she'd betray me.

Ed joins us and Michel hands him the slip of paper. Ed reads it, rubbing his chin.

"Fuck me," he says. "I hate bad guys with brains."

THE RAIN now falls in grey sheets between the buildings as we return to the car. Michel's silent for the rest of the trip and I don't interrupt his reverie. I know he doesn't want me to meet Julien, but now, I'm even more desperate to do so, see what else he can tell me about my mother.

Ed stops in front of my apartment and I turn to Michel but he says nothing, just takes my hand for a brief moment and squeezes, then pulls his hand away. I want him to come up with me, I want to be with him, but this is something I have to leave up to him.

When I get into my apartment, I stand at the window overlooking the street, the water running down gutters to the drains, and I wonder who it is who's out there, watching me.

CHAPTER 11

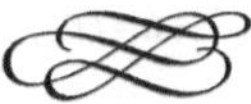

"Ye shall know the truth and the truth shall drive you mad."

Aldous Huxley

I get up the next morning and dress and the first thing I think isn't about how nice it is that the sun is finally shining or that I love the smell of roasting coffee coming from the coffee shop on the street below my apartment.

I think of reading more of Michel's story.

What I read was upsetting, but I can't keep myself from the manuscript and pick it up after doing my usual routine of showering and dressing and munching down a bowl of bran flakes. I take it with me to the coffee shop and get my cup of Organic Medium roast coffee with cream and sit in the back corner – my usual spot for studying when I want to get out of the flat.

Do I feel guilty reading this?

Yes. Incredibly. This is so personal... It's the chronicle of a tragedy. It's the very emotional story of these brothers and their death and rebirth as vampires. It's a record of their enslavement to Marguerite and her murder. He hates it so much he wants to burn it.

Will this guilt keep me from reading on?

No. I'm as drawn to it as I can be and there is no force on this earth that could keep me from reading it.

A sense of disquiet settles over me as I turn the pages to the next section. The section opens with a painting of a heart with a sword through it and I wonder what it represents. Is it the heart of Jesus? Or is it the heart of a man?

"MICHEL CAN'T RESIST VISITING Danielle once more before we leave. He caught sight of her on the battleground at night as we made our way there in the hopes that we'd find a dying soldier or knight and give them a peaceful quick death instead of slow from some other cruelty.

She was there nursing the dying and when Michel saw her, he hid in the shadows, unwilling for her to see him as he now was – a vampire, undead, having betrayed his vows and no longer a priest other than in his own mind.

She was a lovely woman, even now, a decade after we both first met her, with long fair hair and hazel eyes that were fringed with thick lashes. A real beauty, with soft curves and softer lips.

We were both infatuated with her when we were seventeen, and after a long courtship where she couldn't choose between the two of us, she finally chose Michel – the soulful one – instead of me, the hot-headed and impetuous one. When I realized she loved him more, I gracefully moved aside. Michel and I would be starting seminary the following year and so this was our last few months of freedom. I didn't want any hard feelings between us over a girl, even one as pretty as Danielle. Besides I had lost my virginity several years earlier while Michel had planned to save his for God.

I talked him out of it and there are times now that I blame myself for everything, for if he hadn't met Danielle, perhaps everything would be different today. But back when I was seventeen, I thought I was a man and knew my own mind and the ways of the world.

"You have to make a sacrifice to become a priest. If you've never made love to a woman, how can you know the depth of your sacrifice? At least I know what I'll be giving up."

Michel thought that was a reasonable argument for losing his virginity, but he was very picky, always looking for a woman who met his high standards of moral conduct. She had to be a virgin, like he was, and she had to be a good Catholic. One who would do her penance for having sex with him before being married. Oh, he was so idealistic! So wide-eyed and full of faith in the possibility of chastity, believing that God would be enough.

He and Danielle met in a barn in the countryside and lost their virginity to each other in a hayloft, and spent the next few months in a heated romance, their youthful passion never completely slaked no matter how often they met. I thought it might make him change his mind about the priesthood, but I was wrong. While my commitment to it waxed and waned with every pretty girl I met and romanced, Michel's was steadfast.

There were tears that fell when it was time for us to leave for Toulouse and the seminary. He told me that I was right – having lost his virginity and having had a true sexual relationship with Danielle gave him something to sacrifice when he took his vows. He was almost happy to feel the pain of separation from her. The pain made him feel closer to God in some way, as if he deserved pain and heart-break for some wrong he had committed, but if he had committed a wrong, I was never aware of it. He'd always been so good, so loving, so forgiving.

So it was with some mixed feelings that he saw Danielle a decade later, after he'd gained and then lost the Bishophood and became a vampire. For her part, the lovely Danielle had never married and might as well have committed her life to Christ the way Michel had, considering her own chaste life. Perhaps she never recovered from Michel leaving her. Perhaps she just never met another man whom she loved as much as Michel.

He saw her and I think his heart broke. She was still lovely of course, but she had aged and time had worn lines of care and sacrifice into her face.

"Go to her," I said, urging him on from the shadows.

"I can't," he said. "She'd be terrified to see me this way."

"She loved you. She'd be happy to see you, Michel."

And so it was I who was truly responsible for her death, not my poor brother, still so young and inexperienced in the ways of vampires.

He did go to her one night, knocking at her door where she lived still with her aging parents, the spinster daughter who kept their house.

"Michel!" she cried when she saw him. She stole out from the house to meet him, so happy that he'd returned after all these years that she barely noticed how pale he was or how cold was his skin. She fell into his arms as if they'd only parted the previous day. He was, of course, in heaven being with her again. Sentimental Michel, the soft-hearted one. The idealist. Washing away the memory of Marguerite's depravity with Danielle's pure love.

He thought he could drink her blood without killing her, drinking only so much and then letting her recover for a few days so she could once again be healthy. They went on this way for some time, and it was the happiest I had ever seen Michel since we were turned. Everything seemed to be going well for us – Marguerite was nothing more than an uncomfortable memory, we were in our familiar haunts, and the continued crusade in southern France kept us in blood.

Danielle wanted to become a vampire to be with Michel, but of course, he wouldn't agree. He felt guilty enough about drinking her blood and being her lover, let alone creating another vampire. And so a month and then a year passed in this way, with the three of us living in a house we rented, and Danielle offering Michel some solace after his ordeal with Marguerite. Here was a woman who loved him, who was, if not his equal, then a willing partner.

When a new vampire came into town, killing townspeople at will, seemingly not caring if there were rumors of a monster at loose, my first thought was that this was Marguerite's Sire come to find her and take her back under his wing. Michel and I were so naïve at that time. Neither of us knew much about our own kind as Marguerite had no time for teaching us nor did she know much. So we had no idea that the strange sensations we were experiencing were just our heightened senses detecting the presence of another hunter in our territory.

He found us.

One night he turned up at our doorstep and we made our first acquaintance with an Ancient.

Ancients are not like ordinary vampires. They were born that way, made of the union of Nephilim and mortals and were the first vampires, infected with a curse that would turn any who drank their blood into their servants, addicted to blood.

Soren was magnificent, unnaturally beautiful in a cold cruel way, tall, with pale hair, white skin and eyes that were red even when he wasn't feeding or hunting. A man of the Northern realm of ice and snow, he had been made by a Nephilim and had grown up and killed his own maker, drinking his blood and becoming more powerful than all other vampires.

We knew none of this when we killed Marguerite. We learned only too late.

Danielle made the unfortunate mistake of admitting him when he said he knew Michel and wanted to become reacquainted. He came in and went directly to Michel, grabbing him by the neck, demanding to know where Marguerite was. Of course, Michel couldn't hide the truth from him and Soren demanded reparations. He demanded that Michel turn Danielle over to him in blood price. Michel pleaded for her life but Soren was not moved by his talk of how virtuous Danielle was and how much he loved her.

"Either you give her to me and I kill her," he said. "Or you do it yourself. You choose. Either way, she's dead."

Michel was helpless to fight Soren, being only a few years a vampire rather than several thousand.

"Me, then," Michel said. But he couldn't do it, stopping well before she was too weakened by blood loss.

Soren then compelled Michel to kill Danielle, and he did, draining her in front of us, only realizing what he'd done when he finished and she lay dead in his arms. Before her body was even cool, Soren tore her from Michel's arms and threw the body over the city wall, onto a pile of refuse as if it were nothing more than trash.

"Now we're even," he said to Michel but of course, we weren't for Marguerite was a vampire, and Danielle was only mortal. Then Soren compelled Michel to join him, travelling across France and then north to England as his servant.

The night Danielle died, after Soren had retired to his room with two young women, I searched around, looking for Michel and he was nowhere to be found. I went out and scoured the city looking for him, fearing the worst, but instead I found him in the cemetery just outside the city gates, digging Danielle's grave. He'd left our rooms and gone to retrieve her body from the garbage heap outside city walls and carried her to the cemetery, digging the grave beside our family crypt with his bare hands.

And so it was that we buried Danielle and left Carcassonne. One more wound to my brother's heart that I fear will never heal. He and I have killed so many mortals. Most we tried to ensure were already dying but this death was hard and Michel has not yet forgiven himself for putting Danielle at risk.

"I should have walked past her home that night and never seen her again," he said and sat on the ground beside the grave, his head in his hands. He looked up at me, his face wet from tears. "Everywhere we go, people die, Julien. We are God's punishment on mortals."

Our time with Soren was to prove his words truer than either of us knew.

My brother escaped one hell for another, having only a brief respite when he and Danielle were happy together and the wounds Marguerite inflicted on him had healed.

Unable to refuse Soren, Michel rationalized his servitude.

"This way, brother, I can learn the secrets of our kind. Marguerite never told us anything that would be of use in destroying vampires but Soren is very old and knows everything. I must go with him so that I will know as well. Come with me," he begged. "Once we know his secrets we'll kill him."

I CLOSE the manuscript and think of Danielle with the hazel eyes and fair hair. I can't help but suspect that part of the reason Michel's attracted to me is because I resemble her physically. If so, that would be a bad omen. Then I realize both of us resembled Marguerite and I feel sick.

The story I read of the Nephilim intrigues me – biblical creatures created when angels came to earth and mated with human women, according to the Gospel of Enoch, which isn't really part of the standard bible. Of course, I don't believe it for a second. What the bible stories describe is some kind of genetic mutation that people at the time couldn't explain without resorting to gods, angels and demons – nothing truly paranormal.

I make a mental note to check my mother's files to see if there's anything about this because it could prove to be important when I start doing my own medical research. Vampires are immortal. The properties in their genetic makeup that give them immortality could be used to extend human life and is an avenue I would have to explore if it exists.

And then I think maybe Michel's afraid. I remember what Julien wrote about Danielle and how Michel felt responsible for her death. Perhaps he feels that way about me as well and this might explain, at least in part, his need to protect me.

I sit in the coffee shop, waiting for Julien to show. I debated with myself all afternoon whether I'd meet with him, but in the end, I feel I owe it to myself to meet him and hear what more he can tell me about my mother and this whole world.

LATER, I sit in the coffee shop, waiting for Julien to show. I debated with myself all afternoon whether I'd meet with him, but in the end, I feel I owe it to myself to meet him and hear what more he can tell me about my mother and this whole world.

I get a text from Michel before sunset.

Eve,

I can't force you not to meet with Julien. To be honest, if I could compel you not to meet him, I would. I can only ask that you don't. I can say that he'll tell you things you may not want to hear. He and I — there's still an animosity between us because of our past history. But he's still a good man at heart so I can't tell you he's evil or out to hurt you. Neither of us would do that because of your mother.

So, meet with him or not, it's up to you. If you are going to be my Adept, it would be a show of faith if you didn't meet with him.

I'll leave it up to you.

Yours,

Michel

Yours, Michel…

I can't deny the appeal of that for me. I'm sorely tempted not to meet with Julien just to please him, but I feel I owe it to my mother to hear Julien out at least. See what he says. Michel's been quite reticent to speak about my mother. He's focused on his mission and everything seems to be subordinate to it.

In the end, I can't resist meeting Julien and sit in my favorite corner of the café and wait, my back to the window as I watch the door to see him.

He arrives, looking just as beautiful as always, with his long black trench and scarf. He takes off his coat and sits across from me. The waitress comes over right away and smiles at him like he's a rock star. He orders an espresso and turns his attention back to me.

"Lovely Eve," he says. "I can see why my brother wants you all to himself."

"You're very different from him," I say, ignoring the compliment. "You're even different from your manuscript."

He shrugs. "I wrote it a very long time ago. I was so serious back then. Eight hundred years has cured me of being all melancholic for what can't be, unlike Michel. I live in the moment now. It's a good way to be. Listen, Eve, Michel needs to lighten up. Maybe now that he's got you, he will, but I doubt it. He's a lost cause."

"What do you mean?"

"Come on, you know what I mean..." he grins suggestively. "You've seen him. You kissed him..." He gives that lopsided grin, which is entirely too suggestive. "The man's uptight. In need of some redemption. If he had you, I imagine he'd be very happy. Relaxed for once. I'm just surprised he found you so easily."

"I posted a message on a message board and he had a service –"

"Yes, that's what he told me, too. I think it's rather suspicious. I think he knew where you were all along."

The waitress brings Julien his espresso and he touches her hand as he thanks her, and she blushes. He likes the effect he has on women.

I frown and take a sip of my coffee. "What do you mean by that?"

He watches her as she goes behind the counter and then drags his attention back to me, shaking his head quickly.

"Just a little theory I'm working on. Check out his wallet," he says and sips his espresso.

"Why?"

"There's something you might like to see."

"Tell me!"

"Nope," he says. "If you want to know, you can check yourself. Better yet, ask him to show you. See if he'll tell you the truth."

"He said you'd say things I might not like to hear."

"I'm trying not to. You must find some things out yourself. So," he says and leans even closer. "What do you think about my little brother?"

I shrug my shoulder. What can I say? That I want him more than anything?

"He's not really your little brother. You're twins."

"You're in love," he says, smiling. "I can sense it."

I blush extremely hard at that.

"Oh, that blush gives you away. You are in love. Just know this," he says and leans closer still. "My brother is fucked-up big time in the romance department."

"Because of Danielle?"

"No," Julien says, making a face. "Other than the fact he killed her,

Danielle was good for him. Just like you'll be. No, I mean Marguerite," he says and takes a sip of his espresso. "She really did a number on him. Then he killed her. Gotta have a bad effect on a man's soul – his more than others."

I just look at him, amazed. He's so different from Michel. Polar opposites.

"What about your soul?" I say. "You were also enslaved by her."

"My soul was already a lost cause," he says and grins at me. "I was already a killer and seasoned lothario when she killed me so I wasn't scarred by Marguerite the way Michel was. I was tough, kicked and beaten so much by my old bastard of a father that I could shut it off. Michel couldn't, despite the act. His heart was too tender. He was damaged."

I try to change the subject, a sense of disquiet settling over me from his words.

"Why did you leave the Church?"

He leans back. "I joined because he wanted to so I was never really committed to it. When I saw what was going on in political terms, I left. The whole Cathar bit did the trick."

"What about the Cathars? Why were they so dangerous? What's in the manuscript Michel didn't want me to read?"

"You have it," he says. "Read it and find out. Your mother seemed to think it was important, but I expect the really good stuff is in her files, not in my melodramatic story."

"Michel took out half the pages."

"You have her files. I'm sure it's in there because I told her the whole story."

I glance at my watch. "I have to go," I say. "I'm due at the SCU in fifteen."

"Can I give you a ride?"

I hesitate. "Sure," I say and smile. We finish our drinks and he leads the way out of the café, holding the door for me, then opening the door to his car.

As I get in and do up my seatbelt, I catch sight of a flash of grey in the alley beside the café as we drive off and turn around, thinking I saw a vampire, but there's nothing there. Must have been a reflection, or lights flashing. Then I wonder if Michel hasn't been hanging around listening in to my meeting with Julien. Surely he couldn't hear our conversation from outside the café...

"How good are a vampire's ears?"

He glances over at me. "What do you mean?"

Should I say something?

"I thought I saw a vampire in the alley beside the café. If it was Michel, could he hear our conversation from outside the café?"

Julien laughs. "I wouldn't put it past him to spy on us. He's probably really worried that I'll say something I shouldn't."

"Like what?"

"I can't say," he says. "Because I shouldn't."

"That's not fair," I say, angry that neither brother is willing to tell me everything. "If you know something I should know, tell me."

"Life's not fair, Eve. Anyway, I know a lot of things. How do I know what's important and what isn't unless I know you much better?"

He smiles over at me, wagging his eyebrows suggestively. When I frown, he laughs.

"Oh, Eve. Lighten up. I'm just having fun. If it was Michel in the alley, he could probably hear what we were talking about if he focused really hard. The older you get, the better you are able to focus your senses."

We drive through the city towards the Foster Building.

"What are you doing now?" I say, curious about his life.

"Oh, I've taken some time off and have been living at the monastery outside of the city. I worked for the US military for a couple of decades once I left England after the Second World War. Vietnam, Korea, Iraq, Afghanistan, you name it. Did a lot of bad things, saw a lot of shit happen, and I figure I deserve a break. Maybe a bit of redemption myself."

"You fought in Afghanistan and Iraq?"

"Yep," he says, driving, one hand on the wheel. "Once a knight, always a knight, I guess. I was part of a clandestine team who did the really black ops. Black interrogations, renditions, assassinations. Us vampires make great warriors. Hard as fuck to kill."

"Where did you work most recently?"

"Basra, southern Iraq. That is, until my group of fellow warriors was taken out in an ambush, the whole lot of my men staked and decapitated, dumped in the Euphrates. After that, I basically came back and decided I'd drop out for a while. Went to live at the monastery."

Something about his story makes me frown. "They were decapitated?"

"Only way to kill a vampire permanently."

I turn to look at him and then I see it – a tattoo on his neck only visible because his scarf has fallen away. I feel a chill go through me. A Lorraine Cross.

"Tell me about your tattoo."

He turns to me and frowns.

"Oh, this?" he says and fixes his scarf. "It's the insignia of my unit. After the Knights Templar."

"Why them?"

He shrugs. "Just a group we admired."

I get the very strong impression he's not telling me everything. "Some of the bodies in the River Man case had that tattoo."

"Oh, really?" he says, his voice light. "Isn't that an interesting coincidence…"

"If you know something, tell me," I say quietly.

"I don't know what you're talking about, Eve." He turns and looks at me pointedly.

We arrive at the Foster Building and he stops the car and gets out, opens the door for me.

"Hey, listen, Eve," he says and stands close to me when I reach the stairs. "I know I give him a hard time, but Michel's really a good man. He hasn't been corrupted, despite everything. There's a part of him that's still pure, that still has hope, that still believes. Me?" he says and shakes his head, his hands in his pockets. "I'm jaded as hell. I wish I was like him, but I'm not. Physically, we're identical, but emotionally?

We're opposites. He was always softer hearted. My father hated him because of it. Thought he was weak and tried to beat strength into him. It was up to me to protect him so I got hard, fast."

He says nothing for a moment, and I'm completely absorbed in what he's saying, thinking of this bond between these two brothers. He reaches his hand up to my face and strokes my cheek with the backs of his fingers, the way Michel has so many times and I feel a surge of warmth from him.

"You have to know I'd do anything for him. Anything. Even give you up. You can tell him that. Tell him to stop worrying."

Then he turns away and goes around to the car, opens the door and gets in. He drives off without another word, leaving me standing on the sidewalk.

CHAPTER 12

"Being deeply loved by someone gives you strength, while loving someone deeply gives you courage."

Lao Tzu

"I'm glad you're back," Ed says when I enter to the SCU. "I have a present for you." He hands me a box. Inside is a pair of thin leather gloves – exceptionally thin. So thin, I can pick up a dime off the counter. "They'll protect you from intrusions when you touch objects that might have been connected to a murder."

"Thanks," I say, slipping them off and putting them in my coat pocket.

"Most Adepts wear them. Once you start working, doing cases, you'll be more attuned to the traces left in crime scene evidence. Helps keep the crazy images and visions at bay."

I smile at Ed and take in a deep breath. Michel comes to my desk and examines the gloves.

"There's a development in Montana," Ed says. "A similar case. Same

MO. Seems as if our killer's gone inter-state in his killing spree. I want you both to come with me and investigate."

"You want us to go where?"

I can hear the frustration in Michel's voice and see it in the lines on his brow. He shakes his head.

"Montana," Ed says, as if he's unconcerned. "There's a similar murder. We need to investigate the connections."

"I don't like the idea of leaving Boston when Eve isn't fully trained," Michel says. "Not a good idea."

Another murder. I shrug, trying to appear calm at the prospect.

"Here," Ed says and places a paper bag on the desk in front of me. "We use the FBI for our cover. Your badge, your jacket and your permit to carry a weapon. You can go to weapons later and get yourself one. You won't have time to actually do your firearms training, so your magazine will be empty but we can't have a Special Agent walking around without a weapon on their person."

I take the badge out and hang it around my neck. I inspect the jacket. It's a blue windbreaker and has the letters FBI in yellow on the back and the insignia on the front. It feels like a costume rather than a uniform and I feel like an actor, not the real deal.

"Sounds interesting," I say, trying to feel confident in my abilities. Truly, I would have preferred to spend a few more days reading and just becoming familiar with SCU procedures but I understand they want to find the killer.

"Fill out the requisitions," Ed says to Michel, "and I'll sign them to approve your travel expenses."

I'm not really sure I want to go to Montana but it will be a chance for Michel and I to work together as a team. I get to do some real work, and so, I'll put extra food in my cat's dish and pack my bags once more.

I can tell Michel isn't happy but he shrugs and gives in. Later, when we're finished making arrangements, he pulls me over alone in the hallway.

"Eve, I don't like this. I don't like taking you out of town when you're not trained. You'll be a liability."

"That's nice to know."

"It's not your fault. I don't know why Ed's insisting, but we have orders from Headquarters. Please," he says, and tightens his grip on my arm. "If you're serious about being my Adept, this is the time to just obey me."

He's so serious, his face so dark, I nod my head.

"OK," I say and take his hand. "I am serious. I will."

He brushes my hair from my cheek.

"Too bad I didn't make this speech earlier and then maybe you wouldn't have met with my brother – again."

"Michel, he said not to worry. He said he wouldn't try to take me from you."

Michel shakes his head.

"I'll believe that when I know you're mine completely. And even then, maybe not."

"You don't trust him?"

"Not in this, no."

I sigh, never having expected to get caught between these two brothers.

THE NEXT DAY, we charter a Council jet that's specially designed so that Michel will be protected from the sunlight. We fly to Helena in the afternoon, arriving just after sundown, going straight to the hotel once we arrive. It's close enough to the airport that I can stand at the lobby window and watch as a small plane lands.

Ed signs in first, flashing his FBI badge. He scopes out the hotel, asking for certain rooms and the clerk complies with all the requests. I feel safe knowing he and Michel will be in the rooms on either side of me and that if I need them, they can just open the door and be there.

We sit in my room and after I get my laptop set up and internet connected, we go over the details of the current murder. The Helena Valley Regulating Reservoir is about four miles from the airport.

That's where local authorities found the decapitated body and after checking in with the local police, it's our first destination.

We drive to the Helena Police Department's Criminal Investigations Building, a newer square brick building on 11th Avenue. Ed introduces us to the officer in charge of the case, Detective Brent Fletcher. Fletcher's in his early forties and has that clean-cut All-American look to him, as if he just stepped out of a Wheaties advertisement.

"Nice to meet you," he says in a soft Mid-Western accent. We walk down the hallways leading from the security desk to the administration offices at the north side of the building. Fletcher takes us to his corner of the open office and we sit down to discuss the case. His office area is small and filled with bookshelves, filing cabinets, his desk littered with papers, files and half-empty Styrofoam cups of coffee.

"An older guy known as 'Fishman' found the body. A vagrant who fishes in the reservoir for his food. Guess he doesn't appreciate the food at the local shelter." He grins at us.

We discuss the cases in Boston, and it's only now, while going over the cases there, that I learn that there are more in other states. Montana is only the latest in a series of states with similar murders. This killer has a wide range.

We drive to the reservoir to check the dumpsite. After the detective explains where the body was found and the way the witness had come forward, we linger behind so I can do a little psychic sleuthing. I take off my gloves, and touch the rocks lining the shore but there's nothing I can find connected to the killer.

Next we go back to the precinct to watch tapes of the witness interview. "Fishman" is in his forties, with long dark hair that looks like a horsetail down his back. He has a scraggly beard shot through with gray and red, and wears several layers of rotting and frayed clothing, thick with body oils. I can only imagine his stink.

He'd been prospecting for bottles left behind by teens who parked along the reservoir at night for some action, and was there when a man carrying a large burden arrived and dumped the body on the shore. Fishman hid behind a trashcan and watched as the man rolled the body into the water, and then placed the severed head in the corpse's arms, just like all the others.

When the killer left the scene, Fishman checked the corpse's pockets for money before making his way to the precinct to inform police of what he'd seen.

"I figured the dead guy didn't need it," he says plainly. "But there was 'nuthin there."

I examine the crime scene photographs and it doesn't take me long to note the gloves on the corpse's hands. Thin leather. I show it to Ed.

"So why hasn't the killer targeted me?"

"Maybe he has. Remember the note. We don't know yet what connects these Adepts. That's why we're here. Looking into each of their pasts is going to give us an idea. Maybe use it to predict his future targets."

WE VIEW the body at the morgue but there's nothing to see that we haven't seen before. Body bled out then decapitated. Dumped on the shore of the reservoir. Head in shackled embrace. The Adept is a younger man with dark curling hair that's plastered to his pale forehead. When the technician's busy speaking with Ed, I touch the body quickly to see what I can glean but there's nothing. Just a sense of darkness, stars overhead breaking through the clouds. In my mind's eye, a blackness spreads over the sky above and then nothing. Apparently, as time passes, the memories caught in synapses fade, leaving little for Adepts to find. I turn his head to the side and there it is – a tattoo like Julien's. A Lorraine Cross.

"Look at this," I say and point to the tattoo.

Definitely linked to the others," Ed says. I use my iPhone to take a picture of it when they turn away.

We have dinner at the hotel and take a brief rest, for our real work starts later. Michel is being unusually distant, as if he still disapproves of my being here. We're going to the sheriff's office in a small town in

Montana about an hour's drive to the north. We're there to watch an interview with the owner of the private security corporation that trains people for duty in the Middle East and Persian Gulf. The dead man worked for the owner. Fletcher thinks there may be some connection.

$\sim$

THE NIGHT'S SO COLD. I shiver as we walk from the parking lot to the Sheriff's office. After another round of introductions in which Ed flashes his badge, I sit at a desk, going over my own notes on the small laptop, waiting for the dead man's boss to arrive and answer questions. When he walks in the office, my back's to the door, so I hear him, feel his presence before I see him. I turn slowly, not wanting to betray my anticipation. He has white skin and eyes so pale the iris resembles water, the pupils huge, much larger than normal. Platinum hair.

A vampire.

Michel stands and almost knocks over his chair, his expression one of shock, his eyes wide. The man smiles at Michel. He makes a hand signal as if telling Michel to sit and he does.

What the heck is going on?

I turn to Michel but he won't meet my eyes. If a vampire could flush, Michel would have at that moment, and I reach out to touch him to see what's wrong. He pulls his hand away and shakes his head quickly.

I turn back to the vampire. He wears a beret and black suede coat with a lambskin collar, and looks to be well over six feet tall. He removes his coat and beret and sits down on the chair the Sheriff's deputy offers him.

He looks around the room, waiting for the Sheriff to get off the phone and begin his questions, his fingers tapping impatiently on the tabletop. A thick gold signet ring circles his index finger. When those ice blue eyes come to rest on me, I have to fight with all my might not to look quickly away. I merely nod and wait for him to break the eye contact between us. He finally looks away, his eyes closing briefly, a small smile on his lips as if he knows who I am and why I'm here. The thought makes me nervous.

The Sheriff finally puts down the phone and comes to the desk, extending his hand to the vampire, who according to my file, is former Marine, retired Colonel Anders Henrickson. Late thirties, long pale hair pulled back in a ponytail. He rises briefly and shakes the Sheriff's hand, then seats himself once again.

"Thank you for coming down so quickly to meet with me to discuss the recent death of one of your members, Cpl. Conrad," the Sheriff says, consulting a file in front of him. "A former Marine, and according to his membership card, a lieutenant in your organization."

"Yes," Henrickson replies, his voice deep and sonorous with a hint of a Norwegian accent. "Such a shock to us all, so tragic a loss - Conrad was one of my best officers."

The Sheriff nods. "I spoke to his family in Georgia - they seemed pleased he was a member of the group - says it was the first time he's been out of trouble in years. You had no problems with discipline? Any enemies he might have - someone who might want him dead?"

"None that I know of," Henrickson replies, shifting in his chair, waving his hand in dismissal. "I was pleased with him. I'm sad to lose him."

Henrickson sits patiently, waiting for the Sheriff to continue. His legs are crossed casually, his hands resting on the arms of the wooden chair. He's calm under the Sheriff's questions - totally at ease with the situation, no hint of nervousness. His air of absolute command makes the rest of us look pale and insignificant in comparison.

"As I say, there was a witness report about another man present at the scene when the Lieutenant died - a tall man with pale hair and skin. The man was driving a late model GMC truck. I remember from our last meeting that you own such a truck."

Henrickson raises his eyebrows. "Yes. I do, but there must be dozens in this area of the country. Any leads on who the man might be?"

"No, we think it's just the witnesses' vivid imagination. Not a very reliable fellow. Just for the record, Colonel, can you tell me your whereabouts in the early morning hours around 0300 hours?"

Henrickson looks down at the floor and then nods. "Yes, I was with my ... girlfriend, in my quarters. She's my secretary, Jane Beauregard. I can give you her number and address if you require it."

"Thanks, Colonel. You understand we have to check it out," the Sheriff says, downplaying the seriousness of the issue. Henrickson waves his hand and shrugs, taking a pen out of his shirt pocket and writing something on a slip of paper.

"No problem. I understand protocol."

The Sheriff takes the slip of paper and nods, then stands up and extends his hand once again. Henrickson rises and shakes it, then shrugs on the coat over his strong form before looking at us all, me last, and nodding good-bye. He pulls a beret over his head before he leaves.

"Is there anything else?"

The sheriff shakes his head.

"Good day, gentlemen," he says, his voice almost jovial. "Lady." He nods to me. "Let's hope there's no more reason for me to visit your pleasant office again." His eye catches mine before he leaves and a shiver goes through me.

We gather around the Sheriff's desk and discuss the case - the Sheriff's unconvinced of Fishman's statement. Michel still looks to be in shock but he says nothing.

"I'll check out the Colonel's alibi but it's highly unlikely that Henrickson himself would do the dirty work. More likely one of his staff." The Sheriff looks at me and shakes his head. "Sorry, I just don't buy it. There's no motive, no evidence."

Ed nods.

Another dead end.

ONCE WE'RE outside the building, Michel grabs me and pulls me aside.

"We have to get you out of here, fast. That was Soren."

"What?" A shock of adrenaline goes through me, making my legs weak.

Ed comes over. "What's the matter?"

"That was Soren Lindgren, that's what. How did we end up bringing Eve to him? Who told you to come here?"

"Headquarters."

Michel shakes his head. "I don't know what his game is, but she's in danger. We have to leave right away." He grabs my arm and drags me to the car as if he fears Soren's lurking around, preparing to grab me.

We drive to the hotel and Michel calls to order our flight to prepare, but there's been a mechanical problem and it's out of service for at least a day. He calls to find out when the first flight leaves, but it doesn't leave until early morning.

"Listen," Ed says as we sit in the hotel room. "I still think we need to check his place out tomorrow."

"You can do that on your own," Michel says. "I'm sending Eve back on the first flight out of here. I can't believe we brought her directly to Soren. *Merde*," he says and rakes his fingers through his hair. "I can't believe it."

He sits and stares at me as if I'm going to disappear before his eyes.

Then, his cell rings and he checks the caller display.

"Damn," he says, his eyes closed. Then, he taps the icon and answers. "Yes," he says, his voice low.

"I can't do that."

He listens.

Silence.

"I'll be with her the entire time. That's my one condition."

He listens some more and now I wonder what bargain he's striking. He ends the call and shakes his head.

"This is insane. This was a set-up," he says to us, his voice on edge. "He just wanted to get Eve alone somewhere and meet her. I have no choice but to take her to him or he'll kill Julien."

"What?" Ed says, looking between the two of us.

"I'll meet him," I say, not really knowing what that means. "I don't want Julien dead because of me."

~

WE HAVE a late meeting at the compound where Soren trains his recruits. It will mean a late night before Ed's and my early morning flight, but we have to go. Ed drives the rental car and we arrive half an hour early, hoping to spend some time wandering around before the meeting, and are met by a young man dressed in combat fatigues at a guardhouse who requests our names and some identification. I pull out my badge and he looks it over and checks my name on his roster. He nods to Ed and Michel, keeping our ID and asks for our weapons.

I hand him my empty revolver and both Ed and Michel do the same.

The young man gives us directions and Ed drives to a low hangar-like building that looks like it would house small planes. I'm surprised at how little activity there is, and how freely we're able to move around.

Ed parks the car and we go into the small building, which houses Soren's private offices and find ourselves in a small reception area. There's no one there to greet us but we hear the murmur of voices off to the rear of the building. While Michel and Ed check out a door to the north, I step to a partially opened door in the south of the hall that leads to the back of the building and listen - the unmistakable sound of a male and female laughing intimately.

A deep voice - Soren, and a high female voice - perhaps his secretary - I can't tell. I peer through the crack in the door and am shocked at what I see. In the darkness, with only faint light from under the door illuminating the scene, I see them. Soren's pants are undone and are half-way down his muscular thighs. He's leaning over a young woman who is herself bent over a desk, her skirt hiked up, her legs spread. But what shocks me is what I see in the darkness behind him —a pair of huge black wings. I gasp and in an instant what I thought were wings transform into shadow and Soren turns his head towards the door where I hide.

I turn and walk back to Michel and Ed, not knowing what I saw or what to say.

"I saw him," I say, almost choking on my words.

"Where?"

"In an office in the back. With his secretary."

A few moments later, the young woman enters the hall and goes to the reception desk. The only sign that she's had sex is her still-flushed cheeks. She smiles sweetly when she sees us and asks for our names. She picks up a phone and speaks into it.

"He'll see you now," she says, and leads us past the desk where the two had sex and points to an office with an impressive leather chair and ornately carved mahogany desk.

Soren enters the room from an adjoining one - the bathroom, I suppose. He's wiping his face on a towel.

"You caught me at a bad time," he says, a smile on his full lips. "I was just washing up." He raises his eyebrows suggestively at me. Did he know I was there earlier?

I saw something strange – wings. Could they have been just shadows?

He finishes drying himself off and throws the towel onto a table before sitting down at his desk, motioning us to be seated as well.

I sit in a chair with Michel standing behind me as if to claim me. Soren sits with his palms held together almost in prayer.

Is he mocking us? I can't suppress a shudder.

"Cut to the chase," Michel says. "You wanted Eve here. Here she is."

Soren smiles. He gets up and comes to stand directly in front of me, just a foot away, his hands on his hips. He's so tall and powerfully built and beautiful in an unnatural way, the way Julien's manuscript described him. Every feature is perfect, symmetrical, as if he were a Greek statue come to life.

Behind me, Michel leans closer and rests his hands on my shoulders possessively.

"She's mine," he says.

"Technically, she's no one's seeing as you're too pure to claim her."

"She's Natalia's daughter."

"And she was meant for Julien," Soren says. "But I just wanted to see her for myself. You're willing to fight for her?"

"You know I can't beat you, but I will fight you even if I die."

"Relax, Michel," Soren says. "I just wanted to see her. Get to know her. After all, there's been so much to do about her. I wanted to make sure she's worth it."

"She's gifted," Michel says. "But she's not trained. We'll train her, get her ready."

"I'm sure you will." He turns to me. "How's Julien?" he says and smiles down at me. "I hear you've met both brothers. How to choose between them? That must confuse you."

"Leave Julien out of this, " I say.

"Ah, so sweet that you care about a vampire's well-being, given you want to kill them. Isn't it so sweet? I especially love it when humans fall in love with vampires. So tragic. Why, I bet you could love them both. Identical twins? How could you not?"

He steps closer, and Michel's hand tightens on my shoulder.

"I said relax, Michel. I'm not going to take her. At least, not yet. I just want to see what all the fuss is about." He tips up my chin so that I'm forced to look in his eyes. "She's pretty. I like petite blondes. You remember Marguerite, Michel." He reaches out his hand to me and I hesitate.

"Don't touch her," Michel says and his voice is low.

"Don't even think of threatening me, Michel," Soren says. "I could kill you all in the time it takes you to take a breath. I'll do what I want."

He holds his hand out, palm up.

"Stand up," he says.

I stand and he pulls me towards him so that I'm about five inches from him, our hands joined.

Then a wave of something rushes over me, a sense of a powerful questing mind searching out my own, looking for something, but I can't tell what it is. He goes all the way back to my childhood in Europe, to Budapest and the salon where I took music lessons. I'm sitting there in the ornate building at a grand piano, playing for my father and his colleagues. It's the year before my mother dies. The year before we moved back to Boston.

Then, he's at that day, and I'm sitting in the corner of my mother's office at the university, reading National Geographic magazines while she works in the lab that adjoins her office. I hear a commotion, hear glass breaking, hear a muffled sound, and then I go into the room only to find her on the floor and there's blood on her neck and it's frothing out of her mouth...

I cry out, my emotions overwhelming me because the memory's so real I feel as if I'm there in the moment, and tears bite at the corners of my eyes. Then calmness descends over me and my tears stop. He lets go of me and I almost fall back into my chair, Michel catching me, holding my shoulders. Soren goes back around the desk and takes a seat, staring at me over his steepled hands.

"So what is it about you that Michel likes so much, Eve? Is it your fair hair and hazel eyes? I think you remind him of someone he was once in love with." He looks up at Michel. "Danielle if I recall?"

"Eve is her own woman," Michel says, and the hatred in his voice is so clear, I'm surprised that Soren doesn't respond.

"Yes, and she has such a sweet mind to inhabit, doesn't she? Such a tragic past. So breathless for you, and yet fighting it with all her might, as if her life depends on it. And her life does depend on it, doesn't it, Michel? I can see why you want her. Is she that strategically important? Or can you just not bear the thought of me having her?"

"I love her," Michel says and it sends a wave of emotion through me.

"Oh, you love her, do you?" Soren says, his voice mocking. "She's not quite given in to you yet, has she? You haven't yet won her over, have you? She's still too fixated on finding her mother's killer. But give her time. She will be yours. You just can't wait to claim her, can you Michel? To claim her completely."

Soren smiles such an evil smile that I hate him even more if possible.

"I love it," he says and chuckles. "I love a good romance. Maybe one day, she'll have you both. Just like old times? She's attracted to him, too, you know. Even thought about it already, fucking him? But you already know that, don't you, Michel. It must just tear at your heart."

"You're a bastard," I say, and I don't know what's gotten into me. I should be afraid of him but I hate him right now so much I can't hold back.

Michel squeezes my shoulders. "She didn't mean that," he says quietly.

"I did mean it."

"Shh," Michel says.

Soren seems amused more than angry, his arms crossed, a smile on his face.

"To answer you, Eve, technically, yes," he says, "since my father and mother never married, I am a bastard but then, that kind of convention doesn't really apply to the gods."

"Gods?" I say, unable to stop myself. Michel squeezes me again and then he touches the skin on my neck with his hand and he must do something to my brain hormones because I feel a rush go through me. I can't speak, my eyes closing briefly from the intensity.

"Can we go now that you've seen her?" Michel says, his voice soft.

I open my eyes and watch as Soren purses his lips and finally nods. "Yes, by all means. Go back to Boston. Train her in the secret arts of the Adept. I suspect you're going to have a lot of fun with her. She's not likely to obey very easily. But you should get her ready for war."

Ed's been silent through all this.

"If there's nothing else?" he says, rising up. "We have work to do before Eve and I fly to Boston."

Soren nods. "I'm on my way East as well," he says. "Are you taking the flight in the morning? I heard the Council jet had some mechanical problems."

"Yes," Ed ads. "Michel has to stay until the plane's been serviced because he can't leave during the daylight. Eve and I will take the 5:30 a.m. flight."

"Tell you what," Soren says, and his voice has this conspiratorial tone to it. "I've got a spare couple of seats on my plane, and you're all welcome to come with me tomorrow at a more reasonable time. I'm leaving around noon. We'll take you all to Boston."

"We're fine with the arrangements we've made," Michel says, butting in.

"It'll save the Council some money. Come on," Soren says, smiling. "I'd enjoy the company."

Ed purses his lips and seems to seriously consider the offer. Is he crazy?

"What do you think, Eve?" he says and turns to me.

I still can't speak, and just sit there.

"It's my call, not Eve's," Michel says.

"No," Soren says, his voice firm. "It's my call. Isn't that right Michel?"

"You've seen her. That's what you wanted. Just let us go on our way."

Soren comes around from his desk and stands in front of Michel. He reaches out and cups Michel's cheek and Michel's eyes close briefly before opening again.

"I said, it's my call. There's nothing to worry about. I won't take her. She's still yours. You'll join me."

"We'll join you," Michel says, and his voice sounds flat, like Soren has compelled him.

"All right then," Ed says and extends his hand to Soren as if he's just another professional. "What time do you want us here?"

Soren shrugs. "An hour before would be fine. One of my drivers will pick you up in Helena in a UV-protected car."

He turns to me.

"Nice to meet you again, Eve," he says and bends down to me, taking my hand, kissing my knuckles. I can't respond, sitting there like a lump. "Until tomorrow."

I'VE NEVER BEEN SO glad to be away from someone.

On the drive back to Helena, I slowly recover from the effect of whatever endorphin Michel's released in my brain.

"Do you really think it's a good idea to fly back with him?" I say.

Michel says nothing. He's staring out the car window, chewing on his bottom lip as if lost in thought.

"He forced you to agree, didn't he?" I say, taking Michel's hand. "He can compel you to obey him."

Finally Michel turns to me.

"There's nothing to worry about," he says. "He's not going to take you." He leans over to me, his hand tangling in my hair, and he kisses me. He strokes my cheek with his thumb. "You're still mine."

"Do you even know that he's compelled you?"

"Don't worry, Eve." He kisses me once more and turns back to the window, but he takes my hand in his, threading his fingers through mine as if his mind is afraid he'll lose me, even if part of it assures him he won't.

Ed looks at me in the rear-view mirror. "What did you think of him?"

I shake my head and gaze out the window at the stars above the hills. "I think he's very dangerous."

"He's powerful, that's for sure. All this firepower and money." Ed's thinking of weapons and soldiers. I'm thinking of his power to manipulate people's minds and of the shadows that looked like huge wings sprouting from his back. It was probably the play of shadows in a dark room. If I repeat that enough times, I might start to believe it.

~

CHAPTER 13

Edwin Arnold

We arrive back at the hotel before 10:00 P.M. I go inside my room
and immediately flop on the bed. Michel enters the room from his
adjoining room a few moments later.

"You should get some sleep," he says. "I'll just watch news headlines.
I'm not leaving you alone."

He's truly worried, despite Soren's compelling him not to. I nod
and get my nightgown and toiletries and go to the bathroom, do my
nightly routine of cleaning my face and teeth. I come back into the
room and he's on the other bed with his shoes off, and is flipping
through channels on the television. He glances at me when I go to my
bed, his eyes moving over my body. I remember what Soren said –
that he's attracted to me because I resemble Danielle, and that he
wants me because of her.

"Julien told me there was something in your wallet I should see."

He frowns. "I told you he'd try to stir things up."

"Can I see it?"

He hesitates and then sighs, reaching into his jacket pocket to remove a thin leather wallet. He opens it and flips through it, then hands it to me.

"Go ahead."

I take it, feeling bad that I'm snooping but I don't stop. I open the wallet, which is made of fine leather and is smooth to the touch, black, with an inner fold for cash in a money clip and then a spot for credit cards and ID. Inside an inner pocket, I find a tiny picture of me as a girl, maybe ten, the year before my mother died. I sit on the side of the bed and just look at it.

I remember the day this was taken. The ten-year old me stands in the wings of a stage in an auditorium, waiting to perform in a recital. I'm wearing a black velvet dress with a big white bow tied in front and my long hair is up in a bun, tendrils falling around my face like a proper little lady. My face has this dreamy look to it, as if I'm staring off in the distance, lost in thought. It's me, just with a softer face, smaller features.

He crawls over to me, and looks at it over my shoulder.

"Where did you get this?" I ask, not knowing how I feel about this.

"Your mother gave it to me."

"Why?"

"Because I supported her wish to keep you out."

"What do you mean?"

"To train you as a musician and wait until you were an adult before you were offered the option to join the Council. I helped her and your father hide from the Council."

"Michel," I say and turn to look at him. "Why didn't you tell me this?"

He shrugs one shoulder.

"I thought it would upset you to know."

"It upsets me that you didn't tell me." I look on the back and see my name written on the back with the year. My mother's handwriting. "Did I ever meet you?"

"That night," he says and points to the picture. "It was the recital after your Grade Six Royal Conservatory examination in London. After the event was over at the reception, I stopped by to congratulate you and we shook hands."

"So you knew my parents well."

"No," he says. "Not well at all. I was merely an intermediary between my group and your family. I didn't know your family had gone back to Boston until a year later. Before I could reestablish contact, your mother died. I did my best to ensure the Council didn't get you in their clutches."

"So it was you who lost my file?"

He doesn't say anything for a while.

"I had a contact in the normal child welfare system who was supposed to find you a good home, and I did lose track of you as soon as you went to live with your foster family. I didn't want to know where you were or who you were with. I wanted to forget about your existence completely, to protect you from the Council. And I succeeded, until you were looking for a translator. I had no idea Julien gave the manuscript to your mother. I asked him for it and he said he'd given it to a collector."

I just sit and look at the picture, my memories drawn back to that time of my life, travelling with my parents through Europe that last year before we moved back to Boston.

"Why?"

He frowns. "What do you mean? Why did I help?"

"Yes. You say how strategically important I am. I thought your mission was the most important thing to you."

"You were different. I hated the thought that your talent would be wasted. I wanted you to have the chance to develop."

"I wish you would have told me. I would have felt differently."

"What do you mean?"

"If I'd known you knew my parents and helped our family."

He shakes his head.

"I didn't want you to feel any obligation. I wanted it to be your own free will as much as possible."

I hand the picture back to him and I feel so sad now, grief just under the surface. He touches my hand when he takes the picture back.

"This upsets you," he says. "I'm sorry. I told you that Julien would stir things up."

I go back to the other bed and slip under the covers, staring at the ceiling.

He comes over and sits beside me on the bed, leaning down to kiss me, but nothing more. Then he goes back to the other bed, turning back to the television.

I turn over and face him, wondering why he's not going to sleep with me, wishing he would, but I try to be obedient, letting him decide what happens and when.

"Good night," I say quietly.

"Good night, Eve." He clicks off the bedside light and there's just the flicker of blue light from the television.

SOMETIME LATER WHEN the sky is still pitch-black, I wake to find Michel in bed with me, spooned against me, his arms are wrapped around me, and he's kissing my neck. My body responds immediately to his touch, and I gasp when he turns me over and his mouth finds mine.

"I thought he'd take you from me," he whispers, his voice so fearful even now. "I can't lose you."

Then I feel his teeth on the skin of my neck and I know he's in hunter mode for I can feel his fangs. They don't break my skin, just remind me that he's a vampire and that he could take me if he wanted. I want him to but he doesn't.

Then he rises up and it's not Michel. It's Soren. I gasp and try to push him away, but he's too strong...

My eyes fly open and I'm alone on the bed. It was just a dream. After a few moments of deep breathing to calm my racing heart, I get up and open the curtains to look at the airport. It's still dark out.

Michel isn't on the other bed beside me and so I assume he's gone back to his own room. It's 4:00 a.m., and if I'm going on the early flight, we have to leave in half an hour. I need to get up.

I dress quickly and decide to go down to the restaurant, get a cup of coffee at the coffee shop. I slip on my jacket and boots, then leave the room. I go down the elevator but the hotel coffee shop is closed. I'll have to go to the one next to the hotel and out through a side door to the coffee shop. Before I get to the door of the well-lit parking lot, I stand for a moment and face the airport. A lone plane takes off directly overhead and for a while I just stand and stare up at the sky. The stars are bright enough despite the city lights that I can make out Cassiopeia and the Big Dipper.

I walk with my head up, not paying attention to my surroundings, letting the feelings of relief at leaving Helena fill me, when I bump into a person walking in the opposite direction who grabs my arm.

"Oh, hell," I say, when I realized it's Julien. He's barely visible, wearing his long black trench coat and black fedora.

"What in God's name are you doing walking around alone while it's still dark?" he says, his voice almost a hiss. "Have you no sense?"

"I was just getting coffee."

"At four in the morning?"

"Julien, Michel and Ed have agreed that we're flying back with Soren. I want to go on the first flight. I don't want to go back with Soren."

"Soren's not going to hurt you."

I shake my head. He must have gotten to Julien as well.

"Soren's compelled you, too."

"Quiet," he says, his voice low. He pulls me over between two parked semi-trailer trucks and pushes me against one. He presses his hand over my mouth and shakes his head quickly.

A lone man walks through the parking lot towards us. Julien pulls his coat around me as if to hide me from sight. I glance up at his face. He speaks in a quiet voice, his tone flat. "Don't say a word."

I try to get hold of myself, realizing that I'm in danger from whoever might be following me. I stand with Julien's arms around me until the man has gone to one of the other semi-trailers and then I try to pull away.

"No. Just keep quiet for a minute."

I just stand there, waiting and Julien buries his nose in my hair and neck, inhaling deeply.

"Christ, Eve," he says. "Why in hell would you think of going out alone? Have you learned nothing about the danger you're in?"

I frown at him.

"I'm in danger from Soren, and you're all convinced he won't take me."

"Soren's not going to take you." He shakes his head. "Eve. You must be extremely careful. You simply can't go out alone," he says, brushing hair off my face. "This was the worst time possible to be brought into this life, but there was no choice. You just have to accept reality."

I look around, trying to avoid his eyes because I'm so frustrated at Soren's ability to manipulate them all.

"I hate this," I say. "I hate you, and Michel and Ed and everything."

"Hush," he says, his grin lopsided. "No you don't. You don't hate me. You don't hate Michel. In fact, you like us both a little too much." He takes my arm, gently escorting me towards the coffee shop. "It's not what you imagined, but it's reality. You're a survivor, Eve. You just have to accept things for what they are and cooperate."

He squeezes my arm and I tug it away, but it's futile.

"You enjoy this, don't you?" I say, angry at his possessiveness. "This sense of ownership you and your brother have over me."

"No," he says. "I don't, Eve. Actually, I'm mad at you. You have no idea how much danger you put yourself in by coming out here."

"You're all putting me in danger, letting me go back with Soren on his plane."

"Don't worry, Eve. He's not going to take you."

"You keep saying that. Don't you realize he's compelled you?"

We reached the door to the hotel.

"You go on in. I'll get you a cup of coffee. Medium roast with cream, right? I'll be up in about fifteen minutes. I have to make a call first. I don't know how Michel let you out of his sight."

He pushes me forward and I enter the hotel with my keycard and go to the bank of elevators. I get in the elevator and go back to my room.

∼

I CHECK Michel's room but there's no answer. At 4:30 a.m. Julien still hasn't come to my room so I knock on the door adjoining my room once more and call Michel's name.

There's still no answer. I call down to the front desk and ask the night clerk if she knows where Ed and Michel are.

"Oh, he and Special Agent de Cernay left for the airport twenty minutes ago. They left word that you were flying back with a Mr. Henrickson later this morning."

"What?"

The clerk starts to repeat herself but I cut her off.

"They're gone?"

"Yes, I called a cab for them. They left for the airport."

All I can think is that this is a nightmare and soon I'll wake up and see that none of the preceding happened – it's all been a bad dream.

"Can you tell me what room Julien de Cernay is in?"

She pauses on the other end for a moment. "I'm sorry. We have no guest registered with that name."

I sigh. What the hell?

"Can you call me a taxi? I have to make it to the airport for the flight."

The clerk frowned. "Well," she says slowly, "that might be a bit hard since it's already taken off."

"What?" Damn.

"Agent O'Neil said he sent you an email," the clerk says, her voice hopeful.

"Thank you," I say and hang up.

I open my cell and check my mail. There it is:

Eve,

Michel and I are going back now on the Council jet. It's fixed and we'll be gone at 4:30. Colonel Lindgren will send a driver at 11:00 so you can catch a ride out to his airstrip in time for his flight. Glad you decided to fly back with him – you looked really tired when we spoke last night and I agree – some sleep and a later flight will be good for you, given your recent experiences. Take the rest of the day off and see you at work tomorrow night.

Ed.

What? I talked to him? I have no memory of talking to him. Soren must have compelled him, too. I sit on the small sofa in the room and try to decide. I can't even get a rental because I don't have a credit card so I grit my teeth and will fly back with Soren. I have a feeling it will be quite a test, whatever happens.

THE CAR PICKS me up at 11:00. A black limo, the driver tips his cap and opens the door for me before loading my bag into the trunk. It takes just under an hour to arrive and I'm glad for the plastic partition that separates the driver from the passenger.

We drive through the countryside to the base, the driver sailing through the guardhouse checkpoint without even rolling down his window. The limo stops at the hangar and the driver opens my door, ushering me over to the hanger door. He brings my bag out and I wait for someone to come and get me.

The pilot opens the hangar side door and shakes my hand. He's a very young clean-cut man, red-blooded son of the Mid-West, who introduces himself with that familiar soft drawl that's not quite southern Cowboy, but not Northeastern that I'm more used to hearing.

"Come this way," he says. "Colonel Lindgren is already on the plane."

I follow him, steeling myself for the experience of spending a couple of hours in his presence – alone. I climb up the steps to the door and enter. Next I step through a heavy draped doorway and into the cocoon-like interior. It's been remodeled and has four plush armchair-like seats. The window shades are closed and the room is lit by soft yellow lamps along the cabin bulkhead.

Soren is seated in one of the chairs reading a file when I enter.

"Eve, how nice to see you again." He stands and like a gentleman, comes and shakes my gloved hand. He lays his other hand over it, clasping my smaller hand in his. "I was glad that at least one of you could fly with me. Agent O'Neil sent me a note to let me know you'd had a difficult couple of days and would sleep in, take the later flight with me. Glad I could be of service."

"What a load of bullshit," I say, unwilling to play this game of pleasantries between enemies. "You compelled Michel to let me come alone with you. Probably Julien and Ed as well."

He smiles. "You have a saucy mouth," he says. "I love saucy, Eve, so don't think that will put me off. Eternity's so long and I do love a challenge. Now, take a seat. We'll be taking off shortly. If you don't mind, I have a bit of reading to do. Help yourself to a magazine or newspaper while we wait." He points to a table at the side of the cabin.

I take off my coat and gloves, hanging them on the back of the seat and go over and select The New York Times. I need something to distract me for I hate small planes. In a large jet, I can pretend I'm on a bus or train, the ground firm beneath me. In a small plane, I'm unable to maintain the premise.

"What's that sigh for?" Soren says after a moment. I didn't realize I made any sound. "Don't like small jets? Or are you just tired?"

Is he reading my mind at a distance?

"I prefer larger jets, actually, Colonel," I say, hating to admit fear to him.

"Please call me Soren. Eve, my pilot is very skilled. Ex-top gun, former member of an aerobatics team."

"I'll be fine."

The engines start as the pilot goes over his pre-flight check, their whine signifying the inevitability of this trip. I breathe deeply and look around, trying to distract myself from the flight. I try to pretend I'm on a small bus. Deny that it's a plane - that I'm flying on a cushion of air. I can do it on a 727. I suspect I won't pull it off in this Lear jet. I'd need a drink or two for that.

Soren stands and comes over to me, bending over me, his face close to mine, and tethers me in before I can move to stop him. His skin is so pale, long blond hair pulled back as before. He's handsome in a cold way. He has me strapped in so quickly, I can't even protest. He pulls the shoulder belt, keeping one hand in between the belt and my chest to ensure comfort, looking at me closely as he tightens it.

"There," he says, standing up, keeping his eyes on mine as if to gauge my response at what he's about to tell me. "My pilot informs me that we're in for some turbulence between here and Boston. Might get pretty choppy, so you'll need to keep this on."

I swallow, hating turbulence and the feeling that's growing in me - my heart pounding at the prospect. I'm afraid of looking foolish more than death. Death is inevitable - looking foolish likely is too, but at least one could fight that.

"Would you like a drink? It might help calm you."

"Isn't it a bit early?"

Soren laughs. "As we say in the forces, the sun is always over the yardarm somewhere in the world."

"What have you got?" I ask, my voice a bit shaky.

"Very good cognac. Here," he says and goes to a small bar, pulling out a bottle of the liquor. I watch as he un-stoppers the bottle and pours the amber liquid in crystal snifters, turning the snifter on the side to gauge the amount.

"Perfect," he says, handing me one of the snifters. "Do you drink cognac?"

I shake my head. "My father did. I rarely drink. When I fly, at social gatherings."

He nods. "Hard to lose a father."

I frown. "He's not dead."

He glances up. "Might as well be, considering you haven't seen him for so long."

"Why are you bringing him up?"

"You're the one who brought him up." He holds up a hand. "Please, relax." He sits down in his seat, strapping himself in and then takes the snifter in his hand. He holds it up and nods to me. "Cheers." He takes a sip, smacking his lips and letting out a sigh of appreciation. Another sip and then he places his snifter down and opens his briefcase. "I've got a lot of work ahead of me," he says, and opens a file thick with paper. "I'm afraid I won't be very good company, Eve."

I nod, glad that he's going to be busy with work. I open a National Geographic and begin exploring the issue, but soon close it and my eyes, leaning my head back, planning to read once we level off. After a few moments, I feel the plane move and open my eyes.

"Well," Soren says, putting down his papers and leaning his own head back. "We're off."

The speed increases and I look at the window, glad in a way that the shutters are pulled. This way I can pretend I'm still in the limo and we're just driving really fast and up a steep hill.

The plane rises and falls softly as we climb higher. I hate that feeling, preferring the bumps of a firm highway beneath tires.

After what seems like an eternity, we level off and one of the pilots comes back to us. He's dressed in fatigues, his dark hair cut very short, his brown eyes set in a face of such innocent youth I wondered how he can be old enough to fly this plane.

"Miss," he says, nodding at me then smiling at Soren.

"James," Soren says, smiling and putting his papers down. The young man leans against the desk and looks at Soren.

"We've reached cruising speed and altitude. We'll be in Boston on schedule. Your flight leaves at 2030 hours. Is there anything you need now?"

Soren shakes his head. The pilot returns to the cockpit and I to my magazine. It's as I'm contemplating Soren's identity that I feel the first bumps of turbulence. Small at first, like riding in a small craft on a choppy sea, they grow in intensity and soon, Soren downs his cognac. He picks up another document, though, and reads it over, flipping pages as he scans the material, unconcerned.

Of course, I'm fearful and likely white as a ghost. The pilot's voice comes over the intercom.

"Colonel, we've got a system in front of us. I'm going to ascend and try to clear it, get out of this turbulence."

"Please do," Soren replies, flipping the page of his document. Then, I feel a huge drop followed by several moderate bumps as we hit a pocket of air. Soren's snifter falls to the ground, and rolls around on the soft carpet.

"Don't worry," Soren says, as if sensing my growing fear. "We'll be over this in a few moments, and it'll be a lot calmer."

I close my eyes and can't help but mouth the Twenty-third Psalm in my mind. Despite my atheism, it's something even I resort to when under extreme stress – like when flying.

"Are you Catholic, Eve?" he says softly.

How did he do that? Is he reading my mind at a distance? I nod, repeating the psalm, gaining some comfort from it even though I don't believe any of it. I feel our ascent but the turbulence only seems to worsen and all at once I feel an incredible drop. My neck jars from it, my teeth grinding together.

"Shit!" I can't help but cry out.

"The pilot has to dive to get out of the worst of it - pretty bad - he was unable to clear through it. We'll have to drop down below it."

He takes my hand in his and his touch is cool, his skin dry and smooth against my damp palm.

"Don't worry," he says. "We'll be fine."

This act of kindness, this attempt to calm me, makes me thankful for contact of any kind, even with him, and yet I hate him. He has Michel under his control and can do what he wants with me. I wonder if I can beat him in a fight if necessary.

As the turbulence worsens, I turn to him. I don't know what I think he'll do - save us from crashing? If he's some sort of fallen angel, I feel certain he has powers to do such a thing, and I can't help but hope he will, almost willing to beg him to stop this, stop this terri-fying descent.

"Do something," I whisper, closing my eyes.

He squeezes my hand again and after a very long moment, I feel the plane level out, slowly at first, then more rapidly until we're almost level. I open my eyes and look into his pale ones – he's been watching me. He doesn't smile; he doesn't say anything. Just lets go of my hand, but before he does, a sense of familiarity sweeps through me at his touch. I can't identify it, but it feels as if I know him. When he turns back to his closed briefcase, to retrieve his document, I understand the source of the feeling.

He's the River Man.

Soren puts down his paper and unfastens his belt. He picks up his snifter and then retrieves the bottle of cognac, pouring more for himself and then coming to my side, standing directly in front of me holding the bottle up. "More?" he asks.

I look away, the realization that he's the killer filling me with dread.

"I said, did you want some more?"

I nod. The liquid sloshes in the crystal glass and I drink it down quickly. He then fills it once again and sits back down.

I drink that down, too, and lean back, the warmth of the liquor comforting, heat burning down my throat and in my belly. We sit in silence for the rest of the trip, Soren reading his documents. My mind is unable to be blank, and I wonder if he'll let me go. Will he let me leave the plane, return to Michel or will I be a captive?

I remember the dark wing-like shadows that spread out from his shoulders from the previous day. I've always accepted that there are such things as vampires. Am I now going to have to accept that there are also fallen angels?

The liquor makes me drowsy and I must have fallen asleep for when I blink awake, we're descending towards a small airport near Boston.

"See," Soren says. "That wasn't so bad. I let you sleep. I figured you needed it after everything that's happened."

Once the plane taxis off the runway and over to the terminal, we disembark into the dusk, the sun having just set.

I follow him, watching the way he exudes confidence, as if he owns the world. We reach the entrance to the hangar and there's a limo waiting for me, the driver at the open door.

Soren extends his hand to me and I'm glad that I've put my gloves back on before we left the plane. Yet, I hesitate. I feel like a fraud to be shaking his hand, as if we're just a couple of professionals who shared a flight and are not enemies.

"I'm sorry," I say quietly, turning my face away from him. "I can't pretend to be your friend, considering who I am and what you are and that you have both Michel and Julien in your control."

"Oh, Eve," he chuckles, putting his briefcase down and grabbing me in a hug. I feel stiff, startled to be pulled into his embrace. "You think you know what I am," he whispers in my ear, his cheek pressed against mine. He squeezes me tightly, one hand going to the small of my back, pulling me against his body. "But you're wrong. You don't even know what you are."

He slips a hand into my jacket pocket and I feel something hard and heavy slide to the bottom of it, clinking against my keys and change. Then he kisses my cheeks, one after the other, his tongue touching my skin the way Michel kissed me, and he's off, his briefcase in hand.

I watch the swell of people close around him as he makes his way into the terminal. He's tall enough that I can watch him, his pale head bobbing above the crowd. He makes such a striking figure with his white skin such a contrast against his dark clothing. I see him bend down to someone and hear his deep mellow voice laugh out loud, jovial, full of exuberance.

I slide my hand in my pocket and pull out a piece of fired red clay, cuneiform lettering stamped into its surface and a figure carved on it in relief. It appears to be a piece of broken pottery. Egyptian? Or even earlier – Mesopotamia? The figure depicts a half-lion half-bird. I rub my thumb over the rough edge of the semi-circular piece of clay. Soren has given me a clue of some kind - he wants me to know who or what he is. He claims to know my true identity.

My mind turns these facts around as I step into the limousine for my drive back to Boston and Michel, wondering whether I'll see him tonight. When I'm almost home, I get a text from Ed, telling me I can take the rest of the night off and just go home.

Thank God. I feel like crap after that hellish flight, the cognac and the stress of being with Soren.

All I really want to do is go home and have a hot bath, then go to bed. Soren, the case and this whole business with Michel and Julien will be there in the morning.

CHAPTER 14

Emily Dickenson

Once back at my apartment, I run a hot bath, needing to soak the chill out of me. Rain pelts at my window and I wonder when the storm will break and we'll finally get nice weather. I fill the tub with bubbles and a drop of my perfume that Michel liked so much, then lie back in the tub and relax, trying to blank my mind of everything and just let the heat soothe me. Of course, I can't blank my mind. I'm on edge from the trip with Soren, wanting to speak to Michel about it, find out if he was compelled and what he thinks about the meeting, but I'm exhausted and a bit lethargic from the cognac on the plane.

Of course, I can't keep my mind blank and it moves back to Michel. I no longer know what I feel about anything. I thought I'd be doing my mother's life work, finding a magic bullet to kill all vampires so I could get my revenge and eradicate their plague from the face of the earth. Instead, I'm falling in love with one and all I want is to have him, to be his, to be whatever I can be to him and it feels like a betrayal of my mother and myself.

Michel and Julien are not what I thought about when I imagined vampires. I saw them as monsters, evil, bloodsuckers. Instead, I see them now as humans who met a tragic end that didn't kill them. Now, they must face an eternity addicted to blood and trapped by night, their senses heightened, acutely aware of everything – sound, sight, scent, touch, their emotions magnified. They have forever to regret their mistakes, superior to humans in strength and senses, and yet loving us – loving that which they inevitably either kill or watch die from old age.

I think of him, so beautiful and so soulful despite what he thinks of himself, how he mourns his lost innocence and how he mourns the Church he lost that day when he thought his beloved brother was dead.

I want him so much…

Lying in the warm water, I can't help but let my mind wander back to Michel. He's just so intense and I want him so much, my body warming to the thought of him lying on top of me on my bed the other night, his kiss so passionate…

I lie in the warm soapy water and feel sad that we won't become lovers unless I pass some test. I imagine him holding my hands like he did on the bed, his lips on mine, his tongue touching mine…

A knock at the door brings me right back to reality and I sit up.

Who the hell is bothering me at this time of night?

"Eve," Michel calls out. "It's me, Michel."

Oh, damn…

I don't say anything, my mind flustered that he's caught me imagining being his lover.

"Eve, I can tell you're in there. I can smell you…"

Oh, hell… That admission just does something to me.

"I can't come to the door," I say, my voice quivery from being so close to an orgasm. "I'm in the bath."

I hear the key in the lock. Oh, *damn*. I forgot he has the duplicate. My heart flutters for he's coming in and the bathroom door is open. I don't have time to get out and put a bathrobe on, so I sink down into the bath and try to hide under the bubbles. I hear his boots on the hardwood, and then the sound of them dropping on the floor as he removes them. Then he's in the bathroom standing in the doorway, looking at me like a lion looks at a baby gazelle and I can barely breathe. Some part of my still-functioning brain knows I'm in trouble even if I want this.

His coat is open, the shoulders soaked from the deluge, and he's wearing a black sweater underneath, his gold cross dangling around his neck. His wet hair hangs in his eyes, his black lashes clumped together from the rain, his blue eyes riveted on me.

He looks – *desperate*.

"You're back," he says, his voice soft. "I was so worried about you..." He comes to the bathtub and stands over me, staring down, and there I am, naked, my hair soaked, my cheeks red, my body only somewhat covered by the last remaining bubbles and only moments away from a self-imposed orgasm. Then he reaches down, stroking my cheek with the backs of his fingers, his eyes closed. I feel the connection, the walls between us falling away, and all I can think is that he almost caught me. My body is so ready, my heart racing, my cheeks hot. Then he senses my masturbatory fantasy about him just moments earlier before he knocked and how close I am.

"Oh, God, *Eve*," he says and reaches down, grabbing me under my arm, his other arm under my legs, pulling me out of the tub, splashing water all over everywhere as he lifts me and carries me naked and dripping to my bedroom, his mouth already on mine before I can even gasp in shock.

He lays me on the bed and lies on top of me, his coat still on, his mouth never leaving mine, one hand holding mine above my head and he runs his other hand down my naked wet skin, over my shoulder and down to my breast and then lower between my thighs, his fingers finding my clit as he kisses me, his tongue insistent, his breathing so fast. I feel his lust now, feel his flesh so hard, the ache of desire in him as he kisses and touches me. Then he breaks the kiss and moves his mouth down over my chin, down my neck where he pauses at my throat. For a few seconds, I hold my breath and wonder if he's going to bite me and I don't care, almost wanting him to and there's nothing I could do to stop him, he's so strong and has me confined.

He makes a noise deep in his throat like agony and pulls away, breathing heavily and when I look at him, his face has changed to the hunter, his teeth longer, his pupils huge now, and a mix of lust and fear floods through me.

He doesn't speak, releasing my hands above my head. He moves lower, sucking each nipple as he squeezes my breasts. His sharp teeth slide over my nipple, but he doesn't break my skin and jolts of pleasure go right from my nipples to my clit and deep inside of me. I don't know how much more I can take I'm so ready. He moves even lower, spreading my thighs, his mouth covering my sex, his tongue finding my clit and stroking, fast and firm, and I cry out loud it feels so good, my hips grinding against his mouth.

He slips fingers inside of me, and makes that throat sound, and I feel the sweetness building deep inside as his fingers and tongue stroke me. Just as I think I'm over the edge, he pulls his fingers out and moves up, kissing my neck as he's fumbling with his pants, unbuttoning his fly.

When he's finally free, he shoves himself inside of me, fully. He's so thick, he fills me up and the pressure is so intense. He thrusts inside me, grabbing my hands over my head and he's kissing my throat, his other hand on my breast, squeezing my nipple and I feel his lust and mine combined so that the waves of pleasure build until I'm gasping, my body arching, my muscles clenching around him.

I'm coming as he thrusts harder and faster and I feel his climax on top of mine, his cheek pressed against mine, grunting with each thrust. It's as if he's holding me there, right at the top not letting me fall. I feel his body spasm as if it's my own, and it *is* my own, the pleasure such agony and it goes on and on and I'm completely drowning in it...

❧

WE LIE THERE, recovering, our breathing slowly returning to normal. He moves off me, slipping out of my body and then he's lying on his side looking at me. He touches the skin on my shoulders and hips where his coat has rubbed against my skin, leaving fabric burn, his mouth soft on the raw spots. He tongues the wound on my shoulder, which weeps just a bit of blood and his tongue on my skin feels so good, so tender, so intimate. But even that small amount of blood brings out the hunter in him again and his eyes become bloodshot, his pupils now huge.

I'm a little in fear of him right now. He senses it and stops licking my wound, exhaling slowly and rests his head on my breast, his breath on my nipple.

"Don't worry," he whispers. "I won't bite you."

I don't know if I'm worried or in hope, and the thought makes me feel like such a traitor. I turn my face away, but in truth, somewhere dark and deep, I want it. I just don't want to admit it. I lie there, surprised at how I'm both scared and attracted to him in hunter mode.

"That was so *fast*," I say, still a bit in shock at how quickly it all happened.

"You were so ready," he says, and now Michel is back, and the hunter recedes. He's smiling that lopsided grin of his. "I could have prolonged things. I usually prefer it long and slow, and I would have preferred to confine you properly, but you were just so *close*..."

My cheeks burn at the memory and how he knows I was masturbating just before he knocked on the door.

"Don't you *dare* be embarrassed," he says, leaning over me again, staring into my eyes. "Do you have any idea how erotic that was? To find you like that, naked, wet, ready? All my plans for self-control totally laid to waste..."

I smile at him, and touch his face, push his hair back behind his ear and out of his eyes. God, he's so *beautiful*...

"What plans? Tell me, oh Genghis Kahn, what your plans for total dominion over me were?"

He cracks a grin, but then becomes serious.

"Oh, Eve..." he says and rolls onto his back, rubbing his eyes. "I fucked up."

"You regret this?" I say, a feeling of numbness spreading through me. What – is he going to take it back now? "It's not a really good thing to tell a woman you just had sex with that you regret it."

He sits up and then removes his coat and lies on his side, leaning over me, resting on one elbow, his gaze moving over my naked body and I remember what Julien wrote about vampire stamina.

"Regret isn't the word. I'm angry with myself for being so weak. I shouldn't have come in, but I had to see you. After Helena, after meeting with Soren I felt so," he shakes his head. "Afraid for you when Soren saw you, knew you were back in play. I didn't intend to have sex with you, and certainly not like this, but you were so ..." he says, and hesitates as if searching for words. "You were so there how could I not? It was like the laws of the universe would be violated if I hadn't."

"Spacetime itself would be disrupted?" I say and smile, but I'm still not sure where this is going and whether I'm going to be sad or happy when he finally explains. "What's so terrible about what happened?"

He rolls over on his stomach and rests on his elbows, his fingers laced together, his gold crucifix dangling. He looks over at me, and I'm just lying there, naked as the day I was born, but I don't move to cover up. He's seen right into my mind and heart. What's my nakedness in comparison?

"It shouldn't have happened until I knew if we can work. If we can form that bond. If I can claim you completely as my own. Vampires are used to controlling humans using our powers of compulsion. Adepts and their vampire partners included. You and I," he says and reaches out to touch me. "We can kill each other. We can protect each other. That's why I'm so torn. I feel guilt about it because this is going to be very dangerous, and I hate that I'm putting you in danger, but from the moment I saw you in the office that first night, I wanted you as my Adept. My," he says, hesitating. "My protector."

I frown. "Your protector?"

"You can kill vampires. Who better to protect me?"

I lie there for a moment, absorbing this revelation.

"I thought we'd work cases together."

"We will. But this is a military operation, Eve, not a police action. We're preparing to fight a war. I need you to be my protector because you can kill vampires and that's who I'll be fighting."

"Tell me about the war."

He shakes his head. "I can't tell you more, Eve, or risk putting you in more danger. Please trust me on this."

I inhale. Trust.

"So you need to know if we can form this bond of trust? How will you know?"

"Only when you're able to be completely obedient to me. To completely trust me with your life. Not ask questions, not doubt my commands. Then, I can trust you with *my* life."

Trust me with his life? That does something to me, making me swell with emotion.

"Only then would sex between us not complicate the bond. Sex too early and it's harder to establish. If we were just a normal couple, then it would be different, but we're not."

"This is life and death," he says. "In a military relationship, as your superior, I make the decisions about what we do and when and how. As my subordinate, you're responsible for carrying out my commands exactly as I specify. It's essential when we're on missions for you to obey me without hesitation, without thought. I have to know you'll do what I command at all times. There can be only one leader."

"Why not partners?"

"Because partners can argue over decisions, each one pushing their own agenda, and in that space of time, people will die. I've seen it happen."

"So you want me to be your servant?"

"Names are just words," he says. "Whether I call you my lieutenant or my servant, you are my subordinate and can't be anything else. The power I have over everything is so much greater."

"I don't know what I want. I don't like the idea of being anyone's servant."

He rolls over closer to me, his finger touching my bottom lip. "If we form this bond," Michel says, running his finger along my arm. "We would be more than married, Eve. This bond is so deep, it transcends what an ordinary mortal feels with another. We would truly know each other at the deepest level."

I have to close my eyes for a moment and breathe deeply. To have someone know you that deeply. He leans over and kisses my shoulder.

When I open my eyes, he's serious again.

"Eve, you and I? This relationship? We do it to stay *alive*." He looks at me with those so-intense eyes. "You turn over your will to me. The mission is first, and our own will exists only to complete the mission. I am the leader and you're my right hand."

"So having sex first does what?"

"It complicates things. Lovers often put their own needs and that of their lover first over the mission. There can't be that kind of dynamic or one of us – or both – could die."

I stare at the ceiling. "Why not two people who are committed to the mission? Working together?"

"Because of how power works," he says. "It's a zero sum game. It's based on making decisions and being able to react to conditions on the ground. Only one person can do that." He leans over me, his eyes so intense. "This is war. A war for dominion. Who will win? Humans or vampires? If humans are to win, those of us who fight for you must be in perfect unison. We must be committed completely to winning. You think vampires are very strong, and we are, but we're also vulnerable in daylight and rely on humans to protect us."

"You have guards," I say. "Why not use them?"

"Where we'll go, I can't always take guards with me. But I can take my pet."

"I'd be your pet?"

"That's how you'd be seen."

I inhale and consider.

"Do all vampires have pets?"

"All of those with power do. Some have a harem."

"Not you," I can't stop myself from saying it out loud.

He laughs. "No, not me, Eve. I am a former priest. Harems really aren't our thing."

"You keep saying you're a priest, but you're not really. Otherwise you just broke your vows."

"I'm a priest here," he says, and points to his heart. "No matter what."

"So do you have sex and just feel guilty?"

"Yes." He cracks a lopsided grin. "Intensely. I do penance."

"Hair shirt?" I say, smiling. "Flogger?"

"Sore knees from praying."

I reach out and stroke his cheek.

"Poor Michel." And I mean it. I can't understand this devotion to the Church, but it's just part of him. "So you wanted to wait until you'd established that bond with me before having sex."

"Exactly. Then you had to put that perfume in the water. I could smell it on the street, and it smells of you. I *had* to come in…"

"And you really think you wouldn't have had sex with me if I'd been dressed and sitting on the sofa reading a book? You looked," I say and hesitate. "Desperate. Like you're worried something is going to happen to me."

"I needed to see you, talk to you, see you smile and it would make me feel better."

"Do you?" I smile, flashing my dimples at him. "Feel better?"

"Much *much* better," he says and kisses my shoulder and even that makes me feel warm inside, makes my body respond. He touches my face.

"Eve," he says. "Not that I think we can put the genie back in the bottle, but I have to be sure. Will you commit to become my Adept?"

"I can try," I say, frowning, not sure if I can when he puts it that way.

"Like Yoda said, there is no *try*. There is only do or do not."

I shake my head. "I can't believe a vampire watched Star Wars and can quote Yoda."

"Eternity's very long. Cable television helps." He grins that grin I love so much and I can't help but smile back, my heart swelling, and I reach out to touch his face.

Then he's serious again, the grin gone, his blue eyes intense once more.

"Eve, with us, it's all in or all out. I'll be your mind and you'll be my heart. There *is* no other option. Not if you enter our world. Humans are never equals with vampires. You're always our servants."

I watch him for a moment, staring at his beautiful face, remembering his touch, thinking of his history, and I know what my decision is.

"All in, then."

He leans over me and kisses me softly, tenderly. I run my hands up his back under his sweater and over his shoulder. My body's ready again and I want it long and slow.

"Oh, *Eve…*"

CHAPTER 15

"FEAR MAY INDUCE the show of submission, but love only can truly subjugate a haughty spirit."

Mary Cowden Clarke

I wake while it's still dark and he's not beside me. I hear him in the bathroom and he's wearing only his boxer briefs, washing his face when I go in to join him.

"Time to go?" I say, admiring his physique, sad that dawn has to part us.

"Time for bed," he says and when he's finished drying his hands, he grabs me and pulls me against him, my hands in one of his behind my back, his grip tight. Why does that send such a thrill through me?

"You must sleep as well. Training starts tonight. I want to show you how to kill vampires up close and personal, so you'll be able to defend yourself. Make sure you're well-rested."

I frown. I wanted to speak with him about Montana, the sense of unease I've felt since we met Soren surfacing.

"Michel, I want to talk about Montana."

"Tomorrow night, Eve. We'll do a full debrief. I don't have a lot of time right now and you need to get some sleep."

I nod and lean against him, looking up into his eyes. "I think I'm going to have a very good sleep."

"You were already sleeping like a baby." He kisses me, softly.

"I wish you could stay and sleep with me."

"I know," he says. "Can't risk it. My home is designed to protect me from the sun. Besides, Vasily will be getting really bored out in the car."

"You have a guard outside?"

"Have one posted at the front and back door. I have to be safe. But soon, you'll come to my place and sleep with me all day if you want."

"I want," I say. Then he lets my hands go and he puts his watch on and pulls his sweater over his head. I stand naked, watching him dress, and he glances at me and smiles.

"What a lovely way to start the morning," he says and comes to me when he's dressed, lifting my chin with a finger. "A naked Eve, smiling, displaying her dimples. The way my day should always start." He kisses me. "I want you to move in with me and I want you to be naked at all times when we're alone in our suite."

"When I *move in* with you?"

He nods. "Yes," he says, taking my shoulders in his hands. "You'll live with me and protect me, as I said. We'll be together at all times, even when I sleep."

I frown. "What about my apartment?"

"You can keep it if you want, but you won't need it."

I smile, but I don't know if I like this – moving in with him so soon. "We've only just met," I say, unable to hide the hesitance in my voice. "I have cats."

"Eve," he says and pulls me into his arms. "Remember – all in or all out. I'd say you could bring your cats, except I have several Dobermans who patrol the house. We'll make sure your cats are cared for."

I force a smile. "I said all in. I meant it." Of course, then I think about meeting Julien in Montana when I went outside early in the morning to get a cup of coffee.

When Michel kisses me, then he must sense my thoughts for he pulls away, frowning.

"He was there?"

I clench my fists, a surge of guilt and frustration flowing through me that I'm unable to control his access to my mind.

"Don't be upset with me. I have no control over what Julien does."

Michel shakes his head, clearly upset. Finally, he leans his forehead against mine and exhales. "Of course you don't. I'm not upset with you. I just wish Julien could let this drop, but he's stubborn."

Then he pulls away and stares in my eyes as if searching for my feelings for Julien. Yes, Julien is beautiful – like Michel – but he's *not* Michel.

He's completely different.

It's *Michel* I want. As if he senses that, Michel leans in again and kisses me and I'm once more completely unwound by his touch and by the connection we share. I feel his need for me to be his, and his alone, totally under his control. It makes me weak, but also a little fearful.

Then he's gone and I'm alone again. I creep into my bed and pull the covers over my head, wondering what tonight will bring.

I GO to the office the next evening, expecting to see Michel there waiting for me, but Ed tells me Michel's not in yet. I'm relieved and sad at the same time. I thought he'd be there when I arrived. I hoped he hadn't got second thoughts after last night.

"I have to talk to you," I say to Ed. "Soren's the River Man."

"What?" he says, making a face. "You're crazy. We already cleared him of the murder in Montana. He had an alibi."

"Ed, I read him on the plane. He's the one. I know it."

"Did you see his kills?"

I frown. I didn't see his kills. But I know he felt the same as the one who touched those items I did – the beach glass – the slip of paper with my name on it.

"No, but I read him, Ed. I know he's the killer. Maybe he ordered them or maybe he was there, but he did it.

"Sorry, Eve. You need to see him doing it for it to stick as a blood witness. Otherwise, it's not evidence."

I sit alone in the room and wonder what it was I felt. I spend the first part of the evening just reviewing the case, mulling it over in my head. Other than the building manager, I'm alone in the main SCU office after Ed leaves for the on-call room down the hall because he pulled an all-day and nighter. Terri had a lecture earlier that evening and reception afterwards and wasn't coming in so I'm alone.

I glance over at Terri's office, which is beside Ed's. The door's ajar and so I go in and turn on the light, wondering if Terri has any less-dry reading material on the cases they'd prosecuted in the past. Julien said everything was in the files here and in my mother's files, and so I'm tempted to go sleuthing. Several filing cabinets are off to the side of the room and so I go to each and open them up, checking to see what they contain. Two of the three open, and contain a lot of material but none of it looks really interesting. The third is locked.

That's the one with interesting material, as Julien said. I open the top drawer of Terri's desk, fishing around in the assortment of paper clips, glue sticks and pens for a key to the file cabinet. Sure enough, there's one stuck to the side of the metal drawer with one of those magnetic key holders.

Bingo.

Breathless, knowing I shouldn't really be snooping, I go to the filing cabinet and open it up. Inside are personnel files dating back to the inception of the SCU almost thirty years earlier. The files are old and faded, the edges frayed, and a slightly musty scent wafts up when I pull a file out.

Some research papers on Adepts. One looks especially interesting, describing a new research program to use gene therapy to induce mutations using vampire DNA. Taking it makes me feel uneasy but because it's so old, I doubt anyone will miss it. I go and get my back-pack so I can take it home with me when I leave.

Then, I flip through the files in search for something about Michel.

Sure enough, there's one and what's most interesting is that he's had two partners over the past ten years that worked at the SCU. The first lasted seven years – a Michelle Joyce. She died on a mission and had a Do Not Resuscitate order on her file, so no one could save her by making her a vampire. The second died less than a year ago, killed as part of the River Man case. Neither of the two Adepts could fight and it was that inability that contributed to their deaths.

No wonder they want Adepts who can fight and beat a vampire. Every single Adept that worked for the SCU since its inception has died on the job. I pick through the files, checking each one, numbness filling me.

Damn. It's like open season on Adepts.

Then, I look for my own file. There's a folder in the drawer with my name on it. The file's new, and there are several images of me dating back to when I was just a child. A shiver goes through me...

How did they get these? From my father?

One when I was three and taking my first piano lessons.

One at eight when I was performing at a recital. I played Fur Elise.

One at nine when I was in a competition for young pianists and won.

One of me at eleven, after my mother's death when I was at the funeral with my father, who already looked as if he was on the way to the psych ward.

One of me when I was taken into protective custody after he crashed and I spent the night on the porch. I'd been mosquito bitten and was sunburned from wandering around in the summer sun without adequate protection, unable to get inside because he'd been on a alcohol and drug bender and never came home.

One of me in the hospital. What?

There's a tube down my throat as if I'm ventilated.

How come I don't remember?

I barely remember that period of my life. John and Vanessa Barnes, a couple with Council connections had been appointed to take custody of me and become my legal guardians but the Council lost track of me when my file went missing and I was given to another couple not in the system.

A whole lot of darkness followed that – a darkness I take pains not to remember.

Attached to the back of the sheet on my background were a few papers stapled together on my mother. She moved to Boston and went to school there, getting a Masters and PhD before joining the Council to work as a researcher. She met and married my father, Sean Hayden, a concert pianist, in 1988.

Then a line in a legal document signed by my mother and father:

"Subject accepted implantation on August 21, 1989 of three enhanced embryos. Two registered to the Council and one for the subject and spouse to raise. In the event only one embryo survives to birth, that surviving child will be property of the Council's Enhanced Adept program, to be turned over to the Council's liaison at three days of age, to be raised by foster parents and trained to become part of the program..."

That's the contract Michel referred to that first night.

Another report from a hospital where it was found I was the only surviving triplet implanted in my mother's womb. The other two embryos failed to implant, as shown on the ultrasound at sixteen weeks.

I was genetically enhanced... I'd always thought I was a freak of nature and that my skills were a fluke. But I was made?

The transfer to the Council's liaison never happened. Before I was even born, my mother ran with my father, disappearing on a transatlantic flight before anyone knew. She only relented once I turned ten and she decided that it was better to prepare me for the life, in case someone found me. That must have been when she met Julien. She returned to Boston and that's when she got the manuscript.

I sit in the chair at Terri's desk, reading over the lost details of my life – the true details and a sense of shock settles over me like a shroud. A bit lightheaded, my limbs feeling numb, I cover my mouth and bite back tears.

Here I am, after everything my parents did to prevent me becoming an Adept, working for the Council.

A sound draws my attention away from the file. It's Ed, standing in the doorway. I close the file and put it on the desk in front of me, not meeting his eyes.

"Eve, what are you doing?" He comes to me and reaches down, picking up the file.

"Finding out the truth." I stand and turn to face him, my cheeks burning.

He picks up my backpack and removes the file on adepts and examines it for a moment.

"Eve," he says disapprovingly. He picks up his cell and dials a number, then shakes his head. "Where the fuck is Michel when you need him?" He waits and then speaks on the phone.

"You better get back, soon. Like tonight. We have a major fucking breach in security and I need you to answer your fucking phone." He hangs up and goes to the door.

"Come with me," he says and I follow him into his office like a truant student in the principal's office. Ed sits across from me, his hands folded. He's mad at me, but I'm even more furious with everyone.

"Why won't you explain things to me?" I say, angry that he's apparently ignoring me.

"Terri will speak with you tomorrow, since it was her files you broke into."

"You know the answers," I say, unwilling to stand down. "When were you ever going to tell me that I'm some kind of test project? Never?"

"You're angry. I get that, Eve. Let me enlighten you about something. This is a military operation," he says and pounds a finger onto the desk. "There's a chain of command and people get information on a need-to-know basis. You have to learn to take orders. Period."

He sends me home and I take a cab, retreating into my flat to nurse my wounds. Michel will be mad. He said Julien would try to stir things up, and he was right. I'm mad as well, confused about what to think and what to believe.

CHAPTER 16

"AT THE TOUCH of love everyone becomes a poet."

Plato

The phone rings in the middle of the night, waking me up out of a dead sleep. I grab it and check the caller ID – O'Neil, Ed.

"Eve speaking."

"Hey, sorry to wake you so soon, but something's happened. You have to come back in."

"What?" I rub my forehead, still barely awake.

"I'll be there in ten to pick you up. Buckle up, Eve. This one's gonna be a hell of a ride."

"Tell me," I say, eager to hear what's up.

"Can't," he says. "Security. Just be outside."

He hangs up the phone and I get up and run around the apartment, trying to pull myself together. I grab my coat and shoulder bag and run down the stairs. The car is there and Ed opens the door to the sedan.

"Get in. Prepare yourself."

I sit and fasten my seatbelt, thinking of his words. Buckle up, Eve.

"What is it?"

He clicks on the overhead light and hands me a fax sheet. As the sedan speeds off into the dark Boston night, I examine the fax and have to look twice at the image.

Michel. But then I see it's not him. The hair's too short and there's the long scar on the side of his head.

"Julien?" A shock courses through me and I feel dizzy. I turn to him.

He nods.

"Someone took him out. He's dead, but he's recoverable."

"What does that mean?"

"It means a load of pain for Michel."

At first, I feel faint because I thought it was Michel, but I also feel close to Julien, having read his words and his story and now having met him and spoken to him. I stare at the image of him. My first thought – a crazy thought – is that it was Michel, but it couldn't be him.

"It was Soren," I say.

"No," Ed says, making a face of disbelief. "He told Michel that if he brought you to see him, he'd spare Julien," Ed says.

"I can't believe you'd accept what he says. He's a killer and a manipulator."

Ed shrugs. I stare at the fax and feel incredible guilt that Julien's been staked because of me. I realize I've been warming to Julien. I examine the photographs taken of his body, which show him lying on the grass in a park outside the cathedral, a stake through his heart, his beautiful face contorted in agony, his blue eyes half-open, his hands around the base of the stake and I'm shaken that he's dead.

"He's not really dead dead, right?"

"Technically, he's dead dead, but just not destroyed. He's still got his head, so he can be resurrected. If the killer had cut off his head, he'd be unrecoverable."

"How do they recover him?"

"Only with the blood of an Ancient and unless Michel has connections, they're few and far between. Only about two-hundred spread out around the world and as a whole, they're nasty fuckers. Although Soren seemed like an OK guy."

"OK?" I say, shaking my head. "He's a monster. He has Michel firmly under his thumb. He compelled you, Ed. Can't you see?"

"He said he wouldn't hurt Julien. Someone else did it."

We drive across the bridge to the cathedral grounds where they found his body. The old stone building sits surrounded by trees, its turrets reminding me of castles in Hungary where my father conducted a string quartet when I was a child.

The murder took place in a small copse of evergreens near the corner of the grounds a short distance from the entrance to the Holy Cross Cathedral. We stop at the side of the road and I leave the car to stand beneath the huge boughs of one tall evergreen. Police have cordoned off the area with yellow tape, which flaps in the wind. Ed speaks with the detective in charge as he leaves. He ushers me over. From where we stand I can make out a dark stain on the ground. Blood. Julien's blood.

"Our suspect must have arranged to meet him here and then staked him."

"Where's the body?"

"Being taken to the SCU morgue. I've claimed jurisdiction."

"Any witnesses?"

"One. They're transferring him to the SCU to be interviewed. He's a derelict. Seems pretty crazy. Homeless guy who hangs out around the cathedral hoping for handouts."

Several bystanders crowd together on the sidewalk across from the crime scene and speak together. A uniform keeps them away from the church grounds.

"Any other witnesses?" I say, glancing at the crowd.

"Ed shakes his head. "Naw, it was really late. Everyone was asleep and no one admits hearing anything out of the ordinary." Ed turns to me. "Do you want to look around, see if you can find anything?"

"Sure," I say and duck under the tape. "But I already know who did it." I take the flashlight and point it around. I run a hand over the dirt where the bloodstain was located but nothing turns up. There really isn't much to see – just pine needles and a few bits of old newspaper. I touch the paper just in case, but get nothing from it.

I return to Ed and hand him the flashlight. "Nothing jumps out. Maybe if I come back tomorrow, I'll find something in the daylight."

He nods. "OK, I'll have someone protect the scene. I've tried to find Michel but he's not answering his cell or responding to texts. The two of you seem intent on violating the rules tonight."

I say nothing. What can I say?

"Let's go and interview the witness, then we'll see the body once I find Michel."

I sit in the seat, totally numb from the events of the evening.

TERRI MEETS us in the hallway outside her office.

"I just heard," she says, her voice shaky. "He's recoverable?"

"Technically," Ed says. "But Michel will have to find a willing Ancient."

"The witness is in the main office," Terri says and makes a face. "He's pretty crazy. I don't think you'll get much useful information out of him. Oh, and I advise you to stay back," she says and plugs her nose.

Ed nods. "You get what you get. The guy left witnesses," Ed says to me as he opens the door to the main office. "He wasn't very clean in his kill. Guess he's not so smart after all. This is his first slip-up and so we may be close to finding him."

THE OLD MAN has an air of madness about him. It shows in his wide rheumy eyes, and the filthy hair that hangs in long mats from his head. His smell is so intense that Ed refuses to interview him in one of the small interrogation rooms. Instead, he sits in the middle of the office, alone on a chair, as far away from anyone in particular as possible.

A light rain has fallen all night long and the man is soaked to his skin. As he sits and waits for Ed's questions, water puddles beneath his chair. In the warmth of the room, steam rises off his worn clothing as if the man is burning up like the ember of his cigarette.

Police found him crouched against the wall that circled the cathedral just a few dozen feet from where the murder took place. He'd run to the cathedral priory and reported the murder and then slipped away in the confusion. Now, while Ed tells him who I am, I fear that his testimony will be like Terri said. Useless.

I cross the room to the window and open one pane to let in some fresh air. The streets are deserted, as they should be at this time of night. Only the incessant drip of rain breaks the silence.

I turn at the sound of a chair being dragged across the floor and watch as Ed perches on it across from the witness.

"Tell me, Antonio, what did you see?"

"I see them everyday," he says with a thick Italian accent. "The priests. I know them well, each by face and name. I knew this one, Julien de Cernay. When he came close and gave me a coin, I knew it was him. I saw his aura." Antonio's voice comes to me as if we're under water – muted, dull. He sits back as if satisfied that he's delivered the most important part of his message.

"His aura?" My voice is distant and my throat feels choked.

"*Vampyr.* They exist in two planes, one of spirit and one of flesh. I see their spirit."

I sit at the desk against the wall and flip open the case file while Ed questions Antonio about his place of residence. Ed's hand-written notes are barely legible, but they confirm what I already know and provide more information on Michel's brother.

Julien de Cernay, age thirty-five when he was turned in 1224. Lives at the monastery outside of Boston although he owns property in the city along the waterfront. He assists a priest in the Diocese with services on occasion. Why is he out so late dressed in full clerics? It seems as if the brothers have switched roles, with Michel acting as the warrior and Julien as the priest.

"Did he say anything to you?"

"No." Antonio shrugs as if he wishes he had more to offer. "He merely dropped a few coins in my hand and mumbled a blessing. He seemed in haste to get to his destination. I watched him walk through trees towards the main buildings and then disappear around a corner. I thought it odd for him to be out so late at night. Something was up," he says and nods as if in agreement with his own assessment. "I arrived at the edge of the cathedral gardens but it was dark and I could see very little. After a few moments, I saw him, or rather, them. Julien and another taller man. I couldn't tell who had joined him, but when Julien knelt before the man, I moved closer, careful to remain silent. Who knew what they were doing?"

I frown. He only claimed that he saw the body. What's he doing?

"Wait a minute," Ed said. "You didn't say you saw the murder. You said you found the body."

"I was upset," Antonio said, waving Ed's protest away with a flick of his hand. "I have just only now remembered."

"Only now?" Ed turns to me and rolls his eyes.

"Yes. The fright must have clouded my memory. But I remember now. They appeared to be praying. The larger man was also dressed in clerics and had pale skin and fair hair. He laid a hand on Julien's head as if offering a blessing. Another priest killed him." Antonio says plainly.

A knock at the door tears my attention away from Antonio. A tech pops his head inside and looks at Ed.

"Someone in Arlington wants to speak to you."

Ed rises and glances at me.

"I'll be right back." He turns to Antonio and points. "You – keep quiet until I return."

A sense of dread fills me that I can't explain. I do not want to be alone with the witness. When Ed leaves the room and closes the door, that familiar feeling of time standing still washes over me and I brace myself. The air feels as if it's been sucked out of my lungs. Yet, Antonio speaks, as if he's in the same time frame as I am. His voice is soft, conspiratorial.

"I waited to reveal what I saw to someone who mattered. I knew as soon as I saw you that I could trust you."

"Why me?"

"You're special."

"How am I special?" I say but he ignores me.

"I saw them together, and before my eyes, he changed. I shook my head as if to clear it and blinked away the mist, but the apparition persisted. Darkness spread out behind them and then I could see him – his great black wings unfolded so that they blocked out the light from the cathedral."

That sends a wave of shock through me, my blood like ice in my veins as I remember Soren in Montana.

"You're supposed to wait until Agent O'Neil comes back." I close my eyes and rub my forehead. I don't want to think about him mentioning black wings. "Besides, I thought you said he was a vampire."

"Julien, yes. But the other one. He was *Strigoi*."

"A demon?"

"Yes. An Ancient with great dark wings. All my life I've read about such beings." Now Antonio seems to warm to his subject and leans forward, his face almost beatific. "I am a true believer but still, to see a Fallen so close . . ." He slips a hand into some fold of his filthy clothing, retrieving a rough wooden crucifix on a leather strap. "I delivered the exorcism to chase the demon off. In the Name of Jesus Christ, our God and Lord," he says, his voice wavering at first, then growing louder, "strengthened by the intercession of the Immaculate Virgin Mary . . ."

I glance at the door, wishing it would open. "Are you a priest as well?"

"No, never ordained. Merely an Exorcist. But I'm trained. Now it's my duty to watch over the flock, protect them from Him."

This is clearly so absurd that I might as well stop the tape and shoo him out of the SCU but I play along.

"What happened next?"

"I stepped even closer, delivering the prayer of exorcism even though my knees were shaking, and my voice was barely a whisper. Mother of God," he says, his eyes wide. "Mother of the Blessed Michael the Archangel, of the Blessed Apostles Peter and Paul and all the Saints, and powerful in the holy authority of our ministry. . ."

A drip of spittle falls from his lips as he stares off into space as if watching the scene in his mind's eye.

"The demon raised his eyes to me, baring his teeth, but I persisted." He holds up his wooden crucifix. "We confidently undertake to repulse the attacks and deceits of the devil."

"Then," the old man says, his face crumpling. "Julien pulled free of the demon's embrace and turned towards me. "You can't have him,'" I shouted. Then the demon held me down as if by some invisible power. I could do nothing but watch as the monster staked Julien like so," he says and mimics the action. "He picked Julien up and threw him across the clearing towards me as if he were nothing more than a bundle of rags." Antonio bends down over his knees and weeps, his face in his filthy hands.

"I no longer cared for my own life." Antonio looks up at me, his face wet with tears. "I dragged myself to him and felt for a pulse but there was nothing. I knew what I must do. I whispered the last rites into his ear even though I am not a priest, but I know God will forgive me. Into thy hands, Lord, I commend my spirit." The old man makes the sign of the cross. "Mary Mother of grace, Mother of mercy, do thou protect me from the enemy and receive me at the hour of my death."

I hand him a tissue and he wipes his eyes.

"When I looked up, the demon was gone."

I shake my head. He appears so crazy for he completely believes the story he just recounted.

"You must stop him. You and Michel."

"Me?" How does he know about Michel?

Then the door opens and the moment passes as if a gust of wind has blown it away. The clock begins to tick loudly once again as time returns to normal, and the coffee pot hisses as an errant drop of moisture falls on the exposed burner. Ed apologizes to us and takes his seat across from Antonio. I examine the tape recorder on the table but I know that when we play it back, neither Antonio's words or mine will have been recorded.

"So," O'Neil says, "when I left, you claimed to have seen the murder itself. Please, describe what you saw."

"It was dark." Antonio shrugs, now seemingly unwilling to recount his story.

"But you saw the murder? You saw the murderer?"

"I saw two shapes in the darkness, heard hushed voices. I couldn't see anything clearly. But I heard a scream and ran like the Devil himself was after me." He glances at me and winks.

"That's everything? You left the park and ran to the cathedral?"

"Yes." The old man nods and with a furtive hand, tucks the crucifix away in a pocket.

"You never told the rector that you saw the murder."

"Eh," he says and shrugs. "I had a lot to drink."

Ed turns to me and rolls his eyes. I get the sense Antonio is trying to appear insane, but that only makes me more anxious. We're being played. The question is, by whom?

I sigh. Once we find Michel, we'll have to tell him of his sibling's death. My heart goes out to him. He's somewhere right now, ignorant of what's happened. To be told in the early hours of a rainy morning that your brother has been staked on church grounds is cruel.

I doubt if anything can make such news less painful.

CHAPTER 17

"LOVE IS my religion - I could die for it."

John Keats

Dawn is still a few hours away when we take the interstate, going directly to Michel's home outside Cambridge, an historic property, and it's then I realize that Michel has money. From the looks of the property, lots of it. But of course, his forefathers were Vicomtes back in the day.

Ed drives up to the security gate and waits for his car to be waved through. Finally the gate opens and Ed drives up the semicircular drive and parks in front of the door. The old mansion is a colonial with stately columns and lush landscaping. I can't begin to imagine how old or how expensive it is nor can I imagine Michel living here.

We get out of the car and I glance around. There are security cameras everywhere and a guard greets us at the front door. He's wearing a suit and has an earpiece like I've seen on Secret Service personnel. This place has a lot of security.

Ed speaks with the guard and the guard goes back inside, leaving us on the front driveway. Finally, the guard returns and waves us in. I enter the house and can't help but be curious, but at the same time, I'm afraid of how Michel will react to the news.

"He's in the library. Follow me," the guard says and points to a set of double glass doors. He leads the way and we pass through into a huge room with wall to ceiling bookshelves. There are thousands of books and the shelves are so high, there is a ladder on rollers for access. The room is grand and a huge fireplace is a focal point to the room.

Michel's sitting in a wing chair, reading. He's dressed in black jeans and a black sweater and the darkness of the fabric contrasts with his white skin and dark hair. He glances at me briefly, but his face is unreadable.

"My Lord," the guard says. "Agents O'Neil and Hayden to see you."

My Lord?

"What's the matter?" Michel says, closing the book. "You wouldn't come to my home unless this was important. Do we have a suspect?"

"Why the fuck haven't you been answering your phone?" Ed says. "Regs stipulate that you must be in phone contact 24/7."

"I left you a note about a personal trip I had to make and that I'd be out of phone contact for twenty-four hours at least," Michel says, his voice clipped, impatient.

"Where were you? The dark side of the moon? There's no reason for you to be out of phone contact."

"I sent a note, Ed. Surely you can do without me for one day."

"I didn't get any note. We've been trying to get in touch with you all night."

Michel's jaw tenses. "What's so important?"

"Well, first, Eve was snooping around in Terri's files. The personnel files and she found her own."

Michel turns to look at me, and instead of mild disinterest, he appears concerned.

"How much did you read?"

I shake my head. "That's not important." I turn to Ed. "Tell him."

"Tell me what?"

Ed sits on the couch across from Michel, who grips onto the arm of the sofa and his book slips out of his hand onto the floor. "Julien?"

Ed nods and stares at Michel.

"Staked. We found him just after midnight. He's intact, but he's dead."

I watch Michel and his eyes close, his nostrils flaring as he absorbs the news. He covers his eyes with a hand and my heart clenches for him.

Ed clears his throat. "He wasn't working on some clandestine operation we didn't know about?"

"Not that I know of," Michel says, his voice barely audible. "We've only recently begun speaking again."

"You'll have to find someone to revive him."

"Of course," Michel says, and bends to pick up his book. I reach down for him, glancing at the title. Aquinas, *Summa Theologica*. I hand it to him and our fingers touch for a second. A surge of sadness fills me from him and I want to take his hand and feel more, but he quickly pulls his hand away from mine as if avoiding my touch. He glances at his watch.

"I'll have to make arrangements..."

"I'm sorry about this Michel," Ed says, his earlier anger gone, replaced by patience. "We should go to the morgue," Ed says, standing. "You need to identify him. Take possession."

Michel slips the book onto the table and follows him. I take up the rear and walk behind Michel. He's being amazingly calm, considering but I can tell he's very upset by the stiffness to his body and his movements, as if he's holding himself in, desperately trying to control his emotions. I want so much to comfort him, but know there is nothing I could do or say. We stop in the entry and Michel speaks to a servant, who brings him his cassock-coat, helping him with it. I note the way all the staff treat him with deference, keeping their eyes downcast.

Michel speaks with the guard who greeted us, and when we drive away from the grounds, I notice there's a car tailing us.

We drive to the morgue in silence. Michel is seated beside me in the back of the sedan. I glance at him and he's looking down at his hands, which are in fists, his hair partially covering his face. I want so badly just to lean over and put my arms around him.

"You met with him before Montana and once we were there," he says quietly. "Did he say anything?"

"You already know what we spoke about."

"I have no idea what you spoke about," Michel says, turning to me, frowning. "I was away on personal business."

"I'm sorry," I say quickly. "I thought I saw a vampire in the alley behind the café. I thought it was you."

"Spying on you? I was busy all that night until I saw you."

"Michel," I say, leaning in closer, taking his hand, squeezing, needing to touch him. "He has that tattoo – the same as the other victims of the River Man. The Lorraine Cross."

He frowns and turns to me, squeezing my hand back, his grief barely held at bay.

"He does? I haven't seen it but we've been estranged for decades…"

I remember the thick scarf Julien wore the night he showed up. I wonder if he hasn't been hiding it for it was only because Julien's scarf fell open when we had coffee that I saw it.

Michel lets me hold his hand, but I get nothing from him of where he's been or what he was doing. He's just a wall of raw emotion.

"There's a video camera so you can identify him at a distance," Ed says from the front seat.

Michel shakes his head. "I want to see him."

"Michel," I say and pull his hand closer. "When I was with Soren, I read him. He's the one killing Adepts. He's the River Man."

Michel turns to me and shakes his head.

"He can't be. He has an alibi for every murder."

I look at him. Can't he see that Soren can compel anyone to give him an alibi?

"I know what I felt."

"What did you see?"

"I didn't see anything, but if he's more powerful than a vampire, he might be able to block my telepathy. But I know I felt him and he's the River Man."

~

WE ARRIVE AT THE SCU. Michel and I walk hand in hand to the storage area and we wait while an attendant retrieves the body. After a nod from Ed, the attendant pulls the draping back to reveal Julien's white face. The attendant keeps the shroud just above the shoulders, covering the stake.

"Why haven't they removed the stake?"

"It has to stay in," Ed says. "So they can do the rite."

I reach out to touch it and see if there are any memory traces but Ed reaches out to stop me.

"Let me check it," I say.

He shakes his head. "It's obvious this is the work of the same killer."

"But it's my job…"

Michel squeezes my hand to stop me. "Eve," he says, his voice choked. "This is not your fight."

I frown. Michel lets go of my hand and stands next to the table. I glance from one brother to the other. Identical except for Julien's hair and scar.

"He was older by four minutes," Michel says, his voice choking. "The first to do everything – to walk, to speak, to kiss a girl…"

The first to die… I think, completing his thought.

I wonder about the legendary bond that exists between identical twins. It's impossible to explain in purely scientific terms so one has to resort to paranormal phenomena to account for it, but I'm a scientist. I cling to the belief that everything has a material basis – even telepathy.

Michel covers his mouth and leans down, pressing his forehead against his brother's. He grabs Julien's jacket and squeezes, and I fear he's going to lose control.

After a moment, Ed clears his throat, and Michel straightens and wipes his eyes. I feel a surge of sympathy for him when I see his tears, and mine bite at the corner of my eyes in response. Finally, the attendant re-covers the body. I take Michel's arm and lead him out of the room and his hand slips down my arm, threading his fingers through mine.

"Our witness told us what happened, but he's not really reliable."

"A witness?"

"Some old vagrant sleeping in the street outside the cathedral," Ed says. "Probably senile. Always pestering the parishioners for spare change."

"You don't think he staked Julien?"

"No," Ed says. "He was too old and weak. Probably another vampire or an Adept."

Michel's face is grim as we wait for the elevator to the third floor offices. I get in beside Michel, and am almost overwhelmed at the intensity of his grief. He holds it in such control, his body stiff, his face blank, only his hand gripping mine so tightly shows any emotion.

We enter Ed's office and Ed sits behind his desk and Michel sits on the chair across from him. He sinks into it and wipes his eyes. I remain standing at the side of the office.

"I have your brother's personal effects," Ed says, and thrusts an envelope and a sheet of paper towards Michel. "You'll have to sign this release form."

Michel opens the envelope and retrieves a watch, rosary and a ring. He puts them in his pocket but keeps the ring in his hand, turning it over and over in his palm.

"His clothing," Ed says while Michel signs the release form, "his overcoat is being kept as evidence. It's quite damaged."

Michel nods. He examines Julien's ring, and then slips it on the index finger on his right hand.

"I know this is painful," Ed says, speaking in a soft voice, "but do you have any idea who might have done this to him? Any enemies? People with a grudge? Was he trying to take over anyone's territory?"

"No," Michel says, his blue eyes red from tears. "We've made many enemies over the centuries."

"It was Soren," I say to them both, but they ignore me, as if they can't even hear what I'm saying. Ed flips a few pages in his file. A knock at the door draws my attention away from Michel. One of the clerical workers hands Ed a file. He returns to his desk and flips through the contents.

"You should see this," he says, motioning for Michel to join him. Michel goes to his side and leans down to examine the file, which contains several pages of email messages. I peer over Michel's shoulder, careful not to get too close. There I see a research paper on the Cathars. Michel picks it up and reads through the first page.

Ed glances up. "What about any groups your brother might have been involved in?"

"Groups?"

"Yes, you know. Special study groups. Religious sects. That sort of thing."

"We were both of the Order of Preachers, the Dominicans, if that's what you mean, but it's hardly a sect. Julien used to go rock climbing with some of the monks. He volunteered at a local library archives, cataloguing old documents. That's all I know. No groups."

I pick up one of the emails. It's addressed to "In Doubt" and was from someone with the handle "Brother Novae". The body of the email mentions a meeting to discuss "The Pure".

Ed rustles through the printed pages in the file.

"Forensics found some interesting information in your brother's email," he says. Ed holds up an email and reads it. "He had a trip planned for the summer to France to follow the path of the Albigensian crusade. And there were a few email addresses to a group known as 'The Pure'. Do you know anything about that?"

Michel shakes his head. "Trip down memory lane? Julien fought to defend the Cathars back in the day. I sided with the Church against them," Michel says. "It's old news." Michel rises. "If we're done here, the sun will rise very shortly."

"Fine," Ed says. "Take some time to arrange things. But please, keep your phone on."

Michel nods, and now I'm so curious about why he was out of contact for the past twenty-four hours.

"Do you need anything?" I say, touching his arm. "Let me know how I can help."

Michel takes my hand, squeezing it. "I'm fine," he says.

I know he's anything but.

CHAPTER 18

"A WOUNDED DEER LEAPS THE HIGHEST."

Emily Dickenson

The next evening after sunset, I take a cab to the cathedral, hoping to find Antonio and ask him some questions about what happened. Once I arrive on monastery grounds, I go on foot. The noise from the distant highway has faded, and now all I hear is the sound of my thumping heart. A walk will help me relax. The events of the previous night and morning have drained me and I need the exercise.

The streets are still wet from the rain. To the north, the fog distorts the view of the cathedral buildings, deep within a small wooded area. A long wall of stone surrounds the grounds, and there, about half way up the street, sits a figure in a tangle of cardboard and plastic, a hat and muffler obscuring his face. Ed indicated that a few homeless people lived in the area so this might not be Antonio, but I forge on in hope that he is.

I draw closer and slow my pace, my gut knotting when I see

Michel turning onto the sidewalk in front of me. He's facing the other direction and doesn't see me, so I hang back, wondering what he'll do.

When Michel approaches the seated figure, the man looks up and I recognize Antonio from the curve of his nose. He shakes his hand as if demanding a coin. Michel reaches deep into his pocket and retrieves a few coins, then drops them into the outstretched palm. I join him rather than hang back and remain out of sight. I'm worried what Michel might do. It's impossible to predict the behavior of those who grieve.

"*Deo grazia.*" Antonio says as I join them. Michel looks at me and frowns.

"Are you following me?"

"No," I say, embarrassed and insulted at the same time. "I wanted to check out the crime scene. I saw you and came over."

"You shouldn't be out alone, especially not at night. My security team has failed I see."

He turns back to Antonio. The old man counts the coins and then closes his hand around them, placing his hand against his chest.

"Accept my condolences for your loss," he says.

"You were here when he was murdered?" Michel clears his throat as if he finds it difficult to speak. "You saw my brother die? Did you see who killed him?"

"Julien always gave something." The old man shakes his head. "He had a generous heart."

"Who are you?"

"Me?" he says and shrugs. "I'm no one. But my name is Antonio."

"Did you see who killed my brother?" Michel says once again.

The old man closes his eyes and makes the sign of the cross.

"The Dragon has returned and even now walks among us. Someone strong must destroy his minions and send Him back to the pit where He belongs."

Michel shakes his head and turns to me, disappointment clear in his eyes.

I sigh. "We told you he wasn't ... reliable."

Michel turns away, but before we can leave, Antonio reaches out and grabs Michel's pant leg.

"Your brother wanted to fight," he says, looking up at Michel. "He would have killed the Dragon if he could have, but he was not strong enough. It happened too fast and we were not prepared. And I . . ." The old man shakes his head and rubs his eyes. "I was weak. I couldn't save him."

"What are you talking about?" Michel jerks his leg out of Antonio's grasp and strides down the street towards the cathedral.

"Don't be so quick to dismiss what I say," Antonio calls out when Michel's a few paces away. His voice has lost its age and is now strong and firm. "This guise is useful, for it protects me from those who would try to stop me and others like me."

Michel turns back, and I'm also compelled to stay and listen. A thrill goes through me at the sound of lucidity in Antonio's voice.

"What do you mean, others like you?" Michel says.

"Others who are pure. One day, you'll understand – if you survive the trials."

"I'm not pure," he says and shakes his head, his voice catching.

"You have no idea who you are, either of you," he says and points at us. "Still, the Dragon has returned. He must be defeated. We must all watch and be vigilant and those of us who can, must try to destroy Him."

Michel turns away as if he can't bear to listen any more.

"The Dragon and St. Michael have been fighting for thousands of years," Antonio says. "You think you've read church history but you have not read it all, not even close. But don't believe me. After all, I am just an old man, am I not? Go," Antonio says and waves his hand. He picks up a piece of cardboard and places it over his head to protect himself from the rain, which has just started once more. "Be with God."

Michel turns to me. "I have an appointment with the Bishop about Julien. Do you have a ride? It's not safe for you out here alone."

"I'll call a cab," I say and hold up my cell. "Don't worry about me."

"Let me get my driver to take you home." He takes my head in his hands and pulls me closer, kissing my forehead. "I can't have anything happen to you."

"It's OK. I'm just going to look at the crime scene again and then I'll call a cab."

"Just let my driver know when you're ready, and he'll take you. I won't let you go home alone, Eve. You shouldn't even be here."

Michel opens his cell and speaks into it, and his limo drives up.

"Take it when you're ready."

I nod and watch Michel enter the long winding path to the cathedral, knowing there's nothing I can say to comfort him. I want so much to be with him, but he hasn't asked and I know this must be a lonely journey for him.

The rain starts again and so I open my umbrella and walk along the sidewalk towards the crime scene. I stand alone in the deserted garden. The police and forensic units have long gone. Only a lone ribbon of yellow tape flapping in the wind marks the spot as a crime scene.

I enter the enclosure and stand in the center of the darkened garden, trying to imagine what Julien was doing here so late the night before. From where I stand, the lights from the street cast a baleful yellow glow over the area, but it does little to illuminate the enclosure. Tall firs and oaks line the wall and block out most of the light so that it's almost completely dark. The street noises are muted and only the sound of the rain pattering on my umbrella fills the silence. The previous night, the rain wasn't as heavy, but it had been constant. Why had Julien come here at midnight, to meet his killer alone? Was this part of some cult to which he belonged?

I glance up, feeling the odd sensation of being watched. A figure stands in the entry, no umbrella in hand. After a moment, he walks over to me. Michel. He says nothing as the rain falls and drenches him so that his eyelashes cling to each other and rain drips off his cheeks.

"I thought you had a meeting with the Bishop."

"I can't relax until I know you're safe. Have you found anything?"

"No," I say. "Come under the umbrella. The rain's cold." I hold it up, but he declines with a shake of his head.

"Then come over here under the trees for shelter. You're soaked."

"I'm dead," he says, his voice bitter. "What does it matter?"

I take his arm and pull him to the shelter of one of the tall firs. Underneath, only a few errant drops of rain fall through the canopy of needles. I close my umbrella and stand still in the ensuing silence.

I squeeze his arm in comfort.

Michel shakes his head. His hair is soaked and his thick lashes clumped from the rain – or tears.

"He was so good to me," he says, his voice breaking. For a moment, he says nothing, and I can see him struggling with his composure. "Despite everything, he treated me so well."

"He loved you very much, despite how he teased you," I say. "How hard will it be to get an Ancient's blood to restore him?"

Michel sighs. "I'll get Soren to do the rite tomorrow, but the price will be very high." Then he touches my cheek lightly, saying nothing, reaching up to cup my face and I lean into his hand. I realize he's using his powers to take away my sadness, and in that moment, I feel a surge of something for him that surprises me. Whether it was his doing, or just a flash of insight, I don't know. All I know is that he was never a monster, no matter what he's done.

In the darkness, he reaches out and folds me in an embrace, his arms tightening around me. Our skin doesn't touch and so we're just two people embracing, providing each other comfort. I rest my head against his shoulder. He's silent for a long moment and it feels so comforting to be in his arms.

"Soren arranged all this," he says, his voice filled with emotion. "All of it like one big chess game. He wants one of us. He'll want Julien's servitude in return for reviving him."

I can think of nothing to say in response. Then, movement catches my eye and I turn, my heart racing, only to find Antonio standing on the pathway a few steps away from us. Like Michel, he's drenched from the rain.

"This is where they stood," Antonio calls out. The old man points to a spot off the pathway. "I held up my crucifix and tried to stop it, to make it leave Julien alone, but I was not strong enough. Julien was already under its spell."

Michel doesn't move. I'm transfixed as well, imagining it in my mind's eye.

"The demon tried to stop me, but I fought it," Antonio says, his voice gaining strength and emotion. "Then it killed Julien, staking him. It threw him across the clearing as if he were no more than a rag doll. He fell onto the ground here." Antonio points to a tall fir beside the walkway.

Michel moves closer and examines the spot but there's nothing to see. Whatever blood there was has been washed away in the rain.

"You must take up the fight, Michel," Antonio says. "You must follow in his footsteps. Give in to God's plan. But there are sides. Choose carefully."

Michel pushes past the old man and leaves the garden. I follow him to the park's exit and he stops and waits for me.

I touch his arm. "He's a crazy old man. Ignore him."

"Not as crazy as you might think."

"Tell me, then."

"Eve," he says and rubs his forehead. "I'm taking some time off while I make arrangements to revive Julien." He looks at me. "You're not safe. I'm going to have to teach you to look after yourself. I want you to meet me tomorrow night at the dojo. If I'm leaving you unprotected, I'm doing things my way. I have to go to my appointment, but you need to go home now. Promise me you'll use my driver and go home right away."

"Of course I will."

He leaves my side and walks down the lane to the monastery without looking back. When I glance back to the garden, the old man stands in the center where Julien died, still unprotected from the rain that now falls in torrents.

~

CHAPTER 19

"THEY SICKEN of the calm who knew the storm."

Dorothy Parker

Michel's waiting in the dojo when I arrive for my shift at seven, and as soon as I see him, I'm like Pavlov's dog, all excited and breathless. On top of my desire for him, there's a strange excitement in my belly at the prospect of him teaching me how to kill a vampire properly – and as acting as his proper Adept.

I remind myself what he said – that I must obey him, no questions asked about his decisions. That I must trust him completely.

I'm not sure if I can do this. I'm so used to being my own woman, making all my own decisions. I've been alone for my entire life, with no siblings, and most of it without my real parents. I just don't know if I can play this role.

I've dressed appropriately in sweats and a t-shirt, my hair back in a tightly coiled bun like I used to wear when I danced as a girl. I enter the dojo, bowing slightly, and then stand before him, still a bit shy around him after last night's intensity.

"Hello, Eve," he says softly.

"Michel," I reply and I can't not smile up at him, because I'm so glad to see him even after such a short separation.

"Eve…Don't smile at me or I won't be able to concentrate."

I cover my mouth with a hand, trying to stifle my smile, and wait for him to speak.

He picks through his duffle bag and pulls out a red bingo stamp. He hands it to me and I take it and make a face, examining it.

I give a nervous laugh. "A bingo stamp?"

"You've got to show me that you can hit exactly where a vampire's most vulnerable. So," he says and steps in front of me. "Tell me what you think you know about killing a vampire."

I bite my lip for a moment.

"This is standard stuff, Eve," he says, all serious now, his eyes intense. "You should know and would have known if we hadn't lost your case when you were put in the foster system."

"Stake them with wood," I say. "Only thing that kills them. Cut their head off and burn their bodies to ensure they can't be revived."

"Yes, but how do you stake them? Where?" He takes off his shirt and I admire his smooth pale skin and well-developed abs, a trail of dark hair leading down from his navel to below his own sweats. "Show me where. You've taken anatomy and physiology. You know where my heart is."

I touch his chest, and even that makes my heart skip.

"You're heart's behind the sternum, more of it to the left because of the structure of the heart."

"And if you were to thrust a stake right into the sternum?" he says and touches his chest there. "You'd hit a solid plate of bone and only the strongest weapon could pierce it. To stake a vampire, it's best to come up under the sternum and angle your thrust so that it goes towards the center line. Show me with your stamp," he says, his hands at his side.

I can't hold back my smile and tilt my head to the side. "You want me to attack you with a stamp?"

"This isn't a joke, Eve," he says, and I can tell he's trying not to smile back but his eyes soften a bit and he's staring at my dimples again. "Remember what I said last night. I want you to use the stamp so you can see where to hit a vampire with a stake. Go ahead. Do it."

I make a half-hearted thrust at him, pressing the stamp on his skin just below the sternum, but it's hard to take this seriously. He grabs me and turns me around so that my back is facing him, his arm around my shoulders, my hands confined behind my back. His mouth is on my neck, which he bites playfully, tonguing my skin, his fangs retracted.

"And because you weren't really trying," he whispers, his voice only a bit angered, "the vampire now has you just where he wants you and all those freaky vampire hunter skills are useless." He releases me but even the brief moment of his confining me arouses me and I feel all flushed from his touch. "Try again, and this time, take it seriously."

He waits until I've turned back and waves me on. He's trying to get me angry to make me focus but all I can think of is how desirable he is and how even now, I really only want to just feel him on top of me.

"Come on," he says, hands on his hips. "If you don't, I'll have to get rough."

I shake my head and look away, and then lunge at him, and jab him with the stamp before he can respond.

"Good," he says. "That's more like it." He glances down at the mark I've left.

"Slightly off target and you haven't hit me hard enough to drive a stake into me. But it's a better effort. Finally," he says and shakes his head. I smile at him and tilt my head to the side, trying to look coy.

"Stop that, Eve," he says and steps closer. One hand goes behind my head and he presses his forehead against mine, his eyes closed, his expression all serious. "Please take this seriously. My brother has already been killed as have several Adepts. I have to leave you and I don't want you to be in danger. Remember our talk."

"I'll be fine," I say. "I was fine before you came along, and I'll be fine now."

"You won't be fine," he says, his voice firm. "Not anymore. Remember what I said."

I do remember, but something in me fights back, despite my promise.

He steps back, all business again.

"You almost had it. Try once more," he says and takes a blue stamp from his duffle bag and marks the spot I should hit. "Try to hit me right there. Remember to thrust up and to the center, not straight in."

I hit him again, and this time, my aim is more accurate.

"Your strength still isn't there." He grabs me and has me in his arms once more, my hands tightly confined, his grip a bit painful, biting a bit harder on my neck so that it actually hurts.

"You have to hit harder or you'll just make a surface wound, and that will only make a vampire angrier," he says, his mouth now at my ear. "Remember, you'll have to go up under the sternum. The other option is to come down between ribs," he says and demonstrates, "but you need to really practice that one before you can count on it and you need to use your body weight."

He releases me once more and I think he doesn't realize how he affects me. I stand across from him, my pulse increased, breathing more heavily.

"Why not just use a crossbow?"

"They're good," he says and nods. "You should always have one in your weapons cache. But you can't carry one around with you all the time. You need to be ready to fight with whatever you have at any time."

"Why do you think I'm in such danger?"

"You read our personnel files," he says and it's the first time he's mentioned my little breach of security. Then I remember that every single Adept who's worked with the SCU has died. "Now that you're working for the SCU, you're a target. Other vampires will eventually find out you're an Adept and might just decide to steal you from me."

"So I'm your property?"

"Yes," he says, his face dark. He steps closer and cups my cheek. "No, not really. You're under my protection. I told you how this has to work, Eve. All in or all out."

"I want all in," I say, intending the double meaning, smiling and he makes that little throat sound and smiles in spite of himself.

"You are so impatient," he says and grabs me, and pulling me against his body, holding my hands behind my back. My heart jumps, my body responding to his intensity. God, he makes me dizzy just touching me... He kisses me, hard and passionate. Then he kisses my neck, holding his lips there, his breathing harsh.

Then he pushes me away and I'm standing there, my own breathing fast and shallow.

"Now, concentrate. We don't have long."

"How can I concentrate when you do that to me?"

"How can I not do that to you when you display your dimples like some temptress?" he says, grinning.

But then he's back to business and stands at the ready again, waving me on.

"Look around you when you're in a compromised situation," he says. "If you feel under threat, you'll fall into a fight trance. Look for anything wooden you could use as a stake. If you need to, break a broomstick, or anything else wooden. Even a pencil will work if it goes directly into the heart. If there's nothing wood, use something metal. It won't kill the vampire permanently, but it'll give you a few moments to escape while the vampire recovers."

"Why is that?" I say, looking at the stamp in my hand. "Why wood?"

"It's organic. Metals don't kill vampires, although silver weakens us. Our bodies repel metals except silver, which if it remains in our bodies, draws out our strength. Sure, metal weapons create a wound, but that wound heals rapidly, in moments. Unless you stake us with wood first, you can't cut our heads off. Remember – our bones are very hard. All you'll end up doing is making a hideous wound that will heal in a very short time so it's pointless to try," he says, his face dark. "Unless you want just to torture us, and if that's what you want, use silver. It burns and directly saps our strength. Now enough delaying. Attack me once again. This time, hit harder. You've got to push the stake up and into the heart. It takes considerable strength so you might want to use your bodyweight to assist. Jump at me."

He crouches down a bit and waves me on again. I'm embarrassed to have to try this.

"Don't make me get rough, Eve. Believe me, I can and will. This is deadly serious."

"I can't do this," I say and hold up the stamp. "It's too silly."

He stands up straight and sighs, then goes to the weapons case on the wall. He unlocks the padlock, and withdraws a short steel dagger about four inches long. He returns and hands it to me.

"Use this."

The blade is smooth and sharp and short. I turn it over in my hands. "You want me to attack you with this?"

"No," he says. "I wanted you to attack me with the stamp, but it's too silly for you. I thought maybe a dagger would be less silly. Maybe you'd take this seriously."

"I can't," I say, shaking my head. "I can't really stab you."

"Eve, you must. I'm leaving and you'll be in danger. Please understand I won't be here to protect you."

He looks so earnest, his voice so insistent, I feel a lump in my throat.

"Just think of your poor mother dying in front of you," he adds. "Think of the vampire who did it, who took her from you and ruined your life. Use that anger."

I shake my head and stare at the dagger.

"I can't."

"Come on Eve. Just do it." He slaps me, his hand meeting my cheek with a sharp smack, my head jerking away. I wasn't expecting it and it hurts and makes me mad.

His face is dark, his brows furrowed. "I said I'd have to get rough if you don't take this seriously."

"You want me to stab your heart with this?"

He nods. "Do it once, and you'll remember the feeling, you'll know almost how much force you need to use. You'll know how to do it with a stake. Now, come on, vampire hunter. Pretend that's a stake and stab me."

"But it will hurt you…"

He shrugs. "In eight hundred years, it's happened a half-dozen times. I'm tough, Eve. It'll kill me for a moment, disable me for about five minutes, and I'll bleed but I'll heal or I wouldn't let you do it. Go ahead. Do it. Just remember to take the blade out immediately, or it'll take longer for me to recover."

I just stand there, unmoving, a sense of horror going through me. Then he attacks me, slapping me, shoving me, getting in my face so that I stumble back and almost trip. I fall into fight trance without trying, and it's like I'm no longer in the same time dimension he is.

I have the dagger in him, exactly where it's supposed to go before he can even move and I know the blade has done its job. He groans, his face contorting and he falls against me. I try to hold him up with my body but he's too heavy. He slides to his knees.

"Take it out," he manages to hiss between gritted teeth.

"Oh, God, Michel," I cry out when I come out of fight trance and pull the blade out. He slips onto his front, his face smacking against the mat, his eyes closed, and I struggle to turn him over onto his back. I touch his wound, pressing on it to stop the flow of blood, his skin slick with it.

About three minutes pass before his eyelids flutter and in that time, I almost run upstairs to find Ed. When he opens those blue eyes and grimaces, I kiss him, my tears welling up because I killed him, even if only for a few minutes. He just lies there, breathing heavily. Finally, he struggles to sit up.

"Jesus Christ that hurts," he hisses through gritted teeth.

"I'm sorry," I say, my voice breaking. "But you wanted me to."

"Don't worry," he says, cracking a tiny smile. "You did it perfectly. But remember," he says and tries to sit up straighter. "You have to use more force with a stake. A metal weapon is always easier to use but won't kill the vampire. Only wood will and only if it's directly in the heart."

My hands are bloodied and I wipe the tears off my cheeks with the backs of my hands.

"It's OK," he says and brushes my cheek with his fingers. "See? I'm almost all better and it's only been a few minutes."

I shake my head, my throat constricting.

"All this time, I've fantasized about killing vampires – you know, really doing it. Especially the vampire who killed my mother. I never thought about what it meant to actually do it. I don't know," I say and glance away from him. "I don't know if I can do this. I wanted to do research. I wanted to use my mind to find a cure or a poison. Not actually have to stake vampires."

"Hopefully, you won't have to. Hopefully," he says and takes my chin in his hand and turns my face back to him. "You'll spend your time looking at evidence and maybe now and then, reading a vampire to see their last kill and you won't have to ever stake one. But at least now you know you can."

He leans in and kisses me tenderly, his lips soft against mine and I just melt into him, my hands on his chest.

"Come and wash up." He stands up, only a bit hesitant, one hand over his chest.

"Are you sure you're OK?" I reach out and touch his chest where the only sign of a stab wound is a thin red seam and blood that spilled down his chest to his belly.

"All better." He pokes at the wound. "Just a bit tender. Now come with me and let's get you cleaned up. We're going to Franklin Park to look for vampires."

I hesitate. "What?"

He walks off the mats towards the locker room.

"I'm going to take you out so you can see vampires at night. See where they go, what they do. There's quite a few in town and you can bet some will be at the park, looking for willing blood whores. It's illegal but it's not grounds for prosecution. The blood whores need the money and so it's more of a nuisance. The Council mostly looks the other way."

"Will I be in danger?"

He shakes his head.

"Not as long as you're with me."

We wash off in the locker room and then Michel pulls on his t-shirt. Before we leave for Franklin Park, he reaches into a pocket in his jacket and withdraws a small piece of cloth, which had been folded up into a tiny package. He unwraps it and takes out a piece of flesh colored rubber with two red gashes in it – a fake vampire bite.

"Here," he says and tilts my head to the side. He peels the backing off the fake bite and then kisses my neck softly before placing the fake bite there, just below my ear.

"If, for whatever reason we're separated, this is for your protection. I want you to look like you're claimed. Otherwise someone might try to take you. You could beat them if they didn't ambush you, but if there are more than one, you might not be able to fight them all off. That will take further training."

I touch the fake vampire bite, frowning. Then, his face changes, his fangs extending, eyes red-rimmed, and he bites his wrist, daubs his finger in some blood and smears it first on my chin, then some on my face next to my mouth. He actually looks scary when he's in his hunter mode and I frown, touching my face, my fingers coming back bloody.

"What are you doing?"

"Any vampires in the park will smell my blood on you and think I've claimed you. They'll believe that you're my blood slave and they'll know that they'll have to fight me if they want you. I'm one of the older surviving vampires, so they won't challenge me."

I examine my fingers. "You're marking me like a dog marks its territory."

"That's exactly right, Eve," he says and sighs, his face reverting to its more human look. "That's what we do."

I look at my fingers and then to him.

"Why teach me to fight if I'm not going to use it?"

He shakes his head. "Sun Tzu once wrote that supreme excellence consists in breaking the enemy's resistance without fighting. Fighting's dangerous. You could be hurt. If you're ambushed, you might be overcome. If you get too close to a vampire without realizing it, you could succumb to their powers and be helpless to fight. Better not to fight at all." Then, he reaches into an inside pocket in his trench and withdraws a small thin stake with a round handle.

"But if you have to, use this and do what I taught you. Use your full body weight and hit at the right angle. Remember, we're bloody hard to kill, even for an Adept."

I take the stake and feel its weight, passing it from one hand to the other, finally taking it in my right hand.

"Here?" I mime staking him with it. He frowns and steps back for a moment, as if he thought for one moment I'd actually do it.

"That's right," he says, his voice a bit shaky. Finally, he smiles. "Just don't get any ideas."

I don't smile back. "I already killed you once, remember?"

"How could I forget?"

I look at the stake in my hand. "I didn't like it."

He nods. "I'm glad you didn't. Don't get a taste for it. At least not for me."

"I do have a taste for you," I say and smile and that elicits a little throat noise from him and he grabs me once more and kisses my cheeks, his tongue touching my skin and I feel something surge inside of me.

"Lets go," Michel says and leads the way out of the Foster Building.

CHAPTER 20

"THE HEART HAS its reasons that reason knows not of."

Pascal

We take Blue Hill Avenue to Circuit Drive and stop under a streetlamp in the middle of the park. Michel comes around to my side and leans over me while I'm still in my seat and undoes my belt for me.

"Stay close," he says softly. "If anyone approaches us, play it as if you're my blood slave. Act a bit drunk or stoned. That way, you won't have to say anything and if there's a threat, they won't be expecting you to be capable of self-defense. We definitely do not want anyone to know you're an Adept."

He helps me out of the car and a tremor of excitement goes through me at the prospect of being among vampires. We enter the park, and in the darkness, I can see as if through a night vision scope, allowing me to navigate despite the dimness. Ahead, I see only a sea of trees and brush with a faint green glow over the landscape from starlight and ambient light from the city.

We walk on, Michel still holding my arm, and finally, about two hundred feet inside the park, I see two people under a fir tree, facing each other. Neither is a vampire – vampires have a strange color in the dark due to their body temperature. I glance at Michel – he looks like a stone angel in a graveyard, his skin different shades of grey in my night vision, his blue eyes grey, his pupils huge in the darkness.

"Just a couple of druggies exchanging a needle," he says, leaning down close to me, whispering in my ear. "We have to go deeper. Take care with what you say to me. Remember vampire hearing is very acute. Anyone in the park will hear what we say."

He slides his hand down my arm, his fingers threading through mine. We pass the pair and go farther into the park, stopping at a bench beside a path leading to a clearing in the trees.

"Sit here for a while," he says softly.

I sit beside him and he places his arm around me, pulling me closer, turning to face me while his eyes move over the landscape behind me, so we look like a vampire-human couple instead of a pair of Council Agents on a training mission. Of course, we're both.

As I scan the park around us, a question rises in my mind.

"If scientists were able to develop a cure for vampirism, would you take it?" I say, whispering. I look up at his face when he doesn't answer right away.

"There'll be no cure, Eve," he says and looks down at me. "It's not just a disease. You might be able to alter it, but it won't go away."

"No," I say and shake my head. "It is just a disease. It's likely just a set of mutations that are passed through shared blood, like HIV. Maybe some kind of retrovirus that alters your DNA, turning you into a vampire."

"It's not just a mutation," he says firmly.

"I don't believe that religious drivel," I say and sigh. "Remember I'm an atheist."

"Remember I'm a priest."

"Ah, but you left the priesthood."

"Not by choice."

I exhale heavily and close my eyes, trying to feel drugged, but my experience with drugs is pretty minimal.

"So if you could, you'd become a priest again?"

"Without hesitation."

That hurts me. "You don't mind celibacy?"

"I hate it. A priest has to make sacrifices."

"I think celibacy is wrong," I say, wanting to argue with him. "It's unnatural. Humans are meant to be sexual."

"What's natural? Bach is unnatural, if you mean evolutionary development. Humans are unnatural. We don't need to play piano or compose beautiful works of music. We do because we're metaphysical. We create ourselves, we escape our biology, we mold ourselves into what we want to be to reach a higher plane. Celibacy is just one way of exerting control over desire so you can channel it for other purposes."

"Why aren't you celibate now? If you were, you could channel all that desire into accomplishing your mission," I say, trying to be saucy.

"Eve of a thousand questions..." He takes my chin in his hand and leans down and kisses me. "I am celibate," he says, his lips at my ear. "I have been."

My body responds to that revelation, a surge of something going through me. He's celibate?

I pull away and look in his eyes. "I didn't know. I thought you wanted me."

"I do." His face becomes serious once more. "I try to live my life as a priest, even if I'm not officially one. I pray, Eve. I worship. I ask for forgiveness. I'm hoping for redemption."

"What do you have to ask forgiveness for?" I say softly, thinking how God should be asking forgiveness for making him a vampire. He just shakes his head and looks away from me.

"I was very bad, Eve. I have much to atone for."

"That's why you ripped out pages of the manuscript?"

"Part of the reason, yes."

"If there was a God," I say, "and I don't believe there is one, why would he allow people to be killed by vampires? My mother wasn't a sinner. I don't care what anyone says. She was a good person and didn't deserve to die. I didn't deserve to become motherless. You didn't deserve to become a vampire."

"Eve," he says, his voice almost a whisper. "I don't think vampirism has anything to do with hurting humans. We're like collateral damage."

I frown, unable to let the thought go. "What do you mean? God was punishing someone else?"

He nods but doesn't elaborate.

"Who?" I say finally but he shakes his head and looks away. I say nothing. There's no arguing with people on this and I know it.

"Shh," he says and takes my chin in his hand once more. "Just enjoy the night. Quit thinking so much. Besides, you should just drink." He takes one of my hands in his and holds his other wrist out to me. Drink? He must mean that I should pretend to drink his blood like a good blood slave would. I frown and take his wrist and I hold it in front of me, reluctant to go through with the ruse.

I think about blood slaves – humans who drink vampire blood and are addicted to its effect on their neurotransmitters. To me, they're no different from any other addict. To be pitied. But there's something in the whole idea that draws me and I feel just a slight twinge of shame. Like it's illicit, like it's XXX porn, drawing you in, arousing you, but making you feel slightly tarnished afterwards.

Sitting there with his wrist at my lips, his arm around me, other vampires watching us, does something to me that surprises even me. I feel aroused. My body warms at the thought of this intimate act – drinking his blood. I remember how Michel felt when he drank the woman's blood in my shared memory with him. It was so erotic, that connection he felt when he drank, like the joining of two bodies in sex. I kiss his wrist, and then open my mouth, my tongue on his skin and he gasps.

I turn my face up to him.

"What are you doing to me?" I whisper.

"Nothing," he says, his voice breathless. "That's all you."

Then, a strange warmth floods through me and I know I'm channeling him, his emotions. He feels for me, tenderness, ownership – as if I am so valuable, he'll do anything to protect me.

It's then I realize something not in the papers and books I read about vampires. They're humans whose lives were taken from them, usually against their will, and were forced to become killers to survive, their humanity slowly slipping away because of their hunter nature and need for human blood, slowly losing all emotions unless they maintain contact with us through feeding. It is a curse and in that moment, my heart feels as if it's expanding, growing bigger, admitting vampires back into my category of 'human'.

They really are damned – not by a god as Michel thinks, but by a strange quirk of evolution. Now, instead of wanting to find a drug to poison them, kill them all as I once dreamed of in my fantasies of vengeance, I turn my thoughts to a cure. I wonder if a cure is even possible, but I'm certain that vampirism is some genetic mutation in a virus or other infectious agent that evolved thousands of years ago.

"If vampirism is a genetic mutation or set of mutations, there's always gene therapy. How wonderful would that be – to cure vampirism?" I say, looking in his eyes. "To give you back your life? You could be a priest."

"You're wrong," he whispers. "But I love your mind."

I smile, my eyes closed, unwilling to be drawn back to the real world. The drowsy warmth I feel builds, the desire in me building along with it, but I'm helpless to stop it. I don't want to stop it. It's so pleasant here, I let myself just drift on this strange cloud of warmth that seems to go on and on.

Then, it breaks and I startle back to the present. Michel turns his body to me and our eyes meet.

"We're not alone," he whispers as he bends down to me, his lips touching my ear. "Remember what I said."

I instantly become alert.

Michel turns away from me slightly, but I keep facing him. Someone has joined us and is standing close. I can sense him.

A vampire.

"I like her blood type," the vampire says, his voice deep and smooth. "B positive. Mostly Irish but some Welsh. I could smell her across the park. Is she temporary or permanent?"

Michel stands and brings me around in front of him, his arms around me, one across my shoulders, the other still holding my hand. He's tall enough so that his chin rests on the top of my head.

"Permanent."

I keep my eyes closed and lean back against Michel, the back of my head against his chest. I try to act drugged as if I'm his blood slave, and it isn't hard to do. I know he's doing something to my mind to ensure I don't panic and I'm glad.

I peer at the vampire through my eyelashes. He's older, with grey hair and that strange grey skin in the darkness. His lips look almost blue, and his mouth's slightly open, revealing sharp canines. He's in hunter mode.

"You couldn't beat me," Michel says flatly, as if answering an unspoken challenge. "Don't even think of trying."

A surge of adrenaline goes through me and Michel squeezes me as if to calm me. Soon enough, I relax and my heart rate slows once more.

"Don't worry," the vampire says. "I'm not interested in fighting."

Michel doesn't say anything but he does relax his arms around me just a bit.

"She's new," the vampire says. "I heard your conversation and she sounds as if she isn't really your property just yet. That's why I came over. You'll have lots of fun with this one. A real challenge."

"That she most definitely is," Michel says in reply but his voice is brusque and not inviting of any further conversation.

Then the vampire turns and is gone, moving so fast he would have blended into the shadows to a normal mortal, but with my night vision, I can follow him. He's off looking for someone to feed on – some poor blood whore in need of money or a fix of vampire blood.

"You did well, Eve. Congratulations," he says and squeezes me. It feels so good, so comforting. I truly feel safe with him. "You survived your first encounter with a vampire in the field."

He takes my hand and pulls me deeper into the trees. Ahead in the moonlight, I see the same vampire with a woman in his arms.

"That was fast," I say.

"Shh," Michel says. "He can hear you."

We watch as the couple embraces for a few moments and then part, the blood whore going off in the other direction from the vampire. It's a straight exchange – blood for money.

Nothing different from prostitution and it makes me very sad with a sense of moral outrage that women are so vulnerable. Emotion fills me – grief that so many women are compromised, being so poor or addicted, or even just with tragic pasts, that compel them to sell themselves as prostitutes, either for sex or blood.

Michel squeezes my hand. "The oldest profession."

When I think of them, my stomach clenches. Suddenly, I'm fearful because I'm afraid of how easy it would be for me to just lose myself in Michel, become his blood slave as well as his servant. How easily I could become one of these women, desperate, selling myself for it, willing to do anything to get it.

"It's disgusting."

"Why so hostile?"

"I don't like exploitation," I say, suddenly angry.

"You won't become one, Eve. I'd never let you."

"I'm really going to have to figure out how to create mental blocks."

He sighs. "I thought you liked our connection," he says softly. "It's what we vampires do. It's as natural to us as breathing. Just remember that I can't compel you. I can't force you to do anything against your will. You have to choose to be my pet."

"I want to leave," I say, sadness filling me. I wrap my arms around myself.

"We're not done here."

But he follows me, not speaking. When we arrive at the car, he opens the door for me and I get in, buckling my own seatbelt. Once we're driving and I know no one can hear me, I speak.

"Tell me how I can block you out," I say.

"No," he says after a hesitation, his voice soft. "Until this thing between us is settled, I need complete access to you so I can be certain. But one day, after it is, you can find your own blocks. I can't tell you what they'll be."

We drive for a moment in silence.

"Eve," he says and his voice is firm. "I need to know how you are without you screening things, keeping things from me. I need to know what you're feeling so I can judge if you can do the job. If you can do 'us'."

I stare out the window at the darkened streets. As much as I want him, I don't know if I can do 'us' – at least, not in the way I think it's going to be.

"Can you take me home?" I say, emotion filling me. "I don't feel well enough to work any longer."

He says nothing, taking the highway to get back to my apartment, the rest of the trip passing in silence. When he stops the car in front of my building, I go to the front entrance without saying anything to him. I'm seriously freaked about this power he has over me – the power he wants over me and the way it appeals to something deep inside of me.

"Eve," he says and stops me, taking my arm. "Don't be mad at me. I have to do this. I have to know if you're strong enough. If you can handle this world."

"Well?" I say, and try to slip my arm out of his. "Can I?"

He doesn't say anything for a moment, then shakes his head slowly.

"I honestly don't know yet. I only know I want you to be able to do it."

I look away from his too-intense gaze, those bluest of blue eyes seeming hurt by my response.

"I'm sorry." I'm suddenly feeling too tired from it all. "You have to understand how strange this all is." I struggle to find the right words, avoiding his eyes. "Being able to join minds with someone? It's wonderful and scary. I'm afraid that everything between us is leading me down a path I'll come to regret."

"I know," he says and nods. "We have to trust each other

completely. This connection between us – it builds trust. You must trust me with your life. I must trust you with mine." He touches my cheek. "We could kill each other so easily."

We could kill each other. He could catch me unawares and just drink me dry. I could have the stake in his heart in a second. Can I trust him? He's done nothing to raise suspicions in me. He even let me temporarily kill him so that I knew how. The look of concern on his face arouses something in me. Is it fear? Desire? Or is it both?

He removes his hand and stands there on the next step and our eyes are on the level, his face just a few inches from mine and he's so beautiful but I don't know how I feel any longer. The only thing I know for sure is that I want him so much, I'm afraid that I'll do anything to have him.

"Shall I come in?" he asks softly.

"I need to be alone tonight," I say and it's the truth. I need to be away from him for a few hours so I can sort through these emotions.

"I'm going away tomorrow," he says.

"I'm so sad."

He takes my hand and I know it's because he wants to know my sadness.

"I can make you feel better," he says, his voice breathless and his blue eyes narrow. That lopsided grin starts and I close my eyes and can't help but smile in response. He makes that throat sound and takes my head in his hands and kisses my cheeks, one after the other, his tongue touching my skin. I know his thoughts and he wants to touch my skin with his tongue everywhere ... I'm helpless to deny him.

"Eve," he says, his voice solemn. "I want you to stay at my house while I'm gone. You'll be safer there."

I start to protest. "My cats..."

"My servants will take care of them."

I don't want to leave my little apartment, but then I remember my pledge to just obey and I bite back a question, a reason to stay in my own flat.

"OK," I say. "If you want."

"I want." He kisses me. "If you don't, I'll worry about you the entire time I'm away and won't be able to concentrate. We'll go there now. I can send someone over tomorrow to get your things."

"Can't we stop now?"

"No," he says and puts a finger on my lips.

I comply and follow him back into the car.

CHAPTER 21

"THERE IS no remedy for love but to love more."

Thoreau.

We drive out to Cambridge and enter a garage connected to the house. Michel stops and talks to one of his staff, a dark-haired vampire with sharp black eyes and a Hercule Poirot moustache. The man eyes me from under a disapproving frown.

I expect him to take my coat, but Michel seems impatient to take me upstairs to the second floor, where we enter a large bedroom. Against one wall is a huge four-poster bed with a canopy that looks like something out of Buckingham Palace. Michel kicks the door closed and presses me against the wall, pinning my body with his hips, one hand holding mine over my head, his other arm on the wall beside me. I feel his desire for me and it sends a jolt of lust through me.

"I want you, Eve," he says, his voice breathless. "When you had my wrist in your mouth in the park, I thought I'd lose control right there and ravish you."

That sends a wave of desire through me that makes me dizzy.

"You like the thought of me being your pet, being addicted to your blood?" I say, strangely breathy at the thought myself. "I wouldn't want to be addicted to your blood." But even as I say it, the thought does something upsetting to me – it excites me completely.

"You just can't lie very well," he says, staring down into my eyes.

"I know." I remember how I felt when I took his wrist in my mouth. "I can't even lie to myself. But I hate the idea, even if a part of my mind loves it. It would be terrible. It would be a tragedy."

"You don't ever have to do it," he says, his voice quiet. "I admit it appeals to me, but I hate the idea of it as well. I hate the idea that I want it. I have to pray very long and very hard about it, Eve. I do a lot of penance for it."

"Hmm," I say, smiling up at him. "I like the idea of you doing penance."

"Oh, I do an awful lot of it. Speaking of which," he says, trying to frown, but unable to wipe off that lopsided grin. "You kept tempting me with your dimples. Several times you ignored my commands..." He raises his eyebrows playfully.

"I need more training," I say, grinning as wickedly as I can manage.

He makes that throat sound and presses his body against me harder.

"Do you have any idea what that does to me?"

I press back against him. "I think I have a pretty good idea."

He cups my cheek, strokes my skin with his thumb.

"It scares me," I say, swallowing back anxiety. "How omniscient you are. Knowing me better than I know myself."

"But you can know me as well," he says softly. "In a way no normal human can. You'll get better and better at it – listening in, finding things. I've only got an advantage because you're so new at this. I've had eight hundred years of practice."

I look up at him, his blue eyes so beautiful, his dark hair hanging a bit in his eyes, his skin so pale like an angel, and I have to look away. The age thing does something funny to me that I can't immediately understand, and don't want to. I only know it makes me feel weak-kneed and a bit dizzy.

"How do I obey?" I say, barely able to speak, my cheeks hot. "When I'm so used to being in control?"

"Just give yourself permission. Don't question. Don't hesitate. Don't resist. Don't think. Just do."

"But thinking is how I get through the day."

"You don't need to think with me." He takes my chin in his hand and tips my face up, staring into my eyes. "It doesn't mean you're weak. It means you're strong. It means you trust me. A priest understands obedience, Eve. Priests aren't weak because they obey God's will. It makes us strong. That absolute trust provides so much strength and comfort. It's our joy. It could be yours as well."

I close my eyes because this is making me so emotional, my eyes brimming. I feel almost faint, like I'm not getting enough oxygen and I try to breathe in deeply to calm my pounding heart.

"*Mon dieu*," he says, his voice breaking. "You are so beautiful..." He takes my face in his hands and leans down to kiss me, finally, his lips soft on mine, tender, then parting, his kiss becoming more passionate so that my heart races and my body responds. He pulls back and looks in my eyes, and I see so much desire there, so much lust.

"Eve," he says, his voice husky. "I want you."

I swallow back the impulse to be embarrassed. "I want you, too."

Oh, God...

Then I lose myself in him, in his kiss and in his arms. When he carries me to the bed, I don't fight.

I know things will never be the same again.

Afterwards, we lie together, our arms around each other, and he starts to kiss my face, my cheeks, for I'm smiling. Then his mouth finds my neck and I know how much he wants to taste my blood right now, how much he wants to feed, and I feel his teeth sharp and on my skin and I almost tell him to just do it. But the moment passes and he pulls away and rests on his elbows above me, his eyes slowly returning to normal, his teeth retracting.

I glance at him lying on top of me.

"How long will you be away?" I run my hand along his shoulder.

He examines his hands, rolling Julien's ring on his finger.

"It depends on how things go. I must negotiate a deal with Soren to use his blood to resurrect Julien. I won't bargain him away for good, but Julien will be his servant for some good amount of time."

"How long?"

"Could be decades. Because we're among the older vampires, it'll be longer and take more to resurrect him. The Ancients have the power, Eve. The rest of us are children in comparison."

"What are they? The first vampires? What's so special about them? There isn't much written about them or any studies."

He takes in a breath. "I'll tell you but you won't believe it."

"The Fallen Angel stuff? I've read that," I say and shake my head. "You're right. I won't believe it. If they're more powerful, it's likely because they're the first to have the mutations. Maybe the mutations have diminished and become milder as time has passed and that's why you younger vampires aren't as powerful."

He smiles, but it's one of tolerance rather than agreement, like I'm a child that he's indulging.

"I've lived with an Ancient on a daily basis, Eve. I know what they are."

"Soren," I say. "He did this on purpose to get to you, didn't he?"

He nods.

"Yes," he says, his voice quiet, a note of distaste in it. "He's playing us all."

"Go to someone else."

"Eve… He's the only one I have any relationship with. I hate to do it. He's a true monster. But if I don't go to him, he'd destroy me if he found out I went to another."

"Go to someone stronger than him."

He just shakes his head as if I can't understand.

"Even if there was someone more powerful, there's no reason why they'd be willing to go to war with Soren just to resurrect Julien. This is a game of power. He won't just make Julien pay for this. He'll make me pay as well and that's what worries me and why I want you in protective custody."

"Protective custody?" I say and frown. "I don't like the sound of that."

"You don't like the sound of it, but that's the reality, Eve. Get used to it," he says and his voice is harsh. "After tonight, things will never be the same again."

I look at him and the anger in his voice and the darkness in his eyes make me fear for myself.

"They aren't just old vampires, Eve. They're not fallen humans as you think of vampires. They're something entirely different."

I trace his bottom lip with my finger. He's so serious, so afraid of this thing he must do.

"I can't come with you?"

"God, no," he says and shakes his head vigorously. "I'll never let you get within a hundred miles of him again."

"I don't like the sounds of that."

"You shouldn't. Let me warn you now," he says, and reaches out to pull me closer, running his fingers through my hair. "If you ever see him again, run the other way. Don't stop and don't look back. I mean it. He'll have you as his blood slave in a second."

"Why?"

"Because you're an Adept, Eve. You can connect. It's what they crave. It's what we all crave. You know how good it is."

I do know how good it is. "Almost too good."

He nods. "If you were my blood slave, it would be even better. With an Adept, we wouldn't have to even touch."

That sends a wave of something through me. "You said that before. You mean real telepathy? Like spooky action at a distance?"

He nods. "Exactly."

I turn over on my back and lie there, staring at the ceiling, the idea of real telepathy – reading Michel's mind at a distance like some kind of connection at the quantum level. It's disquieting and attractive at the same time. Then a thought comes to me – this thing between he and I – it's been going towards that ever since that night at the university when he held my hand too long.

"Tell me about that night I first met you."

"You were there."

"No," I say and turn over on my side so that I face him. I rest on my elbow and look straight at him. "Tell me what you were thinking." I reach out and touch him for good measure, to see if I can read him. "The truth."

He sighs as if he's been expecting this from me and pulls his hand away.

"Don't pull your hand away." I reach out to take his hand back but he won't let me.

"Trust, Eve," he says, his voice firm. "Do you trust me to tell you what you need to know?"

I just stare at him. I'm not sure I do. He did take those manuscript pages out because he didn't want me to read them. But I said all in, and so I decide to say I trust him even if I don't.

I nod, but don't say anything.

"When I read the message you posted in the forum," he says. "I thought that maybe this was the manuscript. When you called me, and told me the year it was first written – 1224 and that it was by a writer from Carcassonne, I knew it was the manuscript, but I wasn't sure if you were our lost Adept, despite the name. Stranger coincidences have happened to me over the years. When I touched you, I was overwhelmed by your response to me. You suspected I was a vampire and were debating whether to run. Only someone inside, from an Adept family or associated with the Council would suspect that I was a vampire. Then I read you and knew it was you."

He just looks at me, waiting for my questions.

"So," I say, my cheeks heating, upset at what he's saying for some reason. "When you realized who I was, what did you think? Did you think right away that you wanted me as your blood slave?"

He closes his eyes.

"Yes," he says. "That was my first instinct as it would be any vampire who knows what you are. It's what Julien would want as well.

But I rejected that right away and that's why I tried to make you forget our meeting and the manuscript. I don't want it, Eve, at least not here," he says and taps his head. "But here?" He points to his heart. "I can't lie to you. It would be heaven."

"Heaven?" I say, incredulous. "To have me addicted to your blood so that I had to drink it or become sick?"

"I live every day addicted to blood." He glances away. "The heart wants what it wants."

"I know," I say, and a sense of sadness fills me. "I wouldn't wish it on anyone. But I have this fear that that's exactly where you and I are going. Can you deny it?"

"All I can do is try to ensure it doesn't happen."

"There is no try," I say, repeating what he said earlier. "Promise me you just won't do it. I'd rather die."

"I would have preferred death, Eve. We don't always get to choose. Sometimes God chooses for us."

I turn over onto my back and shake my head.

"That's awfully arrogant of you," I say. "Thinking that if a God did exist, he'd be spending all his time ordering the details of your life."

He runs his fingers along my arm.

"God's omnipotent and can do more than one thing at a time, Eve..."

I turn my head and look at him and he's serious. Hell. I pull away so he isn't touching me – so I can think my own thoughts without him knowing it.

How can an intelligent man with so much experience be so trapped by this religious dogma? Of course, he's not just a man. He's a priest. In his heart, if not in reality.

And that really sums it all up. He's a former priest, still a priest at heart, who does penance for his more human nature. He'll have sex with me and love it but feel intense guilt about it. He'll love it but he'll beg for forgiveness afterwards.

He'll make me his blood slave, and hate himself for it, kneel before an image of the Virgin until his knees bleed in penance. But he'll love having me entirely his own, his possession, psychically tied to him by blood. I clench my fists, angry and sad at the truth of it.

He leans over and kisses my shoulder, holding his mouth there.

"Eve?" he says, and moves closer, taking my face in his hands. I dig my nails into my palms harder to try to keep tears at bay. "Eve," he says, a touch of panic in his voice. "I can't read you."

I shake my head, but I'm glad he isn't able to read me, because I'm very upset at these thoughts going through my head.

"You're blocking me," he says, and it's more an accusation than a statement of fact.

"If I am, I don't know how."

He pulls me closer. I don't feel him in my mind. I just feel this pain and it brings tears to my eyes rather than stopping them.

He looks down and sees my fists and takes one hand, opens it. I've been digging my nails into my palms so hard, the corner of one nail has broken the skin.

"You're bleeding."

He looks in my eyes. Then he leans down and licks my palm, licks the blood and the touch of his tongue on the wound takes the pain away. Then he comes flooding in, all concern and panic and fear and I know that I've found one of my blocks.

"Oh, God no," he says, closing his eyes. "Not pain."

That confirms it. I can use pain to block him from reading my mind just as I've used pain to block things from entering my mind for so many years.

"Don't do this. Don't block me, Eve. Don't..."

"You said I'd find my blocks eventually."

"But not so soon. Not until we're ready. Until *I'm* ready." He hangs his head, running his hands through his hair. When he looks up at me again, his eyes are filled with pain. "I need access to you, Eve. Can't you understand that? I need to know how you are, to know when you're ready and when you're not."

"Ready for what?" I say, angered. "There are other ways to tell that..."

"No," he says, grimacing. "Not sex. To be my Adept."

"I think you want access to me. Maybe you'll have to trust me to tell you how I am."

"You won't. I already know that. You lie all the time, Eve. You lie to yourself. You lie to me. If you block me, I can only guess what you're really feeling and thinking."

His words hurt me. I do lie a lot. I lie to myself, just like he says. I have to in order to get through my day.

"You said something about genies and bottles that applies here."

"And you said all in, Eve. This isn't all in. It's only partial if you block me."

I just look at him, and I do feel sorry for his anguish, but what can I say?

"I can't say I won't block you at times. It would be a lie and I don't want to lie to you. I'll try to only block things you don't need to know, like when I have menstrual cramps or something embarrassing, like if the broccoli didn't agree with me and I have gas. You don't need to know those kinds of things."

I smile, flashing him some dimple in the hopes it brings him out of this darkness, but I'm lying even now because I know I'll block him when I don't want him to know how I am.

My smile doesn't lighten his mood. He wants free access, he wants to reach out any time and read me, know my emotions and thoughts. Now he won't be able to and it scares him. He doesn't smile.

CHAPTER 22

"We have to distrust each other. It is our only defense against betrayal."

Tennessee Williams

"It wasn't my fault," I say. "I wasn't trying to block you. I was just upset and it happened without me trying. Don't be mad at me."

"I'm not mad at you, Eve," he says softly and moves closer to me. He leans down and nuzzles my neck. "I'm afraid for you."

"What are you so afraid of?" I squeeze his hand.

"That you won't obey me, that you'll make some foolish and reckless and brave plan and block me from knowing it, that you'll get yourself into trouble, and that you'll get killed," he says with an exaggerated shrug, his voice emotional. "That's all. Nothing really."

"I'm not going to plot and plan. I don't know enough, Michel, to plot and plan."

"Ah, but it's precisely those who don't know how to plot and plan who try it and get into trouble."

"I promise I'll follow your rules to the best of my ability." I pull him down and kiss him and my kiss makes us both all squishy feeling inside.

"Get dressed," he says. "I'll show you the house."

I do, putting on my clothes once more, and Michel takes my hand, leading me through the house to show me every room, stopping first in the library where we gave him the news about Julien.

"That's such a beautiful old Steinway," I say and go to it, touching the keys. "I never asked you but do you play?"

"Yes."

"Play something for me." I take his hand and lead him there.

"You haven't played for me yet, and I asked first," he says, pointing a finger at me.

I smile and sit on the bench. "Any request?" While I play a scale, he sits beside me.

"Play the piece that breaks your heart."

I hesitate at the strange request. The piece that breaks my heart?

"That would have to be Ballade No.1 by Chopin," I say. "I don't play it perfectly. I was learning it when my mother died. It brings back painful memories."

"Play it."

I play the first section, the moderato, well enough, and beside me, Michel sighs.

"Lovely" he says and when I look at him, his eyes are closed and a soft smile is on his lips. "Why does it break your heart? Is it just because of her death?"

"No," I say. "It's just so beautiful and so powerful and so haunting. My psychiatrist made me try to finish learning it as therapy, and it was just so lovely and passionate that I think learning it did heal me but I haven't mastered the end."

I play the middle section, which is the most beautiful and then back to the main theme again but when I get to the coda, I can't continue. It's far too hard without much more practice. I rest my hands on my lap.

"That's as far as I can get."

"You should continue practicing until you master it," Michel says.

"I've been so busy with school, I've let other things slide."

"School is a means to an end," he says. "Music is an end in itself."

Hearing it, playing it, has made my heart ache, but it's a good ache. One that reminds me that I loved my mother and she loved me.

"Your turn," I say and move over a bit so he can play. "Play the piece that breaks your heart."

"Very well." He takes in a deep breath and starts, and I don't recognize it.

"Also Chopin," he says. "We have similar tastes."

"What is it?" I say, feeling the emotion in the piece tug at my heart.

"Nocturne in E Minor. His first, written when he was just seventeen."

"It's so beautiful and so sad."

He nods, and he was right when he said music was one of his passions, because he's playing the piece with such a beautiful and expert touch that I know it is his passion.

"Why does this break your heart?"

"I remember when I was seventeen and my heart was broken."

"Danielle?' I say. "But you chose the priesthood over her. You probably broke her heart."

"I know," he says. "But mine was broken as well."

I listen while he plays, the piece beautiful, his touch so deft.

"You play very well."

"I've had several centuries to learn. You, in contrast, are truly gifted."

The melancholy melody makes my throat close up and tears bite at the corners of my eyes. I watch him play and he's so beautiful, my fallen priest vampire-hunting vampire. When he finishes he turns to me and sees my tears, which I try to blink away, but can't.

"Oh, Eve," he whispers and pulls me into his arms. "What will I do without you?" He lifts my face up, kissing my tears, and I slip my arms around his neck.

"You won't be gone too long, will you?"

"I don't know how long," he says, kissing my neck. "Any time is too long."

Then he sighs and takes my hand, pulling me away from the piano. "I have to get ready. My plane leaves soon."

He takes me on a quick tour of the rest of the house, but now I'm in no mood for it, and take a perfunctory look in each room, the main living room, a smaller sitting room, and he opens a door and lets me peer into an industrial kitchen.

He motions to the dark haired vampire, who follows us back upstairs.

"Sleep now," he says, patting the bed. "I'll think of you lying in my bed all nice and warm and sleepy and I'll be able to relax. I'll let Raymond take you to your flat later this evening and you can gather up your things. Put them in the bathroom. I don't have any female servants, so you'll have to put up with Raymond," he says and points to the servant. "Do what he says because he's very exacting about things and keeps me in line. I'm taking Vasily with me."

"How many servants do you have?"

Michel turns to Raymond. "How many on staff, Raymond?"

"Fifteen, my Lord."

"You make your staff call you my Lord?" I turn to Michel and then look back at Raymond, who clears his throat. Oh, oh, Michel mouths, all wide-eyed faux-panic, his back to Raymond.

"My Lord de Cernay is a Vicomte from a very old and noble family and he was once the Bishop of Carcassonne."

"Yes," I say, "but there are no titles in France any longer. You know, Liberty, Equality, Fraternity?"

Raymond makes a sound in his throat and turns away, pulling back the covers to the bed, which I see have a wet spot on them. Michel finally smiles at me, shaking his head slowly.

"You'll have my staff up in arms if you talk like that while I'm gone."

"You afraid I'll foment rebellion?" I smile, but it's forced because I know the moment we have to separate is coming quickly and I'm getting all teary again.

"Are you sure Lilith isn't your middle name?" he says, taking me in his arms and pulling me against him, kissing me. Raymond makes a face and leaves the room.

"He doesn't like me being here," I say to Michel.

"To him, I'm a priest and so he's scandalized that I have a woman staying in my bed. Since he's been with me, I've been celibate and very priest-like. Give him time."

I pull him against me more tightly. "You said you were celibate earlier. For how long?"

"When I killed my last human."

Holy hell. Over a century without sex? No wonder he was more than ready earlier.

"I feel terribly guilty that I made you break your vows," I say but I'm lying.

"You made me do nothing." He kisses me and I feel his amusement at this line of discussion.

"Why me?" I say, genuinely curious. "Is it only because I look like her? Like Danielle?"

He sits on his bed and pulls me between his legs.

"You do look like her in a way, with that blonde hair and hazel eyes. But you're also different. Your freckles. Your dimples. They're your own and they're what I love about you. And your mind, of course. You have a mind that keeps me shaking my head."

What he loves about me…

He's used love twice in reference to me, saying earlier that he loved my mind while we were in the park. He said it to Soren in Montana. I reach to him, touching his cheek and when I do I feel a deep sense of warmth from him, and it envelops me like a wave and my own emotions swell in response.

"I have to go," he says and pulls me against his body, his face nuzzling in the crook of my neck, his mouth opening, his tongue over my jugular. He's feeling my pulse, enjoying the sensation of it against his tongue. He loves how close he is to my vein, how easy it would be to just bite, and his teeth do elongate and his blood lust increases, but he bears it, loving the sacrifice he makes to keep me pure. He wants to keep me pure, unbroken, untainted.

"I have to leave," he protests, his voice husky. "I don't have time..." He kisses me. "But when I come back, we'll be together for good, Eve," he says, staring in my eyes.

I want him to stay with me. I'm afraid of this price he will pay and what it will mean, but I don't get anything from him. He pulls out of my arms.

"Now go to bed and sleep as long as you want. Raymond will attend to any of your needs. I've told Ed that you'll be on leave while I'm gone because I don't want you going anywhere without me."

"But the case..."

"Ed and Terri are handling it fine without us. Now don't ask questions or protest, Eve. Obey."

I nod and take in a deep breath.

He pulls me once more into his embrace, lifting my body off the floor as if I'm no more that a feather, and of course, he's so strong, with the strength of ten men, and so I am light.

"Stay safe, ma petite," he whispers, his lips against my neck. "My little one."

And then he's gone without looking back.

DURING THE NEXT FOUR DAYS, I spend part of my time playing the lovely old Steinway, learning the Chopin Nocturne Michel played. I want to learn it because he loves it and I want it to become part of me. The rest of the time I spend studying old atlases and maps of the world, drawn hundreds of years earlier that Michel has in his collection, reading books from his library, watching television, and simply lazing around. It is the first real vacation I've had in several years for each summer I've worked and taken classes. It's a relief to just do nothing.

I don't hear from Michel and it hurts a bit that he doesn't think of contacting me, but I try to bite back my disappointment and accept things I can't change.

When Raymond enters the room to bring me tea, I ask him.

"Have you heard from Michel?"

Raymond shakes his head.

"He said he'd be out of contact for several days – maybe a week."

I feel a bit better. He's not deliberately avoiding me then. This is part of his plan, but I miss him and only now realize how familiar his presence has become and how much I desire him, his company, his touch.

That night, as I'm sleeping, I dream of him and it's a strange dream – like something out of a vampire movie with him entering the open window, coming to the bed, his black wings outstretched. He lies on top of me, kissing me with his cold lips, his wings curving around us. I writhe in pleasure under his touch, aching for him. As I do, he bites my neck, his sharp teeth breaking my skin and the mixture of pleasure and pain makes everything even more potent. The feed is short, just a mouthful or two, and then he's gone and not a word is spoken.

I wake up and the dream felt so real, I reach up to touch my neck, but there's no mark. It was just a dream after all…

THAT AFTERNOON, I ask Raymond if someone can take me out so I can visit my apartment and feed my cats, then get a cup of my favorite coffee.

"No offense," I say to him, "but I really like the coffee at a shop just below my apartment. Can someone take me there so I can get a cup? I want to buy some coffee and my favorite dark chocolate at a store beside it. I've been in this house for four days straight and I'm starting to go crazy."

Raymond makes a face and then goes to the door.

"I'll arrange it. My Lord left instructions that any outings should be short, and limited to visiting your apartment to feed your cats. I'll have two guards take you. You're only allowed fifteen minutes. Is that understood?"

I nod, and as much as I like the mansion, I'm happy to be out getting the fresh air. It's sunny and I don't want to waste the nice day.

❧

THE GUARD who met us the first day takes me in a long black sedan and I see a second car following behind us. Talk about security precautions. We arrive at my apartment and I quickly refresh the cat food feeder and water dispenser while the guard named Marco stands like a statue in my doorway, and then we head to the coffee shop for a cup of Medium Blend organic and cream. The side patio is open and so I sit in a chair and enjoy the day. Marco is sitting a few chairs over, his dark glasses on, his hand on a cup of coffee, which he doesn't drink.

I get up to go to the washroom and Marco stands when he sees me rise.

"I'm just going to the washroom."

He nods and then goes ahead of me to check the small washroom out. He opens the door, checks the stall and then nods to me, not a word said.

I go in and have a quick pee and then wash up before leaving. Marco isn't there when I come out, nor is he seated at the table where he was previously. I go to the shop next door to pick up some of the chocolate they sell there – it will go well with the pound of organic espresso I've bought. Surely the driver will see me and will keep an eye out for me for the five minutes I'm in the shop. I go into the tiny store and inspect a half-dozen trays of dark chocolate, selecting several that I'll enjoy after my supper. I glance out the window while the clerk rings the order up and see a strange man staring at me as he crosses traffic. He has his eyes peeled on me, a coat over his arm, and I have a sense that under it is a weapon.

"I'm sorry," I say to the clerk when she hands me the bag. "Is there a back entrance?"

She nods and points to the rear of the store and I leave through the small kitchen. I can circle around the block and see if I can find Marco. Then I hear footsteps behind me in the alley and I remember what Michel said – it's better to avoid fighting, even if you can win. I run, not looking back as Michel instructed. I'm a fast runner, but not fast enough to avoid a gun, a small projectile hitting me in the neck.

I fall and strike my head, and then there is only darkness.

END OF BOOK 1
Book 2: Ascension available at your favorite retailer.

ABOUT THE AUTHOR

S. E. Lund lives on the side of a mountain in the shadow of an active volcano with her family of humans and pets. Besides writing paranormal romance, urban fantasy and contemporary romance, she dreams of living in a warm climate where snow is just a word in a dictionary.

Sign up for her newsletter and get information on new releases, sales and news. She hates spam and will never share your email!

https://www.subscribepage.com/x8t1t7

www.selundauthor.com

selund2012@gmail.com

Drake Unbound

THE MR. BIG SERIES

Mr. Big Shot: Book 1

Mr. Big Love: Book 2

Mr. Big Daddy: Book 3

Mr. Big Deal: Book 4

THE MCINTYRE BROTHERS SERIES

Tempt Me: Book 1

Tease Me: Book 2

Tame Me: Book 3

❧

Military Romance / Romantic Suspense

THE BAD BOY SERIES

Bad Boy Saint: Book 1

Bad Boy Sinner: Book 2

Bad Boy Soldier: Book 3

Bad Boy Savior: Book 4

THE BOYFRIEND SERIES

Boy Toy: Book 1

Man Bun: Book 2

STANDALONE BOOKS:

Matched

If You Fall